THE POWER OF LOVE

Chase Boykins

Paperback ISBN: 979-8-9883289-0-2
eBook ISBN: 979-8-9883289-1-9

Library of Congress Control Number: 2023918840

Cover Design: Deva Digi
Instagram: @devadigi5
Email: devadigi5@gmail.com

Published in the United States of America

Prologue

The Pretentious Palace

Thump-thump. Thump-thump. Thump-thump. The sound of Nadine Jackson-Deville's heartbeats pounded in her ears as she dashed from one end of the master bedroom suite to the other. The lingering effects of her recent bout with COVID-19 forced her to stop periodically to catch her breath.

Tears clouded her vision, and her heart and mind were in a boxing match that was beginning to make her chest hurt and her head spin. Her heart wanted to believe that things would change, but her mind wouldn't let her ignore the facts. She was living, eating, sleeping, and even worshipping with her worst enemy.

Nadine's emotions were running amok. Fear, anger, grief, anxiety, even love … it was all there. How was it possible that this was her reality? She was that girl that most troubled people in the community came to when their lives were falling apart. How did she become one of them?

Nadine's hands trembled, making it difficult for her to even peel open the large trash bags in which she stuffed the items she pulled from her dresser drawers. Sweat that had begun beading on her forehead at the onset of her packing was now sliding down the sides of her face.

For the last couple of weeks, she'd known this day was coming and had even carefully planned for it. But now that it had arrived, Nadine was just as unsure as she was sure. This wasn't like the car she'd bought at the beginning of the year. She had driven it off the lot, taken it home, and driven it to and from her office every day for an entire week. Then she woke up one morning, decided she'd made a mistake, and took it back to the dealership. They honored their warranty and gave Nadine another opportunity to shop their inventory and find the vehicle that would satisfy her desires.

If she followed through with today's plan, that would not be her testimony. There would be no turning back, and the thought of it was overwhelming. Nadine's breath was coming in short pants, and it wasn't due to her rushing. Her nerves were unraveling and starting to get the best of her. Nadine grabbed the bottom of the comforter that draped the bed and blew into it as though it were a brown paper bag that would help steady her breathing. She then used the soft fabric to wipe her face. The sweat and tears were beginning to mix now.

Nadine looked toward the ceiling. "Am I doing the right thing?" Her recessed lighting didn't answer … and neither did God. "Is this your will? Have I heard you correctly? Have I even heard you at all? If I walk out of this house, that's it." She said the last sentence as if she were telling God something He didn't already know.

Damon Deville was not a forgiving man. Her husband was cynical, rigid, controlling, and vengeful. He was arrogant; his sense of superiority could reach frightening levels. If she came crawling back to Damon, he would accept her with open arms just so he could make her life a living hell.

Even knowing all that, the pain Nadine felt was very real. She wasn't leaving because she wanted to; she was leaving because she had to. God had given His answer a long time ago. Damon's cruel behavior and unyielding unwillingness to seek help or even acknowledge a need for change was God's voice.

New tears welled in Nadine's eyes. "It wasn't supposed to be like this!" she muttered in a whisper.

Her mind traveled back to a time that now seemed hundreds of years ago.

"I am one lucky girl," she remembered telling her best friend, Trina Richards. "I think I've met the man who will make me want to settle down and add 'wife' to my resume."

It was the morning after her first date with Damon, and Trina was the only person Nadine had even let in on the fact that the highly respected mayor had begun pursuing her affections. Trina didn't readily share Nadine's enthusiasm.

"That's good and all," her friend responded, "but you need to make sure he's not blowing smoke in your face. You've worked hard to get where you are. I love me some Mayor Deville; don't get me wrong," she quickly added. "He's probably the best mayor the A-T-L has ever had, but that doesn't mean he'll be the best husband. Keep in mind that he's been married before, so there might be some skeletons hiding in that closet of his." Nadine recalled being thrilled to have a ready response for her ever-cautious friend that day. "I'm way ahead of you," she'd replied. "And that's just another thing for me to love about him. He didn't even try to hide anything from me. I was pleasantly surprised by his transparency, especially so early in our relationship."

"So, you asked him about his previous marriage?" Trina's tone said she was surprised too.

"I didn't have to. He's the one who opened the conversation about it, and it was nothing crazy and nothing for me to be concerned about. Every woman doesn't know how to appreciate what a man brings to the table, and Damon brings a lot of great dishes." Nadine remembered giggling at her own choice of words. "And did you know that he is also a licensed minister?" she added.

"Really?"

"Yes, really. So, on top of everything else, he's a man of God! Girl, you know my faith is very important to me, so to know that I'd be equally yoked if this works out is amazing."

The revelation she shared with Trina seemed to calm most of her friend's concerns. By the time their conversation ended, Nadine felt that she'd won over the one person who would probably be her biggest skeptic. If she could convince Trina that Damon was an upstanding and upright man, everybody else should be a piece of cake. But while Nadine had done the initial convincing, it was Damon who made Trina fully drop her guard. When she saw firsthand how he faithfully wooed Nadine, Trina had to admit that it would be crazy for Nadine not to lock in. It was a consensus shared by anybody who saw them together.

From the outside, Damon and Nadine were the perfect pair. Nadine's life and her lifestyle were the dreams of many women and the envy of many more. What woman wouldn't look at her and feel some kind of way? Nadine had nabbed the man who held the highest elected office in Georgia's capital, and whether they were at elite functions or captured on television footage while out and about in the community, every woman everywhere saw Damon treating his wife like rare gold. To the people of metropolitan Atlanta and even beyond, theirs was a whirlwind love story straight out of heaven. People had no idea of the secret hell she had been enduring inside the walls of her pretentious palace.

Nadine snapped back to reality. She scuttled to the nightstand where her cell phone rested and looked at the time. Precious minutes were ticking away quickly. Dashing into the closet, she reappeared with another armful of clothing and shoved them into an open suitcase before zipping it shut. She had to get out of there.

Damon had left to attend a breakfast meeting with some of the other metropolitan Atlanta officials, and mental notes she'd taken from previous gatherings of its kind told Nadine that she had about three hours to make her exit. With as much stuff as she had to pack, that wasn't much time.

To add to Nadine's challenge, she and her husband didn't exactly have an empty nest. While no children had been born inside their union, Damon had moved his widowed father into their home two months ago, after he had a doubleknee replacement. Daddy Deville was an early riser. And since regaining some of his mobility, he got up early every morning to prepare his special coffee blend.

Generally, Nadine didn't care much for the stuff, and she suspected that once she walked out of her home today, she'd never have another cup. However, Daddy Deville added something in the coffee pot after the dripping was complete that made it not only bearable but tasty. Nadine had asked him once to reveal the secret, but he swore he'd take it to his grave.

As a much-sought-after attorney, she rarely had time to prepare a full breakfast before heading to the office of Nadine Jackson & Associates, one of the area's most prominent law firms, so a cup of his brew helped on those days when her workload forced her into overtime. Nadine was an established businesswoman well before marrying Damon, so the sign outside of her office still showcased the last name of the man whose unfailing love she would forever cherish—her father. He had passed away fifteen years ago, and although she was now a full-grown woman on the tail end of her forties, some days she still felt like a little girl who needed her daddy. Like today.

"If you had been alive, I bet you would've seen straight through Damon's fake exterior." Nadine wondered if her father could hear her. "I hope you come down here after I'm gone and beat the mess out of him." She threw in that part just in case he could.

Her steps quickened as she gathered the last of her clothing items, toiletries, and other must-haves and stuffed them in a bag. Nadine hoped beyond hope that her father-in-law didn't have a reason to linger in any of the shared spaces of their home this morning. She couldn't think of one excuse she'd be able to give the man for why she would be filling her vehicle with garbage bags and suitcases that wouldn't raise unwanted questions.

Over recent days, once she finally accepted the fact that this moment was inevitable, Nadine had begun artfully transferring certain personal items to a storage unit her sister had helped her secure. Sophia was Nadine's only sibling and one of only a select few confidants she had even shared her escape plan with, including the location of exactly where Nadine was headed.

"Everybody's going think I'm crazy," she mumbled as new thoughts bombarded her brain. Nadine felt bad that she'd kept this big secret from almost all her friends. Most of them had no clue that she was leaving town today. They had no clue about the torment she had been enduring either.

Her new round of tears was hot and seemed to burn into the corneas of her eyes. "God! Is this what all abused women must deal with?" Nadine felt like she was walking through hell just to get out of hell.

Abused. She hated the word and the reality. Coming to grips with the fact that she was an abused wife had been difficult for her. Her husband had never hit her. In fits of rage, Damon had thrown objects at her in the past, but he'd never struck her with his hands, and she had convinced herself that without that, it wasn't abuse. Nadine trusted herself more than she trusted anyone else, so the lies she'd told herself were the easiest ones to believe.

With her packing almost complete, she walked into her ensuite, turned on the faucet, and filled her cupped hands with water before swallowing gulps of it. Her mouth felt like midday in the Sahara Desert. Nadine took a long look at her reflection in the mirror and barely recognized the woman that returned her stare.

She was just five days away from her fiftieth birthday. Normally, Nadine wore her age very well. But today, she looked like death. Her eyes were red. Her nose was puffy. Her cheeks drooped. And just when she thought she'd been beaten down for the last time by haunting thoughts, more arrived. Not only would the revelation of her leaving blindside Damon, her friends, and most of her relatives, but it was also going to be the talk of the town.

Sophia had already warned her to be prepared for the fallout that was sure to happen when word of the mayor's wife's sudden disappearance hit the news outlets.

Damon certainly wasn't going to tell the whole truth. She could imagine what horrible things he would invent about her, and Nadine knew the media would receive it as the gospel truth. After all, this was Mayor Damon Deville—the man listed in *The Network Journal* magazine among the 21st-century Black leaders to watch. Her face would be plastered everywhere, and her character would be crucified!

What am I doing? Is my life so bad? Is it really worth all the disgrace and embarrassment that leaving will cause? Nadine was certain that what she was now experiencing was the onset of a stroke. She was hot, breathless, and physically weak. Her head was about to explode, and it felt like a brick the size of Texas was sitting on her chest.

Nadine stumbled to her bed and sat on the edge of the mattress. Reaching for her phone, she found the one confidant that she knew would be available to take her call. Olivia was among those who knew that today was "the day"—and she had told Nadine to call her at any moment that she felt the need.

Olivia answered on the first ring, but Nadine didn't give her a chance to say anything beyond, "Hello."

Even to her own ears, Nadine's words sounded like they were coming from a frantic woman who was being held hostage and was terrified for her life. "I don't know what I'm doing, Olivia. I'm scared. This has been my whole life for so long that I don't know what I'm going to do if I leave it. What are people going to think of me? He's gonna lie, and they're going to believe him. I might lose everything. What if …?"

"Stop it." Olivia interrupted Nadine's meltdown in a tone that was firm, but not harsh. She was a pro at doing that. The fact that she was also a believer was what strongly swayed Nadine to choose her as her licensed therapist. "Mayor Deville didn't create you, so he can't destroy you," Olivia continued. "That's the kind of power that he wants you to think he has, but it's all an illusion. Whose report are you going to believe, Nadine?"

"God's," she replied through sobs.

"Whose?" Olivia challenged.

"God's." Nadine's voice was stronger that time, but apparently not strong enough.

"Whose?"

Nadine straightened her back, inhaled deeply, and then slowly emptied her lungs. Thinking about the fallout of her decision was one of the reasons she had endured the shambles of a marriage as long as she had. But it was past time that she stopped worrying about what everyone else would think. She had to consider her own well-being and just trust that the truth would eventually outlive the lies.

"God's!" Nadine exclaimed.

"That's right; God's," Olivia said. "You've ministered to others about His love and His power, and now it's time for you to apply it to your own situation. Trust Him, Nadine. Think about what you've endured. Your husband is just a half-step away from severely hurting you or worse. You deserve better than this, and you know it."

Olivia was right, and it was just the amount of encouragement that Nadine needed to snap her from her moment of insanity.

She had no doubt that Damon would be both furious and insulted at her decision to leave him without even so much as a hint. Furious, because she would have outsmarted him—a man who thought he was more clever than God Himself, and insulted, because she would have had the unmitigated gall to even think about leaving the great Damon Deville, let alone actually do it.

He had spent years chipping away at her dignity, and he had taken special care to plant a deeply rooted fear in her heart. The verbal, mental, and emotional abuse started early in their marriage, and despite her hopes and prayers that it would get better, it only worsened. In the last couple of years, his fiery temperament and erratic behavior had reached a level that sometimes left her in fear for her safety.

Damon's need to control every part of Nadine's existence had reached a level of cruelty that was demented and diabolical. She was sure her husband's intent was to strip her of all self-worth. He would never suspect that she had the strength or audacity to leave—not even in the secret way she was doing it. How dare she rise from the ashes? How dare she break free? How dare she … ?

A sudden noise from downstairs invaded the silence. Was that the front door closing? Had Damon come back home sooner than expected? Terror gripped Nadine's heart, awakening it once again.

Thump-thump. Thump-thump. Thump-thump.

She found the courage to take cautious steps toward the door of her master bedroom. Carefully, she turned the knob and eased out into the empty hall that led to the stairway. Peeking over the second-floor banister, she saw Daddy Deville using his cane for stability as he carefully bent to pick up the book he had dropped on the floor. He must have made a visit to their library and selected his reading material for the morning. That meant that he was done drinking his coffee and was preparing for …

"Physical therapy!" As the panicky whisper escaped Nadine's lips, she closed her eyes and pressed her back against the wall to help steady her buckling knees. In all her careful planning, she'd failed to factor in Daddy Deville's appointment. For the past three weeks, physical therapists had been coming to provide services every Friday morning. This had been added to their weekly routine after Nadine's escape plan had been set in place. She'd forgotten to add it. The pending arrival of his therapists drastically reduced the escape time Nadine thought she had, and with Daddy Deville up and walking around the house, it wouldn't be enough. She was trapped!

"Oh, God. Please … Please …" Anxiety seemed to evaporate all fluids from her earlier thought flow.

"When you don't know what to pray, just call on Jesus. He's all-wise and all-knowing. He'll provide exactly what you need." The words of Nadine's favorite aunt filtered through her mind like Drano. Not like the regular strength Drano, but like the max gel formula. The one that came in the red bottle and was guaranteed to cut through even the most stubborn clogs. Though Nadine had shared a tight bond with her father throughout her life, she couldn't say the same about her mother. Nadine and Rose's relationship had been rather strained, and Nadine had no doubt that God had personally fashioned her Aunt Pat to fill that void. Although they were sisters, Pat and Rose were nothing alike. Nadine could always count on Patricia Solomon; there was nothing that she didn't feel comfortable telling her. Well … almost nothing.

"Jesus, Jesus, Jesus," Nadine began whispering. "Jesus, Jesus, Jesus."

When her father-in-law opened his bedroom door, Nadine could hear the shower running from his adjoining bathroom. Her eyes fluttered open. Daddy Deville had only recently gotten to the phase of his recovery where he could take showers, and he was notorious for taking long ones. That—combined with his movements being impaired by two fresh artificial knees—would give her the time she needed.

A sense of relief washed over Nadine's body. "Thank you, Jesus, and thank you, Aunt Pat," she said.

She scampered to make the most of the time she had left. Nadine waited until she felt sure that Daddy Deville was in the confines of his shower stall before beginning to haul her belongings downstairs. If she was ever thankful for her regular exercise routine, it was today. It took her a total of six trips up and down the stairs, but even with the nagging residuals that COVID-19 had left behind, she got it all done. Nadine even gave Damon the undeserved courtesy of straightening his bed before exiting the room for the final time.

"Cleanliness is next to godliness." That was something else that Aunt Pat had drilled in her, although she was sure that even a neat freak like her aunt would have given her a pass on a day like today.

On her final trip down the stairs, Nadine detoured to Daddy Deville's bedroom door and carefully pressed her ear against it. The shower waters were still running. That gave her some bonus time to grab a few sentimental items that were scattered throughout the house. She hadn't been able to take those earlier for fear that Damon would notice things missing and become suspicious.

By the time she was done loading up, the back, floors, and seating of her SUV were covered. On her way out the door for the last time, Nadine stopped long enough to pour fresh hot coffee into the insulated travel mug that Daddy Deville had left on the counter for her use. It almost seemed cruel to take it since she was abandoning his son. But, hey … she had a long drive ahead of her, and there was no reason that his morning efforts should go to waste.

Chapter 1

Say Cheese

Nadine squealed as her husband hoisted her up in his arms and spun her around amidst the cheers of the crowd. The room suddenly turned red, white, and blue thanks to the colored balloons that dropped from the ceiling and the tiny bits of paper that blasted from the confetti launchers strategically placed throughout the hall.

Damon Deville had done it again! This mayoral race had been tougher than his three previous ones for several reasons, mostly because his opponent not only had a political lineage, but she was also a white female who practically matched Damon's knack for making friends across party lines. Demographically, Atlanta's Black populace outnumbered that of every other race. However, when it came to those who consistently went to the polls and voted, the ratio had been known to narrow, especially when the weather wasn't agreeable.

The leaders of the "Deville Mobile," as they dubbed the re-election campaign, were not only concerned that Wynette Ingalls-Newhouse might get major support from the city's Caucasian residents but also that of its overall female population.

Practically her entire platform had been built on what she would do to even the playing field for working women, and with there still being an imbalance in areas like equal pay for equal work, Wynette—whose late grandfather served three decades as a well-respected Atlanta judge and whose father currently represented Georgia in the U.S. House of Representatives—had been a force to be reckoned with.

Emory University had recently been ranked number twenty-two in the nation by *U.S. News & World Report*, and almost anyone asked would give much of that credit to Wynette Ingalls -Newhouse. She knew how to run a taut ship without ruffling the wrong feathers. The university's president was well-respected throughout the state of Georgia, and Damon's camp realized early on that the election would be no cakewalk. His opponent's initials spelled "WIN," and she used that as the motto of her crusade.

In the end, however, Wynette's promises weren't enough to erase the massive popularity Damon had gained in the twelve years he had already served. People who ordinarily may not have gotten out on a rainy Tuesday and gone to the polls to cast their votes did so today. And indeed, every single vote was necessary. The margin of Damon's win was slim, but it was a win, nonetheless.

Nadine caught her breath as her husband placed her down, and she readily accepted the spirited kiss he planted on her lips while dozens of cameras caught it all on film. She had long ago lost count of the number of raised cell phones whose owners were taking advantage of the ability to live stream the action on their social media pages.

"Congratulations, honey," she said, gently holding both Damon's cheeks with her hands and looking him straight in the eyes. "There was never any doubt. I knew you could do it."

"No … we did this," Damon stressed before kissing her once more. "There is no me without you, baby. I love you!" Nadine always got compliments about her smile, and tonight, it was as wide as she could make it when she and Damon turned to face the nearby photographers and news reporters who had been hanging out with them at campaign headquarters and capturing their every word and action. This election was a nail-biter, with Wynette leading one minute, and Damon regaining the advantage the next. For over three hours, media professionals had been tirelessly providing dramatic live updates for citizens who had been, no doubt, sitting on the edges of their seats ever since the polling locations closed at 7:00 PM.

After enduring what felt like a million photo shoots of Damon and her lovingly interacting with one another and waving at the crowd, Nadine gladly prepared to step away from the spotlight to give her husband sole ownership of the stage. And that's exactly what it was—a stage.

Both she and Damon deserved Academy Awards. Neither of them had ever had an ounce of theatrical training, yet they were A-list actors. But while Nadine despised her role, Damon seemed to love his. He lived for the hoopla that came with their public life. He was like an addict who was always looking for his next high. Damon had started out serving on the local school board. From there, he won a seat on the city council where he served only one term before grabbing a chance at becoming mayor. He often bragged that one day, he would become the next President Barack Obama. Just the thought of something of that magnitude was enough to make Nadine break out in hives. She adored the former first lady. Michelle Obama had made it all look easy. But being the wife of a mayor was tough enough; Nadine didn't even want to imagine anything more.

She was more than happy to oblige when Damon offered one last kiss before giving the nod that granted her permission to fade into the background while he delivered his victory speech. Nadine had no desire to be an active participant in the endless questions that would follow. All the gathered answers would be put to good use in print, television, and online news stories over the next few days, and Nadine would rather not be quoted. She didn't trust reporters any farther than she could throw them.

"Congratulations, girlie! That was a close one, but Damon must be God's favorite because that come-from-behind win was a miracle!" Nadine's best friend hugged her from behind. "Four more years! Four more years!"

"Thanks, Trina." Nadine tried to laugh at the playful chant, but between the absurd thought that Damon could possibly be God's favorite and the pains shooting through her aching feet, she couldn't. Nadine would pay a blackmailer's demand for a chair right now, but Damon had already warned her not to sit unless she saw him sitting. He said it would make him look bad and give the impression that she wasn't enthused about the election.

"What an amazing night!" Trina exclaimed. "I hope at least one of those cameramen captured me in the crowd. If I must say so myself, this dress is the bomb, and it deserves at least fifteen seconds of fame."

This time, Nadine did laugh. It was funny because it was true. Trina's teal and black bell-sleeved dress was beautiful, but then again, pretty much everything in her closet was. She was a sharp dresser who knew how to be classy without being flashy. She'd been that way for as long as Nadine had known her.

The foundation of the two ladies' friendship began during their grad school years in Washington, D.C. Trina Richards was among four girls who had answered the posted ad for a roommate. Nadine had secured an apartment when she decided to go to school there, and she needed someone to share the expenses. Trina was the first to be interviewed, and during the process, they immediately clicked. Everybody Nadine interviewed after her was just a formality. She'd already made up her mind that Trina would be the one.

As colleagues pursuing the same profession, the two students spent long hours together as study mates while at Howard University School of Law. Upon graduation, they initially went separate ways, with Trina finding her first professional break in nearby Maryland and Nadine relocating to Atlanta. But eighteen months later, when Nadine branched out and started her own law firm, Trina was the first person she reached out to. There was no one else with whom she'd rather start on the ground floor. To Nadine's delight, her friend didn't hesitate to accept the first seat on her team, and the two had been practically inseparable ever since.

Nadine Jackson & Associates would soon be celebrating twenty years of success in metropolitan Atlanta, and Nadine owed a lot of gratitude to Trina. She had supported her every step of the way, and not just in business. Nadine and Trina had been through nearly everything together in their adult years. They'd laughed together, cried together, played together, and prayed together. When Trina had her son sixteen years ago, she'd asked Nadine to be his godmother, and when Nadine got married, Trina stood beside her as maid of honor. "I know you have to be relieved that this is all over," Trina remarked while helping herself to two champagne glasses from the tray of the smartly dressed waiter that approached them. She handed one to Nadine, and they clinked them together in celebration.

"Girl, you don't know the half of it." Nadine giggled when she said it, but all the reasons for her relief were not laughing matters. Her best friend wouldn't be laughing either if she knew all the gory details.

This campaign had been grueling, and Nadine learned early in their marriage that Damon wasn't good under pressure. He was an expert in front of the cameras, but away from the eyes of the public, he could be an entirely different beast. When things didn't go his way, it was always somebody else's fault, and Nadine was his favorite person to blame. Sometimes she felt like she couldn't do anything right in his eyes.

As recently as last night, he was stringing together profanities while telling her how worthless she'd been. They had just completed a private, formal dinner that was attended by about fifty of Damon's strongest supporters. The two of them were hosting it as a show of appreciation for those who had worked hardest on the campaign trail. During the entire ride home, Damon charged Nadine with being reserved and withdrawn from his precious allies. He said she secretly wanted Wynette to pull out a victory.

"You'd love that, wouldn't you?" Damon had accused. "You would just love to see my name in the defeat window when FOX5 Atlanta broadcasts the results tomorrow, wouldn't you?"

Nadine had been arguing her case for twenty minutes already. She was tired, frustrated, and just over it. And since she wasn't getting paid for it, like she would if she were defending herself in a court of law, she decided it wasn't worth it. Nadine answered him with silence, and for the rest of the ride home, she tuned him out as best she could. Unfortunately, that didn't make the situation any better.

By the time they walked into their home, the vicious name-calling had begun, and then the accusations continued as they reached their second-floor bedroom. "I should have dumped you a long time ago," Damon barked. "If I threw you out today, do you know how many other women I could have by tomorrow?" Zero, if they have the good sense they were born with. You wouldn't even have me if this was the man you would have shown me ahead of time.

Nadine knew it was best for her to keep those thoughts inside her head. When she walked into her closet to place her shoes on the rack, she stood in the space for a while and enjoyed the quiet it provided. When Nadine finally walked back into the bedroom, she saw that Damon was leaning against the dresser with his arms folded. He was eyeing her as if patiently waiting for an answer to the question he'd posed earlier.

As much as Nadine had hoped his rant was over, his posture told her that she would have no such luck.

"Why are you standing there looking at me like I'm some kind of fool?" he finally asked. "Don't you hear me talking to you?" Nadine wanted to say, "I'm looking at you like you're some kind of fool because you are some kind of fool," but she didn't. Instead, she lied. "That tooth that I had filled last week was throbbing, and the pain had traveled all the way to my head. I wasn't withdrawn tonight. I had plenty of conversations with people, but maybe not as much as normal because I wanted to keep the air from my tooth."

"Oh, shut up!" Damon removed his tie and slung it on the bed. "When I want you to keep your mouth closed, you don't. But when I need you to open it, suddenly, your tooth aches and your head is about to explode. You ain't good for nothing!" He forcibly kicked his shoes off, sending them sailing into the middle of the floor. "I know what you're doing. You're trying to sabotage my campaign."

"What? Damon, why would you even think that? Haven't I done absolutely everything you've asked me to do? I've gone so far as to pass some of my caseloads to others in my firm just so I could fulfill all your requests of me."

"You act like that's doing me a favor or something!" The scowl lines on Damon's forehead deepened. "You're the wife. I'm the husband. God made me the head; not you. You get it twisted because you make more money, but that don't mean nothing to God, and it don't mean nothing to me."

"I have never compared our salaries or tried to use that as leverage against you, Damon. My firm …"

"Screw your firm!" he yelled. "I don't want to hear about your firm or your caseload. You were passing your caseload to them, alright. What you were probably passing them was material to give to that white woman so she could use it against me. All six attorneys in your office are females, Nadine. You think I don't know what's going on? Ain't no telling what kinds of bribes you've been taking from her in exchange for information."

"Come on, Damon; you know I would never do that to you. I know how much your job means to you, and even with all the talk about how there may be an upset tomorrow, I truly believe you're going to win this. Yes, Wynette has done her best to make people question your stance on women's rights, but she didn't get anything from me, and you've had a valid rebuttal for every charge she's made. Anybody who knows you knows that you're not guilty of that stuff."

"Rebuttal? Charge? Not guilty?" Damon scoffed. "This is not a courtroom, Counselor, so don't throw your legal crap around to talk all over my head and try and make me look like an idiot." Damon made menacing steps toward Nadine and pointed directly in her face. "You can stop trying to act like you're riding with me in the Deville Mobile, 'cause I'm not buying it. If I pull out a win tomorrow, it's going to be without your support. If this win happens, it will be all me and my real supporters because you ain't done jack to help!"

That statement was a far cry from the "No … we did this. There is no me without you, baby" remark that Damon had just said to her in front of the cameras.

A roaring cheer from the crowd in campaign headquarters pulled Nadine from her thoughts of last night's dispute with Damon. She downed the rest of her drink and smiled at her friend. "I envy you. You're going to leave here and be able to go straight to bed when you get home. Damon's phone will probably be ringing all night. As tired as I am, and as tired as I know he'll be, I don't see sleep in our future any time soon."

"I gotta admit—I wouldn't want to be in your shoes," Trina replied. She glanced down at Nadine's feet and added, "Unless, of course, we're talking about those shoes. Girl, I have the perfect outfit for those."

"And I'm sure you already have shoes to match it." Nadine knew her friend well.

"This is true," Trina admitted. "But a girl can never have enough shoes."

The women stopped chatting when a group of people from the crowd approached to congratulate Nadine on her husband's win. Trina quietly stepped away and settled in a nearby empty chair. Nadine's feet longed for her to do the same. On an average day, her shoes wouldn't be a stress point, but she had been walking and standing in them for hours now, and at the moment, their cuteness far outweighed their comfort. But duty called for her to remain standing and smiling as one person after the other either filtered by to shake her hand or hugged her while extending their best compliment.

"Congratulations, Attorney Jackson-Deville!"

"You look lovely tonight, Attorney Jackson-Deville!" "God bless y'all, Attorney Jackson-Deville!"

"You must be so proud, Attorney Jackson-Deville!" "I couldn't be happier, Attorney Jackson-Deville!" "I can hardly wait for the headlines in tomorrow's paper, Attorney Jackson-Deville!"

Contrary to what Damon thought, Nadine could hardly wait for the headlines either. Being the mayor's wife was no easy task, but if he had lost this race, she cringed at the thought of how insufferable the atmosphere in their home would have gotten. Reading the many news articles about how the Deville Mobile had run over the Wynette Corvette was bound to put her husband in a glorious mood. Nadine had overheard one of Damon's campaign leaders make that "Wynette Corvette" quip in a conversation several weeks ago. She was certain they would use it in the celebratory days ahead.

Nadine had pacified herself by attributing the election to Damon's vile behavior. Yes, he had been disrespecting her well before his position in government came up for grabs, but the tighter the race became and the closer Election Day drew, everything worsened. So, while tonight's win wouldn't be the answer to all her problems, Nadine took comfort in knowing that this win would at least give her a break from hearing how pathetic she was. And best of all, even if only for a little while, her nickname would return to "baby" instead of being the other "B word" that had become so common in recent weeks.

Chapter 2

Why Can't This Be Me?

"Here you go, hun. Two sweet teas for the best legal minds this side of heaven," announced the server as she carefully placed one frosted glass in front of Nadine and then the other in front of Trina.

Almost every time the attorney friends came to Moe's Southwestern Grill, they enjoyed the services of the same waitress. Miranda was a woman in her early forties, but she tended to look younger. With her slim frame and her hair always in signature waist-length braids, she had the appearance of someone who should be serving free throws on the basketball court instead of meals in a restaurant.

"And you're definitely one of the best waitresses," Nadine complimented with a smile. She didn't really know the woman personally, but four years ago, she had successfully defended Miranda's son after he was wrongfully accused of being the masked gunman in a bank robbery on the city's eastside.

As it turned out, the only two things the then fourteen-year-old had really been guilty of were being in the wrong area at the wrong time and having his mother's genes—which caused him to be very tall for his age. Sharing the real offender's curly black hair and six-two stature had the eighth grader in dangerously hot water for a while. Had it not been for Nadine's impeccable defense skills, he would be serving time for a crime he never committed instead of preparing to go off to college on a four-year track scholarship.

His mother hadn't stopped trying to pay Nadine back yet. Every time she came, if Miranda was on duty, Nadine got the royal treatment. "Anything else I can get you? Y'all sure you don't want appetizers while you wait for your meals?" Miranda offered. "I can give you my employee discount."

Nadine swatted the waitress's arm playfully. "What have I told you about that? You're not giving us any discounts. And we're skipping the appetizers today anyway."

"That's right," Trina added. "We want to have plenty of space in our bellies for the main course."

"Okay, hun. I'll be bringing those meals out as soon as they're ready," Miranda promised, rubbing Nadine's back before walking away.

Moe's had at least a dozen locations in metropolitan Atlanta, but the one at Colony Square on Peachtree Street was the choice for Nadine and Trina, and they met there at least twice every month. The restaurant had been a part of their lives for almost as long as they'd known each other.

Nadine pulled her straw from its wrapping and scanned the nearest walls around where they sat. "You know … we ought to be sick of this place as much as we eat here. Not to mention all the meals we gobbled up near campus. Remember how we would always go to that Moe's in D.C.?"

Trina laughed at the thought. "Girl, yes! If we had good sense, we would have invested in some Moe's stock back then. We could have ditched law a long time ago and been living large on the French Riviera somewhere."

"Perhaps," Nadine said. "But then, what would people like Miranda have done?"

"Touché." Trina raised her glass to accompany her one-word response. "Besides, we're still living the good life. Great husbands, great homes, great careers … and we can visit France any doggone time we want, right?"

"Right." Nadine watched Trina take several swallows of her tea. There was so much that she was tempted to share with her friend. She had no doubt that Trina would keep her secrets secret. Trust wasn't the issue; it was far more about timing.

Nadine was still holding on to the hope that given a little more time, everything would work itself out. The last thing she wanted to do was share something negative that would be remembered long after the problem was solved. While she might forgive Damon for the never-ending emotional roller coaster he'd had her riding over the years, Nadine wasn't sure it would be so easy for her sometimes overprotective friend to do the same.

"So, have things finally calmed down for you and Damon?" It was almost like Trina was reading her thoughts. "It's been a month since the election, so I suspect it has."

Nadine smiled. Things were on a good streak right now both professionally and personally, and she was genuinely happy about that. How long it would last was anybody's guess, but Nadine was determined to enjoy it while she could. "Well, the phone doesn't ring as much, and we were actually able to go out to dinner last weekend without being hounded by the paparazzi," she responded. "Damon's schedule is always busy, though, and being a mayor can sometimes be a stress point."

"I imagine so, but he keeps running for re-election, so he must love it. Mayor Deville thrives off that stress, girl. He just won his fourth term. He's an old pro now."

Nadine shrugged her shoulders. "I guess," she managed to mutter before pausing to enjoy a sip of tea. "But enough about me and Damon. With all the demands of the election, and with you agreeing to step up and take a lot of my workload so I could be available for the campaign demands, we haven't had the chance to really catch up."

"I know, right? This is the first time we've had lunch together, in what? Six weeks?"

"At least," Nadine replied. "So, what's been going on with you and Bradley? I know you weren't very happy about his decision to buy that motorcycle. Do you cringe every time he takes it for a ride?"

Trina sat forward in her seat. "Oh, it really has been a while since we hung out and talked. He decided not to buy it." "What? What happened?" Nadine's eyes widened at the news. Bradley had been firm in his decision to get a bike as a fiftieth birthday present to himself. His birthday was two weeks ago, and Nadine had been sure that he'd gone out immediately and made the purchase to commemorate the milestone. The conversation between the women had to be placed on a brief pause as Miranda returned to their table with their meals perfectly balanced on the tray she carried. She handed Nadine hers first.

"Here is your yummy usual, hun. The Homewrecker Burrito, loaded with veggies and organic tofu, and of course, topped off with pico de gallo and guacamole." Miranda then turned her attention toward Trina. "And for you, the Chicken Club Quesadilla with extra cheese and extra chicken. Can I get either one of you anything else?"

When both ladies shook their heads to indicate their satisfaction, Miranda added, "Well, enjoy. In the meantime, here are some extra napkins, and I'll be back in a little bit to bring those glasses of water that I know you'll want once you're done with that tea."

"Thank you, Miranda," Nadine said while giggling. "You're the best."

"The best deserves only the best," she replied over her shoulder while walking away.

"Now, if that doesn't tell you how much we eat here, nothing does," Trina commented. "That lady even knows that we're going to want water instead of refills on our tea."

"Miranda knows what I want to eat, and she knows my face, but sometimes, I wonder if she remembers my name," Nadine observed. "Have you noticed that she never calls me anything other than 'hun'?"

"Well, at least she calls you something. I don't think she's ever called me anything. In her head, I guess I'm just 'hun's friend'."

The ladies shared a good laugh before taking a moment to grace their food so they could dig in. Nadine rarely got anything other than the Homewrecker Burrito during their frequent lunch-hour visits. She took her first bite and savored its flavor before continuing the conversation they'd started earlier.

"Okay, so finish telling me why Bradley changed his mind. Did he get cold feet?"

"Oh, no; nothing like that." Trina used a napkin to wipe her mouth before continuing. "He came to me the night before his birthday and said that the best gift he could give himself was to know that he had made me happy."

Nadine's hand fluttered to her chest. "Oh my God; are you serious?"

Trina nodded her head. "He gave me a small gift box, and when I opened it, it had the ripped-up application that had been approved for his purchase of the motorcycle."

Nadine sat back in her chair. "Wow, that was really sweet." One thing she knew for sure—Damon would never have done anything like that. If he'd said he was going to get a bike, he would have gotten it regardless of what she thought. In fact, knowing she was against the idea might have made him buy two instead of one.

The importance of Bradley's decision not to get the motorcycle ran deeper than most people knew. Bradley and Trina would celebrate eleven years of marriage in the next couple of months. He had come into Trina's life and won her heart despite her vow to never fall in love again.

Trina's first marriage ended tragically when her husband, Jamal, died from the massive injuries he'd sustained in a motorcycle accident. JJ, their son, was only two at the time. Jamal's death had turned Trina's world upside down. He had been her college sweetheart and eventually followed her all the way to Atlanta. They married in a beautiful, intimate ceremony and enjoyed six years of marriage before the unthinkable ended it all. Trina would often hop on the seat behind Jamal, wrap her arms around his waist, and ride along with him. But as much as she seemed to love the two-wheeler life before Jamal's accident, Trina hadn't even touched a motorcycle since his death. "I had stopped nagging Bradley about the whole thing, so I was shocked when he told me he wasn't going to make the purchase," Trina said. "I prayed about it and left it alone because it wasn't worth the constant debating. Honestly, I had set my mind to just accept that he was going to get one."

"I prayed about it and left it alone …" Trina's words repeated themselves in Nadine's mind as she sat quietly and slowly chewed her food. She had been praying about Damon's and her situation too. They had stretches of good times—like right now, but the bad times seemed to be coming more frequently than ever before.

Nadine knew that God still heard and answered prayers; her aunt was good for saying that every chance she got. Aunt Pat would follow that by announcing, "He may not come when you want Him, but He's right on time." Nadine didn't know what God's clock said, but clearly, it wasn't synced with hers.

"I can't tell you how glad I am that Bradley didn't get that motorcycle," Trina said. "He still plans to get a new vehicle, but now he's looking at a Camaro."

"Okay, this is beginning to sound like a midlife crisis situation."

Trina nodded her head in agreement. "I said the same thing, but you know what? I'm so happy he didn't get the motorcycle that he could buy a doggone cruise ship right now and I wouldn't care."

Every time Nadine had these talks with Trina, she took conceptual notes hoping something that was said might help if she applied it to her own home life. Am I nagging Damon? Is that why things get so heated between us? Do I know when to back down? As the thoughts filtered through her mind, Nadine filed them away. She would recall them later when she was alone and could do a thorough self-examination.

The Richards had the kind of bond that most Atlantans erroneously thought she shared with Damon. Nadine knew there was no such thing as a perfect marriage, but the love Trina and Bradley had for one another was unmistakable. They were a husband and wife that knew how to disagree without being disrespectful. They knew how to argue without accusing and how to debate without defaming.

Nadine accepted the fresh glass of water that Miranda handed her, and Miranda accepted the company credit card that was given to her in exchange. Nadine used the water to wash down her last mouthful of food. It helped clear her thoughts too.

"So, what color Camaro do you think Bradley's going to get?" she asked.

"Well, if this is really a midlife crisis—fire engine red." Nadine tried not to laugh, but after noticing the horrified look on her friend's face, she laughed out loud. Envisioning Bradley driving around town in a bright red Camaro was an entertaining thought, but if any middle-aged man could pull it off and make it look cool, he probably would be the one.

Bradley was a businessman who breathed new life into a construction company that had closed its doors. The business had been a notable one in Atlanta. It had passed down through four generations, but the fifth had no interest in carrying it on. The building had begun to depreciate after sitting unoccupied for five years.

Bradley's dad had been on the staff of that construction company for many years before he retired. Seeing the place die that had once supplied the resources that kept his family off welfare was more than Bradley could sit by and bear. He landed a bank loan that allowed him to remodel the structure, acquire the necessary equipment, and hire a small, but capable, staff. It turned out to be a wise investment. The new company opened under the name of B.R. Builders, and it became an instant success. It was Bradley's construction company that built Nadine and Damon's home.

"Girl, look at the time," Trina suddenly said as Miranda brought the receipt to the table. "Didn't you mention at our morning staff meeting that you had to meet with a client this afternoon?"

"Thanks, hun," Miranda interrupted as she accepted Nadine's signed copy of the receipt, along with a generous cash tip. "And I hope whatever client you're going to see today knows just how lucky they are."

"Thank you, Miranda." Nadine returned the waitress's smile before she walked away to tend to another set of customers at a nearby table. Glancing at her watch, Nadine said, "I still have plenty of time to get to my meeting; I'm going to head there straight from here."

Trina lowered her voice and leaned in close. "This meeting you have … is it with the lady that shot her husband?"

"He's not her husband, he is her boyfriend. And this meeting isn't with her; it's with the boyfriend and his legal representative."

"What do you think your chances are of getting the charges against her reduced?"

"If she's telling the truth—which I believe she is—getting the charges reduced shouldn't be difficult. This is clearly not a case of aggravated assault."

"Even though there was a weapon present?" Trina looked doubtful.

"Yes, because rest assured, there's more going on than meets the eye. There are several instances of calls being made to the police because my client was being beaten by this guy, and she has bruises—both old and fresh—to corroborate those reports. There are even a couple of hospital records I've requisitioned, one with her being seen because of a displaced shoulder, and another where she received eight stitches in her head. That incident happened so recently that the stitches are still there."

"Let me guess," Trina said. "She kept dropping the charges and going back to him."

Nadine nodded. "And police couldn't hold him without her pressing charges. She loved him, so she wanted to believe him when he said it wouldn't happen again. With this shooting incident, he claims that she flew into a jealous rage when she walked in on him and another woman, so she tried to kill him. On the other hand, my client insists that he pulled the gun on her when she threatened to leave him after another one of his infamous beatings. According to her, the gun went off during a struggle."

"Both stories are credible," Trina pointed out.

"Normally, I would agree. But, the bullet struck his underarm area. It would have been nearly impossible for my client to pull the trigger and the bullet to land there."

"What if he raised his arms like he was surrendering to her when he saw her with the gun?" Trina posed. "Could that have given the bullet opportunity to lodge where it did?"

"That's exactly what he claims happened. But if they were positioned the way he described in his deposition, it's still not probable. He said they were facing each other directly. He would have had to be turned toward the side in addition to having his arms raised for that to be believable without reasonable doubt."

Trina drummed the table with her fingers like she was a juror pondering over the testimonies she'd heard. "On the other hand, it would make sense for that to be the point of entry of the bullet if they were tussling over the gun as your client said."

"Exactly," Nadine stated. "In a struggle, the gun could have turned upward in that manner, and either one of them could have pulled the trigger in that case. Add that to the fact that his witness hasn't been identified nor has she come forward to corroborate his story. Where is this mystery woman he claims my client found him with?"

Trina released a knowing grunt as they both stood from the table and prepared to leave. "You're going after getting the charges dropped altogether, aren't you?"

"That's exactly what I'm going for. I believe it's an open and shut case of self-defense, and you best believe that if he forces me into a courtroom, I'm going to make good use of it. I've already subpoenaed his middle school and high school records. His abusiveness didn't start with my client. This boy has been slapping around girls since he was thirteen. If we have to take this to trial, I'm going to make his mama wish she'd never laid down with his daddy."

Trina laughed as they exited Moe's together. "And I know you will. I'll see you back at the office later. I can't wait to hear how the meeting goes."

Nadine returned Trina's wave as they parted ways. With a push of a button, her BMW X5 cranked before she opened the door and climbed into the driver's seat. While she waited for lunch hour traffic to clear so she could pull onto the street, Nadine reminisced about the day, two weeks ago, when she sat down with her client for the first time.

Rebecca was her name. She was a twenty-two-year-old brunette whose beauty could be seen despite her stitches and scars. Rebecca had been in an "on again/off again" relationship with her boyfriend for four years. When Nadine met the young lady at the county jail, she could see the worry in Rebecca's eyes. One of the first questions she asked was whether her abuser was going to make a full recovery. Even after he'd basically tried to kill her, the girl's first concern was for his well-being.

With a clear opening, Nadine navigated her SUV onto the roadway. Her heart truly went out to Rebecca. Poor thing. She was so young when she got involved with her abuser that she probably didn't even realize she deserved better.

Chapter 3

Petty Pride

"You must be Attorney Jackson's husband."

Who knew that such a simple greeting had the power to ignite a flame that would turn into a towering inferno? Nadine sat on the side of her soaker tub massaging her temples with her fingers. She pretended to have to use the restroom just to get some sense of peace, but she knew this argument was far from over. Nadine imagined Damon was standing just outside the door waiting for her return so he could ring the bell to signify the start of round two.

Their argument had been going on for an hour now, and she just wanted to put it all on mute. She could only imagine what her father-in-law was thinking. Daddy Deville's new knees may have made him move slower than normal, but there was nothing wrong with his ears. He never acted as though he could hear their all-too-frequent disagreements, but the angrier Damon got, the louder the volume of his voice rose. It wasn't possible that his father couldn't hear him.

Grudgingly, Nadine stood from her seated position, walked to the commode, and watched the water inside the toilet bowl quickly empty and refill itself when she flushed it. She had no real reason to wash her hands, but if she wanted her little pretense to have a smidgen of believability, Nadine needed to at least let the faucets run to complete the act.

"The fact that you didn't fire her on the spot tells me something right there," Damon said as soon as Nadine re-entered the bedroom. "Some li'l heifer calls me 'Attorney Jackson's husband,' and you stand there looking like a fool—like I don't have a name or nothing."

"She's new, Damon," Nadine said for what felt like the hundredth time. "I just hired Ava a week ago. She didn't know—"

Damon banged the dresser with his fist so hard that the sudden sound of the impact made Nadine wince. "I'm the mayor of Atlanta!" he said, swearing before continuing. "I don't care if you just hired her five minutes before I got there. She knows my name!"

"I will speak with her tomorrow, okay? First thing in the morning, I will talk to her."

"Talk to her?" Damon scowled, and then repeated, "Talk to her? You're gonna do more than talk to her. I want her fired!"

"Fired?"

"Yes, fired!"

"Just because she didn't say your name?" It was Nadine's turn to scowl. He couldn't be serious. "Damon, I can't do that. She's a very good legal administrative assistant. I went almost a month without one after my last one moved to Connecticut. Admins with legal backgrounds don't come a dime a dozen—not good ones. This one is someone that Trina met at a business meet and greet. She left another firm to come to us. I can't just pull the rug from under her like that."

"What kind of wife are you?" he snarled. "You ain't worth the ring I put on your finger. You're more concerned about how Ava's gonna feel than how I feel. Here I am—your husband—telling you that she pissed me off, and you standing there telling me 'bout how you don't want to hurt her feelings. How stupid is that? What about my feelings? Huh? They don't mean nothing to you? You did without an admin for a month before, you can do without an admin for a month again. I don't care what you gotta do. Make up something if you have to, but I want her terminated!"

Nadine took in a deep breath, and then slowly released it. This was the dumbest thing she'd ever heard. Damon was being completely unreasonable. First of all, he had no right or authority to demand that she fire anybody from a business that she built from the ground up. That was her name on the wall, not his.

Secondly, Ava had been a godsend. She came so highly recommended that Nadine had been prepared to go into a salary bidding war with the girl's previous employer if it came down to it. She wasn't about to cut her from the staff because of Damon's petty pride.

Nadine took another deep breath and then tried her defense from another angle. "I wouldn't be able to justify firing her," she reasoned. "Everybody there loves her. This was a group selection. Ava's hiring got 100% pre-approval from the attorneys."

That last part was only half true. Other than Trina, the associate attorneys hadn't even had a say-so in the hiring, but they really were happy with the decision.

Nadine continued. "I can't just make up something on her. It wouldn't be believable. Trina was the one who recommended Ava, and Damon, you know how thorough Trina is. If there was even one bone from a skeleton in her closet, Trina would have—"

"Trina, Trina, Trina!" Damon's tone was snide and mocking. "I get so tired of hearing about Trina. Trina said this. Trina did that. You're too stupid to even realize that Trina is half of your problem."

"What?" Nadine couldn't believe her ears. Her best friend had never spoken negatively of Damon, at least not in her presence. In fact, Trina, like most Atlantans, thought pretty highly of Mayor Deville, and Nadine had always assumed the feeling was mutual. She searched Damon's face for any sign of hypocrisy but found none. Nadine felt the back of her neck heating up. Her best friend was beautiful both inside and out; he had no reason to talk about her in that manner. "What has Trina ever done to you?"

"It ain't what she's doing to me, it's what she's doing to you," he replied. "If you didn't spend so much time with her, you might have a better marriage."

"Trina has a great marriage. How is *she*, my problem?" As soon as the words left her mouth, Nadine wished she could grab them back. But it was too late. She hadn't meant them the way she knew her husband would take them, and she braced herself to hear the bell for round three.

"Oh, so Trina has a great husband, but yours is trash; is that it?" It was posed as more of an accusation than a question.

Damon had been loud before, but now, he might as well open the room door and give his dad a front-row seat.

Nadine wanted to say something to clarify her remark, but she knew it would be a waste of her words and her time. Her heart rate quickened when Damon made a sudden move, grabbed her brush from the vanity, and hurled it across the room in her direction. The brush missed by at least five feet, coming to rest on the floor of Nadine's open walk-in closet. He clearly hadn't meant to hit her, but he'd probably gotten some twisted satisfaction from startling her.

"I ought to punch you in your face!" Damon said through clenched teeth. "This is why wives get slapped around by husbands. I'm too nice!" he barked, using a few choice words in between. "Any other man would put you in a coma for comparing him to some other woman's husband."

"I didn't compare you to Bradley," Nadine said while trying to keep her own emotions at bay. His insults and threats were beginning to take a toll on her, but she didn't know whether she felt sadness, anger, or both. "You said if it weren't for Trina, I would have a better marriage. I was just pointing out that there was nothing wrong with her marriage. I don't understand how she can have a negative impact on mine if hers is good."

"Because, like I said, you're comparing me to Bradley," Damon charged. "You're looking at what he lets her get away with, and you think you can pull those same tricks on me. Don't you ever, ever think you can talk to me like she talks to him. When I say something, it's the law. I don't need you putting in your two cents. It ain't up for discussion. Do you think just because they discuss stuff, I'm gonna do it too? Well, you're wrong," he said, not even giving her a chance to reply. "Bradley's a punk. I ain't no punk."

"I can't even believe you're saying these things. Bradley and Trina are our closest friends. We double-date with them and everything."

"No. They are your closest friends," Damon stressed. "These are people I just put up with 'cause they came with the package. They were already a part of your life when I married you. I was forced to be the fourth wheel on y'all's raggedy jalopy." These were spiteful words Nadine had never heard before. She wanted to think Damon was just saying them out of anger and in an attempt to be hurtful. She wanted to believe that he didn't truly mean any of it. But in her heart of hearts, she knew he did.

"I've never heard them say one bad thing about you." Nadine's words were just above a whisper like she was talking to herself.

"Yeah, right!" Damon's retort came without any hesitation. "I know y'all talk about me when I'm not around. I ain't nearly as dumb as you think I am. All three of y'all think because you have more education than I do, you're smarter than I am. But all smarts don't come from books. I'm smart enough to take my God-given position in this marriage. I'm the HNIC, not you.

You're not the first woman that tried to overrun my authority. It didn't work for her, and it ain't gonna work for you either."

In times like this, Nadine wished she knew Damon's ex-wife. She longed for just one opportunity to reach out to her and find out the truth about what happened in their failed marriage. The longer she was married to Damon the more certain she was that everything he'd told her in his one-sided story was a lie. When their arguments got overheated, he had the tendency to refer to his previous marriage and remind Nadine of times when he had to set his ex-wife straight.

"See, Bradley would've walked in your office and been okay with that chick calling him 'Attorney Trina Richards' husband'," Damon continued, interrupting Nadine's thoughts. "It wouldn't have bothered him to be disrespected like that, but I'm not letting no low-level glorified secretary refer to me like I'm not the head of my house. That's why you like him so much, and that's why you think he's the perfect husband—because he lets Trina walk all over him."

Nothing he said was the truth, but Nadine was tired of the whole thing. An outburst of music from her phone notified her that someone was calling. It was a welcome sound and would give her a perfect opportunity for escape. Even if it was a client that she didn't particularly want to talk to, she was going to answer just to deflect the dialogue she was having with Damon.

Nadine pulled her cell from her purse and felt the instant deflation of her hope at the sight of Trina's image on the display screen. There was absolutely no way she was going to answer. Not only did Nadine not want to deal with Damon's response to her "disrespecting him" by choosing to take Trina's call in the middle of their conversation, but she also didn't want her best friend to detect any stress that might be heard in her voice if she answered the call. Trina had a self-proclaimed sixth sense that Nadine sometimes really believed existed.

She silenced the notification and then sank onto the side of the bed and buried her face in her hands. For the last few weeks, things had been going well. She and Damon hadn't had an argument of this magnitude since the one that took place on the eve of his re-election. They had been enjoying lighthearted days and some passionate nights. Even today, things had been good up until the moment Damon came to her office.

He had stopped by to surprise her by personally delivering a bouquet of beautiful, exotic flowers and taking her out to lunch, but the lunch never happened. Nadine only knew that it was a part of the original plan because she'd read the card on the flowers he'd resentfully left behind. There was no way not to leave them there without raising questions, and Damon never showed this side of himself to the public. He couldn't. He had an image to uphold. Nobody knew this Damon Deville except her.

"I meant what I said, Nadine," Damon insisted.

Nadine changed her posture and looked up at him. "What you said about what?"

"What do you mean, 'about what'?" he responded. Damon had a look of renewed disgust on his face.

"You said you meant what you said," Nadine reminded him. "Which thing are you talking about?"

Damon walked up to her, squatted to her seated level, and placed his face close to hers as if talking to a child who needed eye-to-eye contact to understand his words. He said the sentence slowly like she was in a special needs class and had trouble comprehending.

"I want her fired tomorrow morning. Are you understanding the words coming out of my mouth?"

Nadine returned his stare. For a man who demanded respect, he handed out disrespect like cheap Halloween candy. If she'd ever spoken to him in the manner that he was speaking to her right now, Nadine hated even to think about what his reaction would be.

"I can't do that, Damon. I will talk to her, and I promise I'll make sure it doesn't happen again, but I can't fire her for this."

"What do you mean you can't fire her?" He yelled the question as if they were standing five yards apart instead of five inches. "You own the place. You can fire anybody you want to fire!"

"Yes, it is my place," she said in an exasperated tone. "And because of that, I can also keep anybody I want to keep."

The expression that washed over Damon's face made Nadine shrink back and wish she could have a do-over of the last ten seconds. His nostrils flared, and his eyes became the size of quarters. For the first time in their marriage, and for the first time in any argument they'd had, Nadine braced herself for a physical backlash.

Instead, he swore at her before punching the space on the mattress beside where she sat. Then he handed Nadine a dare that she knew better than to accept.

"Say it again; I dare you."

Nadine felt her insides trembling, and she was sure that her outsides did the same. She swallowed all the words that she wished she had the courage to say.

Damon slowly raised his index finger, bringing it to a stop just a fraction of an inch away from the space between Nadine's eyes. "You will fire her, and that's that."

When he finally stood up and backed away from her, Nadine released a breath that she didn't even realize she had been holding.

"I don't even want to hear your excuses," he warned. "It's not as if I'm asking you to fire your precious Trina. You just met this chick, and you're putting her feelings before mine?"

"This is not about putting anybody's feelings before yours, Damon; it's just that—"

"It's just that, what?" Damon looked down at her as if he dared her to finish the sentence. "You don't seem to understand what I'm saying, Nadine. I'm not asking you to fire her, I'm telling you to fire her. This ain't a multiple-choice test."

"I signed a one-year contract with her, Damon. I can't fire her without legal ramifications."

It wasn't a half-truth. It wasn't even a partial truth. It was a whole lie, but Nadine felt as though she had no other choice. The only way she'd be able to make her husband retract his unreasonable demand was to get him to believe it would hurt him on the back end.

Through his actions and his words, Damon had proven that *he* was the only person he cared about. Nadine's last-minute desperate decision was to convince Damon the firing would be a mistake that would adversely affect not her, but him.

"If I break that contract, she can retaliate," Nadine went on to explain. "She works in the legal industry, so she knows her rights. And, if she retaliates by going to the media, this would be a mess that I may not be able to clean up before it directly affects you. I don't want to see 'Mayor's wife robs single mom of income' in the headlines any more than you do."

Damon eyes shifted to Nadine once more. The earlier annoyance on his face had been replaced by concern. "Single mom?" he asked with raised eyebrows.

Nadine nodded. "Samuel, age four; Rachel, age two; and Joel just turned six months."

"That news headline is all Wynette Ingalls-Newhouse would need to see," Damon mumbled while scratching his chin and pacing to the other end of the master suite.

"That's right," Nadine quickly said. "Her whole platform was about helping women, especially working moms. She couldn't use this to take back the election she lost, but I guarantee you she'd use it to make you look bad."

"It would be her final act of revenge, her last stab in my back," Damon said.

"Exactly. I don't want to be the one to give her the knife she'd use to do it."

Damon's voice broke the brief silence that lingered. "Okay, fine. Don't fire her, but make sure you talk to her and let her know she'd better put some respect on my name from now on."

"I'll talk to her first thing tomorrow."

When Damon turned and walked into his closet, Nadine escaped to the master bathroom again and locked the door behind her. She quickly turned on the shower to ensure Damon wouldn't start talking to her through the door. This discussion had to be over and done with, but as big of a lie as it was, Nadine couldn't help feeling a sense of accomplishment that she'd outplayed Damon at his own game.

Sunday was two days away. She would ask God for forgiveness during morning worship. Forgiveness not only for lying about the contract, but also for creating three children—all under the age of five and all with names from the Bible—that her assistant didn't even have.

Chapter 4

Get Out

Talk about Monday morning blues! Not since the death of her father could Nadine remember crying as much as she had this morning. Her emotional state was so fragile that she felt the need to do something she had not done since establishing Nadine Jackson & Associates; take a mental health day.

"Girl, do you need me to come over there?" Trina had asked Nadine when she called her to let her know she'd be absent from the firm today.

"No, please don't," Nadine told her. "I appreciate the concern, but I'm fine."

"Are you sure?" Trina asked. "Is Damon there with you?"

"Yes, I'm sure. And no, he's not here. He left for work already, and I'm sure he thinks I have too," Nadine said. "I just need you to handle things at the office. I'll be in first thing in the morning. I need some rest today, that's all. I'm fine. I promise."

But Nadine wasn't really doing fine. Since Friday's argument with Damon, her emotions had been on a rollercoaster, except there had been no thrills, and there had been far more downs than ups. But, while she had been struggling with managing the aftermath of it all, Damon seemed to be handling it just fine.

Saturday morning had brought some sense of calm after she convinced Damon, the night before, that the satisfaction he'd get from having her terminate Ava would not be worth the backlash. Along with that calm, however, came silence. Very few words were spoken between them Saturday, but Nadine would prefer that any day over the arguing.

The lack of communication between them on Saturday had been mostly her fault. She'd intentionally made herself scarce to escape the chaos. Nadine spent over two hours at the gym, working out until every single muscle in her body had been tested, and from there, she made a last-minute decision to join Trina and several other ladies in the women's ministry at the church who had a calendar appointment to visit the pastor's aging mother in the nursing home.

The whole time she was serving with the women's ministry, Nadine felt Trina's suspicions. The mask she wore on her face as a COVID-19 precaution wasn't wide enough to block the sensation Nadine felt from Trina's burning stares. Nadine was trying her best not to give any negative vibes, but she was concerned that her bestie was somehow able to see through her happy veneer.

The last thing she needed was for Trina to discern a problem between her and Damon. During Saturday's ministry visitation,

Nadine had gone overboard in her attempt to act "normal" by laughing where laughter was warranted as she fellowshipped with the others. But, in her gut, she knew Trina wasn't fully buying it. Despite that, Nadine was able to get through the day and part ways with her friend without being questioned.

While she was keeping herself busy outside the house, Damon was spending his rare Saturday with no government obligations at home. He didn't like Nadine to be away from the house on weekends if she wasn't busy helping him look good as the mayor. So, her extended absence would likely have started an argument within itself if it weren't for Daddy Deville.

After having been forced to spend long days and nights in bed following double-knee replacement surgery, Damon's dad had finally reached a point where he could get out of bed and move around with the help of a walker. On Saturday, he wanted to walk out of his bedroom and into what had become his favorite corner of their home, the theatre room. It was Major League baseball season, and Daddy Deville loved watching sports with his son on the big screen mounted on the wall there. Damon shared his dad's appreciation for sports.

When Nadine finally returned home on Saturday, she fully expected to be met with Damon's displeasure of her being away. Instead, she walked into the house and up the stairs to their master suite without even seeing her husband. The sounds she heard confirmed that he was still in the theatre room enjoying ballgames. Nadine could hear Damon and Daddy Deville cheering and jeering. Father nor son came out of their recreational area until Nadine called them out for dinner an hour and a half later.

Saturday evening, Damon carried on as if he hadn't been viciously throwing things at Nadine just a few hours earlier. And that night, as they lay in bed together, he proceeded to be intimate with her as if he hadn't callously demeaned her with vile name-calling the day before. Nadine offered no resistance; she never did. She had learned how to go through the motions, and she always hoped Damon's lovemaking was a sign that he was genuinely changing.

They'd gotten up the next morning, showered, put on their Sunday best, and gone to church as normal. Damon looked as holy as holy could look when he took his place among the other associate ministers at the church yesterday. It was his assigned Sunday to speak, and the sanctuary was full.

"If someone says, 'I love God', and hates his brother, he is a liar!" Damon emphasized as he reffered to 1 John 4:20. "For he who does not love his brother whom he has seen, how can he love God whom he has not seen?"

Each time her husband preached, Nadine was reminded that Rev. Damon Deville was just as popular as Mayor Damon Deville. And on Sunday, the reverend in him preached like he was gunning for the pastor's job. By the time Damon was done with his sermon, the audience was in a Holy Ghost frenzy with the ushers working overtime to keep up with the demand.

Nadine tried to be as captivated as they were, but she knew too much. She's seen and heard too much. She'd experienced too much. She had the inside scoop, and as far as Nadine was concerned, Damon's message should have made him search his own soul. He was always talking about God, but almost every time he did, it was to somehow prove his own authority.

Damon used God as justification for his behavior. As far as Nadine was concerned, what she got from him on a daily basis was a long way from the love he preached about.

She thought she'd done a good job hiding what she'd felt on the inside during the service, but when she and Trina came face to face after the benediction, Nadine knew that she wasn't as good an actor as she thought. She also knew her friend wasn't going to avoid the issue again, as she'd done on Saturday.

"Are you okay?" Trina asked when the two of them found themselves alone in the ladies' lavatory.

Nadine had stepped into the restroom to powder her face. Had she known when she first walked in that Trina was the person in the stall who had just flushed the commode, she would have been okay with a little nose shine.

"Huh?" Nadine made a valiant effort to appear baffled that her friend would even ask such a question. "What do you mean?" She was trying her best not to lie. Nadine had done enough of that already. Between telling Damon that her admin was a single mother of three, and then telling him in bed last night that he was the best lover ever, she'd spent half of today's service asking God to forgive her.

Trina used the sink beside Nadine to wash her hands, looking at her in the mirror while she did. "You just seem not quite yourself lately; that's what I mean. I wanted to say something to you yesterday, but we were so busy at the nursing home that I didn't get to steal you away."

"I'm just a little tired, I guess. I had a long workout at the gym that included ninety minutes on the treadmill before coming to the nursing home." It wasn't a lie. Natalie really was tired when she came to help the women's ministry.

Trina looked at her like she wasn't quite convinced. "And today?"

"I don't know," Nadine said with a shrug of her shoulders. "I added some strength training to my routine yesterday too. My body is still a little sore from that, so I guess that's got me moving a little slow."

Nadine wanted to shake her head at herself. Her body wasn't sore in the least. She was doing so well with telling the truth, but Trina just wouldn't let it go. Now, she would have to ask forgiveness for another blatant lie.

Trina delayed her response long enough to allow the air-blowing wall unit to get her hands semi-dry. As soon as the noise silenced, she turned to face Nadine. "Are you sure that's all it is? You know you can tell me anything and I'll—"

Her statement was left unfinished when their privacy was invaded by two other ladies who chose that moment to join them in the restroom. For Nadine, their entrance provided the perfect opening for her getaway.

"I need to go and catch up with Damon," she quickly told her friend, delivering her a quick hug in the process. "I'll see you at the office in the morning, okay?"

She didn't give Trina time to agree or disagree. Damon was still receiving the last of the accolades from congregants who were shaking his hand and patting him on the back about the day's sermon when Nadine re-entered the sanctuary. A few minutes later, he was opening his car door for her to get in so they could head home.

"You're not going to say anything about how I preached today?"

They had barely pulled out of the parking lot when Damon posed the question.

"Oh, yes," Nadine replied. "It was really good."

Even though he was driving, she could feel Damon side-eying her. She hoped her quick response would be enough to save her from another argument. It wasn't.

"It was really good," he echoed in a mocking tone. Damon then released a dry laugh and added, "You make me so sick." Maybe if she said nothing at all, it would fizzle. Years ago, when she and Sophia were little girls, their dad used to say they could avoid an argument if they refused to participate in it.

"A person can't argue all by themselves," Alex Jackson would say. But their dad hadn't met Damon. Not participating in a dispute that Damon was committed to only fueled his fire. "All you got to say is that it was a good message?" he prodded.

"What else do you want me to say? I enjoyed it."

"Really? I sure couldn't tell. You sat there looking stupid just about the whole time I was up there. Other people were standing up, waving their hands, shouting, but you—you just sat there like a concrete statue."

Nadine shook her head in dispute. "That's not true. I was saying amen; I was clapping."

"Oh, well, I guess I couldn't hear your whisper over all the other people's yells, and I couldn't hear your patty cake claps over the other people's enthusiastic applause."

Closing her eyes, Nadine pressed her weight against the back of her seat wishing that she could somehow apply so much pressure that the leather would open and swallow her inside. Her head had barely stopped hurting from Friday night's ordeal. She wasn't expecting another bout this soon.

Her eyes opened at the sound of the safety seal breaking from the water bottle Damon had brought from the church. He took several slow swigs. The sound of each swallow sounded almost threatening. It didn't take long for Nadine to realize Damon was moisturizing his throat for battle.

"You just love trying to make me look foolish, don't you?" he accused. "And in front of all the church folks too. You think I'm the only one that noticed your cold response to my sermon? If you were going to just sit there, the least you could have done was sit in the back so nobody could see you. But you sat in the front on purpose, didn't you? You wanted to be front and center while you sat there with a stone face."

Nadine didn't know if her husband had been imagining things during the worship service or if he was just telling an outright lie. While she wasn't dancing and shouting like others were doing, she hadn't been unresponsive either.

"When the other associate ministers give their sermons, their wives are their biggest cheerleaders," Damon went on to say. "They don't let nobody else, and especially not other women, out-shout them while their man is up preaching. But when I get up, my wife acts like she's trying to send some silent message to the church members so they'll think I must not be worthy of her support."

"Damon, when have I ever not supported you?" Nadine could keep her silence no longer. "This isn't the first time you've accused me of this, but I honestly can't think of anything you've been involved in at any point in our marriage where I haven't supported you. Whether it's in government, community, or church, I've always been there."

"That's the problem!" Damon accused. "All you've ever been is there! Just there, and nothing else. You don't do nothing to show that you appreciate me."

Nadine sat forward and looked at him. "Like what, Damon? I've campaigned for you during your last two elections. I've hosted several dinners that you've had with other church ministers or business constituents at our house. Is that not showing support? Is that not showing appreciation? What else do you want me to do?"

"You can get out on the floor and shout like the other preachers' wives do when they're preaching, for one!"

"Are you serious? You really want me to get out on the floor, play with God, and pretend to be caught up in the Spirit?" Damon released an oath and slammed his hand on the steering wheel, causing the car to swirl a bit. "What do you mean, pretend? Why do you have to pretend? You think all the other wives who shout when their husbands preach are pretending?"

Nadine opened her mouth but closed it again. She wanted to tell him those other wives could probably be real in their rejoicing because their husbands were living what they were preaching. But Nadine knew if she wanted this argument to end any time soon, it wouldn't be wise to speak her mind.

"Is that what you're saying?" Damon persisted.

"No, I'm not saying they're pretending, but if I got out there, I would be. Damon, this isn't some personal attack on you. You've never seen me get out on the floor and shout like that when anybody else preached either. People express worship in different ways, and that's just not the way God moves me."

"Well, I've seen you stand, clap, and wave your hands before."

"Yes; I'll do those things when the Spirit moves me."

"I've never seen you do it when I'm speaking. So, what are you saying?" Damon challenged. "The Spirit don't ever move you when I'm speaking?"

Nadine's voice got caught in her throat. She didn't want to affirm what her husband had said because nothing good would come of that. At the same time, she didn't want to add any more lies to the new list she'd started in the bathroom at church either.

"Why're you sitting there looking stupid?" Damon said, pressing the brake harder than necessary as he approached the red light. "Silence gives consent, you know. Ain't that what y'all say all the time in court?"

"Actors on television might say that, but not real lawyers in real court." When Nadine mumbled those words, she was not prepared for her husband's response.

Damon picked up the open plastic water bottle he'd been drinking from earlier, held it close to her face, and squeezed hard. The liquid inside it rose to the top and squirted in her face before running down her cheeks, chin, and then onto her clothes. Nadine gasped. "Damon!"

"Don't 'Damon' me! You're lucky I didn't slap you! I done told you about trying to throw it in my face that you have more education than I do."

Nadine used a napkin she fished from her purse to try and absorb some of the liquid from the silk fabric of her dress.

"What are you talking about?" she asked. "I didn't say anything about education."

"Lawyers never say that," Damon mimicked. "You think I don't know what that means? You think I don't know that's your slick way of disrespecting me? You think I—"

"I wasn't trying to disrespect you." Nadine dabbed her face with the same napkin, but it was already too soaked to help much.

"I know you didn't just cut me off while I was talking," Damon said. "That's disrespect right there. When I'm talking, don't ever interrupt me. That's some mess that you get from Trina. She does that to Bradley, but that don't fly over here. When I'm talking, you just need to shut up."

"Damon—"

"I wasn't finished!" he yelled. "I said when I'm talking you need to shut up."

"You weren't talking. I didn't interrupt you."

"Get out!" Damon suddenly jerked the steering wheel and navigated his Bentley to the side of the road. Nadine looked at him in disbelief. "What?"

Cursing at her, Damon used the automatic button near his left hand to unlock the doors. "I said, 'Get out!'"

Nadine's hand trembled as she reached for her door handle and opened the passenger side. She turned and looked at him again, hoping he'd regain his common sense. Instead, she looked into eyes that were red with fury. Nadine wasn't going to chance saying anything more. She grabbed her purse and did as she was told. As soon as she closed the door behind her, he drove away.

Nadine looked around. She wasn't lost. She knew Atlanta like the back of her hand, so she knew exactly where she was, but she was too far from home to walk there. There were at least twenty miles between where she was and where she needed to be. A MARTA bus stop was not far away, but everybody knew her as the mayor's wife. If she boarded public transportation, she wouldn't be able to explain it away.

Nadine reached inside her purse and retrieved her phone. She didn't want to do it, but she had no other choice. There was no one else that she could trust in a time like this. There was only one number in her entire contact list that was safe to tap, and on the first ring, her call was answered.

"Hey, girl," the chipper voice on the other end said. "I'm glad you called me because I was going to call you later. What's up?"

"Trina, can you please come pick me up?" It was all Nadine could say before bursting into tears.

Chapter 5

Make The Call

Nadine awakened from a long nap without even realizing she had drifted off. She hadn't gotten much sleep last night once she finally arrived home, so it made good sense that her body needed more. It was now half past twelve, which meant she had been asleep for over two hours.

The last thing Nadine could clearly remember was making a phone call to the attorney who initially planned to prosecute her client on charges of aggravated assault, and informing him she needed to move their appointment to tomorrow. He'd sent her a message that he wanted to talk, but Nadine wasn't at all sure that he'd be speaking her language. If he wasn't willing to drop the charges altogether, it would be "no deal" for her.

Nadine took the ponytail clip off her hair, allowing her strands to break free and come to a rest just above her shoulders. Damon didn't like it when she wore it down; he never fully explained why. But, every time Nadine tried to wear her hair in any style other than her signature ponytail, he would give her a speech about how God intended for wives to maintain an appearance that pleased their husbands. If the style didn't meet his approval, Nadine was functioning in sin as far as Damon was concerned.

The shoes that Nadine had put on early this morning as she prepared for work were still on her feet. She'd gotten fully dressed but decided to stay home after Damon left. She was surprised that he hadn't bombarded her with questions when she arrived home late yesterday evening. He didn't even ask how she'd gotten home. Apparently, he didn't care.

Nadine removed her shoes and eased them onto their wood flooring. She was trying not to let Daddy Deville realize she was still in the house. He'd seen her dressed for work when she walked downstairs earlier to pour a travel mug of his freshly made coffee. He would want to know why she hadn't gone to the office, and the last thing on Nadine's mind right now was answering her father-in-law's questions. If she got hungry, the edibles they kept stashed inside the mini fridge in the sitting room down the hall would save her from having to go downstairs.

Nadine's purse was still resting on the bed where she'd placed it before falling asleep. She slid it toward her. It only took her a moment to find the business card Trina had insisted she take. Nadine's thoughts drifted back to yesterday when she told her best friend the details that led to her being left at the curbside like a trashcan.

"Please don't let Damon find out I've shared any of this with you," Nadine had said to Trina after baring her soul.

"You know I won't," Trina responded. "What I don't understand is why you're taking this crap from him. Who does he think he is?"

"It's going to be fine. Damon and I will get through this. He'd just had a bad weekend. He's the mayor of Atlanta, remember? I wouldn't want that kind of pressure Would you?"

"Well, if he can't stand the heat, why does he keep going into the kitchen? If being the mayor makes him do junk like this, maybe Wynette was the best candidate for the job."

"Oh, please. It would have been stressful for her too."

Trina smacked her lips and rolled her eyes. "Whatever. His job stress is no excuse for his behavior. Who does that anyway? Who squirts water out of a water bottle in somebody's face? What kind of grown man would just haul off and do something like that? That's worse than Will Smith slapping Chris Rock."

Nadine couldn't help but laugh at her friend's analogy. "You're crazy, girl."

"I'm not crazy, and this ain't funny. You'd better nip this in the bud, Nadine. Get him into a kickboxing class or something so he can work out those aggressions. If you don't, this kind of thing can get out of hand. Before you know it, he might be doing more than dashing water in your face. Girl, I swear, if he ever puts his hand on you—"

"Calm down, Trina," Nadine said. "You think I'd let Damon be abusive to me? I wish he would even think about doing something like that. This was just a one-time incident. Don't blow it out of proportion and make me wish I hadn't talked to you."

It was at that moment that Trina walked to her dresser and retrieved the business card that Nadine now held in her hand. Trina had told her to call the number on the card if she ever wanted to speak with a professional. When Trina suggested it yesterday, it seemed like a ridiculous idea. But as Nadine wiped away a fresh tear that rolled down her cheek, the thought didn't seem as absurd.

"Olivia Fields," Nadine whispered the name that was printed in raised lettering on the business card while she pondered the notion of calling.

Talking to a licensed therapist wasn't foreign to her. She knew the importance of mental health and wellness. After her dad passed away, Nadine completed six months of therapy. She had no problem seeking help back then. It wasn't so frowned upon when a person needed therapy after the death of a close loved one, but to talk to someone about her marriage? That was different. How did she know she could trust this stranger? Nadine had only been partially truthful with Trina. She'd left her friend believing Sunday's fiasco between her and Damon was an isolated incident. Trina would have blown a gasket if Nadine had told her how often she'd had to deal with Damon's nonsense. This therapist was someone Trina knew. Their relationship was a therapist-client one, but Trina talked about Olivia like they were somewhat friends as well. How could Nadine be sure that Olivia wouldn't slip out of professionalism and share with Trina the things Nadine wasn't ready for her to know?

"Lord, I don't know what to do." Nadine looked up at the ceiling in the bedroom as if God's throne was right there and He was sitting on it. "I just don't know what to do." She barely finished the sentence when her phone made a sound to alert her of a text message.

I JUST THOUGHT ABOUT THIS. YOU NEED TO TAKE ADVANTAGE OF THIS TIME. SINCE YOU'RE HOME ALONE, THIS WOULD BE THE PERFECT TIME TO REACH OUT TO OLIVIA.

Nadine almost laughed out loud when her eyes scanned the note that popped in from Trina. She glanced back at the ceiling again. "Okay, Lord. I hear you."

She wasn't exactly home alone, but with the layout of their house, Nadine could easily talk on the phone without Daddy Deville hearing her conversation. She still felt nervous though. Nadine trusted Trina's recommendations, but she had so much more to consider than the average woman would. As the mayor's wife, she needed to have absolutely no misgivings about Olivia's ability to keep their sessions confidential. Nadine needed a therapist who wouldn't share their discussions with anyone at all, not even with someone that she may deem trustworthy.

Damon knew far too many people for Nadine to take any chances. He didn't like anyone knowing their business. Damon didn't even confide in his father, and Daddy Deville never quizzed either of them about personal issues. There was no way that he didn't know about the marital problems they had. While Nadine always tried to keep her voice at a respectful level when they had disagreements, Damon, who despite demanding that their private life be kept private, had no filter for his voice level or his vile language when they were inside their home.

Nadine could see a slight tremble in her hands while she dialed the number on the card. At the sound of the first ring, she tapped the icon to end the call. She couldn't hear her own heartbeats, but she could certainly feel them. The pounding that was happening inside her chest was almost painful. Nadine took a deep breath and prepared to give it another try, but before she could begin dialing, her phone rang.

"Did you get my text message?" It was Trina.

God's jokes were continuing, but this time, Nadine felt no urge to laugh. Instead, she could feel tears pushing behind her eyeballs.

"Not yet, but I'm holding her card in my hand right now. I just—"

"Nadine, no excuses, please. Just call her."

"I have every intention to call her. I just need a minute. I don't know this lady as you do. She might be right for me, and she might not."

Trina released a heavy sigh, then said, "Would I have recommended her if she weren't right for you? Nadine, I know you like the back of my hand, and I'm telling you, Olivia is ideal for you. She's professional, she personable, she's honest, she's smart, and she's a Christian. What else do you need?"

"I need to know that what I share with her, stays with her," Nadine blurted. "I need to know that she's not like a lot of other so-called Christian women with loose tongues that gossip and love drama as much as women of the world. I also need to know that she's not for sale."

"For sale?"

"Yes, for sale. I need to know that she's not connected to somebody in the news industry that can slip her a couple of Benjamins. The next thing I know, Damon's face would be smeared on the eleven o'clock news or on the front cover of some rag magazine."

"First of all," Trina said, "you need to stop worrying about how this is going to affect Damon."

"He's my husband. How can I not—"

"Let me finish," Trina interrupted. "I'm not saying you don't need to care what happens to him; what I'm saying is, if you go into your counseling sessions trying to protect Damon, you're going to do yourself a disservice. This can't be about how it'll make him look. Girl, your husband put you out on the side of the road on a Sunday afternoon, just minutes after he tore the church up preaching a message. And for what? Because you didn't shout all over the church like other women do when their husbands preach. What kind of craziness is that? He needs to be talking to a therapist himself, but we both know that's not going to happen. So, the only person you need to be trying to protect right now is yourself. How 'bout you think about you for a change?"

From the start of their friendship, one of the things Nadine loved most about Trina was her candor. She could always count on her best friend to tell it like it was, whether she liked it or not. And right now, Nadine was leaning toward "not." She didn't want to hear what Trina was saying, but deep inside, she knew it was all necessary.

"Call her." There was a tone of urgency in Trina's voice. "I'd stake our friendship on Olivia," she added. "She won't betray your trust. I've shared all sorts of confidential stuff with her over the years, and nothing has ever come back to bite me in the behind. She has a five-star rating and plenty of great written reviews to back that up. If you don't get a good feeling from your initial conversation with her, then just don't call her back. But you have no reason not to take advantage of the free consultation."

She was right, and Nadine knew it. There was no good reason for her not to at least make the phone call. "I'll call," she conceded. "I'll do it right now."

As soon as they ended their call, Nadine redialed the number on the card. Two rings later, there was an answer. "Good afternoon. Olivia Fields's office. How may I help you?" the kind voice on the other end said.

"Good afternoon." Nadine paused to clear her dry throat. "Is she in? Is Olivia Fields in?"

"Yes, ma'am. But she is with a client currently. If you'll give me your name and number, I'll have her give you a call as soon as she's available."

Nadine bit her bottom lip. She didn't want to leave her name because they might figure out who she was. And she didn't want to leave her number because that might give them a clue to follow that would reveal who she was.

"Can you give me an idea of how soon she'll be available?" she asked the receptionist. "I'd rather just give her a call back if that's okay."

"That's totally fine," the young lady responded. "I'm looking at her schedule right now, and it looks like she'll be out of this meeting in about twenty minutes."

"I'll call her back in twenty-one," Nadine said with a nervous laugh.

The receptionist laughed along with her. "That would be perfect."

Nadine tried her best to keep herself preoccupied while the seconds ticked away on the clock. She eased from the master suite and took the short walk to the sitting room where she usually went when she wanted a quiet place to write in her journal. Writing had proven to be therapeutic for her, especially in recent months. It was tough not being able to talk to anyone about the challenges she had been facing in her marriage.

Just the one incident she'd spoken to Trina about yesterday had made her feel better, so this consultation with Olivia was probably going to do her some good too.

"It's a shame that we aren't closer. I should be able to talk to you," Nadine whispered while looking at a photo of her mom. Rose Jackson and Nadine had become a bit closer in more recent years, but not nearly close enough for Nadine to share intimate secrets with her. She and her mom just never had that kind of relationship, and they likely never would. If she were to call Rose right now and tell her that she was preparing to talk to a therapist, her mom would have a fit. She was one of those church folks who frowned on therapy like it was witchcraft. In Rose's opinion, prayer took care of everything, and going to a psychologist or licensed mental health provider of any kind was a sign of weak faith.

Nadine sat in the chair that was positioned at her desk and opened the top center drawer. From it, she retrieved the flash drive case where the key to her "special drawer" was hidden. Using it to open the bottom desk drawer, Nadine pulled out her journal and began writing. She didn't stop until it was time to make her call. By the time she was back in her bedroom and dialing the number, Nadine was already feeling better.

"Good afternoon. Olivia Fields's office. How may I help you?"

Apparently, it was the receptionist's standard greeting. "Yes, I called earlier, and you advised me to call back in twenty minutes when Ms. Fields would be free."

"Oh, yes ma'am. I remember. May I tell her who's calling?"

"I, uh … I'd rather not say," Nadine replied. "She was recommended to me by a friend. I'd just like to have a consultation with her."

"Her consultations are usually by appointment only, but I'll see if she's available. May I place you on a brief hold?"

"That's fine." As Nadine waited, she determined that if Olivia wouldn't take her unscheduled call, it was a sign from God that it wasn't His will for her to speak to the therapist.

"Olivia Fields speaking."

"Oh." Nadine was caught off-guard. "Hi. Uh … Ms. Fields?"

"Yes, but you can just call me Olivia."

"Okay. Hi, Olivia. Is this a good time for a consultation?"

"It is," she replied. "You chose a great day and time to call. Some days, I hardly have room to breathe between appointments, but I happen to have a while before my next session. I guess it was meant for you to call me on this specific Monday afternoon."

"I guess so," Nadine said looking up at the ceiling. God was on a roll today.

"What can I help you with?" Olivia asked.

"Well, I don't know exactly. I've been having some problems in my marriage, and a friend of mine suggested that I give you a call."

"Well, I'm honored. Please thank your friend for me when you speak with her or him again. Relationship issues aren't rare these days. Some of the best marriages have been tried over the past couple of years, so you're in good company. Marriage is challenging enough, but when you add a pandemic to it that causes a major shift in people's lifestyles, it can sometimes feel like things are spiraling out of control."

Nadine wished she could say that COVID-19 had something to do with her and Damon's problems, but theirs started well before the pandemic.

"I imagine so," she said to Olivia. "I, uh … I, uh …"

"It's okay. Take your time."

There was something soothing about Olivia's voice. Nadine found herself relaxing as she sat on the chair at her vanity and looked at her reflection in the mirror. The woman hadn't even asked for her name. It was like Olivia was saying it didn't matter who she was; her focus was to help.

"How long have you been married?" Olivia asked.

"Nine years."

"And in that time, have you ever had to speak with a counselor or licensed therapist before?"

"No," Nadine told her. "The last time I spoke to a therapist is when my father died. That was fifteen years ago."

"Did you find that treatment to be helpful?"

Nadine thought back to that time. All these years later, Alex Jackson's death was still the worst loss she'd ever suffered. If it had not been for the Christian counseling center that she'd made monthly visits to back then, she didn't know if she would have survived the grief.

"Yes," she answered honestly. "It was very helpful."

"That's good to know," Olivia replied. "The loss of a close family member can be quite traumatic. I'm glad you sought help then, and I'm glad you're seeking it now. Many people, for whatever reason, choose not to because they think it's a sign of weakness, or maybe they fear that what they share with their therapist will somehow become public knowledge. I don't know if you struggle with either of those things, but please know that you certainly don't need to."

It was like this woman was reading her mind. Nadine could feel tears rising again. "Thank you," she whispered.

"You're very welcome. You called for a reason, and I'm here to help in any way that I can. Please share with me the issues you're dealing with in your marriage at this time."

The tears were now spilling down Nadine's cheeks, and she didn't bother to wipe them away. "I don't know where to start."

"Well," Olivia began, "why don't we start at the beginning?"

Chapter 6

Mr. Big - Stirring the Pot

I told you! Didn't I tell you?"

"Yeah, you did, you did." Nadine had to give Trina her props when she invaded her office space Tuesday afternoon. "Olivia seems great. We were on the phone way longer than I planned to be. If I were her, I'd send me a bill." Nadine laughed at her own statement, and then added, "I think I took up more of her time than what she usually gives for a consultation she's not getting paid for."

Peering at Trina from over the rim of her reading glasses, Nadine said, "Look, now. I called her as you asked me to. Don't start pressing for me to really go in and have a sit-down meeting."

"What? Girl, you can't stop now. This isn't an overnight fix. If you liked Olivia over the phone, you'll love her in person. You've got to sign up for some real sessions."

Nadine burst into laughter. "I was kidding; don't have a stroke. I already have a session set up with her."

"You make me sick," Trina said while rolling her eyes. "You better stop playing with me."

"I couldn't resist."

"So, when is your appointment with her?"

With the bottom of her ink pen, Nadine tapped Friday's square on her oversized desk calendar. "It won't be in person though; we're going to do it virtually. I'm just not comfortable with the possibility of anybody other than Olivia knowing that I'm meeting with her. I don't want to run into anyone else that might be in her office or in her waiting room. I don't even want to see her secretary. Not right now anyway."

Near the end of their forty-five-minute conversation yesterday, Nadine revealed her identity to Olivia. Not once had the woman asked for her name, but by the time the consultation was winding down, Nadine felt comfortable volunteering the information. She was pleasantly surprised at not being met with any detectible sense of shock. Olivia acted as calmly as if Nadine had said her name was Jane Doe and her husband was the greasy mechanic at the garage on the corner.

"Virtual makes sense," Trina responded. "I think lots of her appointments, since the pandemic, are held over the computer anyway. That's the way I've done mine lately too."

Nadine took her glasses off, placed her pen on her desk, folded her arms in front of her, and looked Trina directly in the eyes. "I have to be honest about something. Yes, I got good vibes from Olivia, but it almost scares me that you're still going to her. It's been years since Jamal's death. I'm not being judgmental or anything," she quickly inserted. "I know how broken you were when you lost him. But the fact that you're still having to see Olivia after all this time is a little bit discouraging. If she's as good as she seems to be, shouldn't you be beyond going to her at this point? I'd hate to think she's stringing you along just to keep billing your insurance."

This time, the burst of laughter came from Trina. "Girl, I'm not going to her because of Jamal, I'm going to her because of you!"

Nadine sat up straight. "Me? What have I done to make you need to see a therapist?"

"You hired me at Nadine Jackson & Associates; that's what you've done," Trina answered through more laughter. "Either I would go crazy, or I'd drive Bradley and JJ crazy with all the venting I'd have to do to them. We deal with some very interesting people and some very bizarre situations in our line of business. We hear the most unbelievable stories, and we have to go through mounds of documents daily—including photographs— that sometimes yield disturbingly detailed information. How you've done this for so long without therapy, I don't know. The money I give Olivia is money well spent; believe me. If either one of us is taking advantage of the other, it's me that's taking advantage of her. She deserves more than I pay her."

Nadine hadn't thought about it in that manner. It probably would have done her some good over the years to have a professional outlet. The disagreements with Damon were increasing in frequency and so were the headaches she got almost every time tempers flared between them. In hindsight, Nadine could see how the combination of job responsibilities and marital stress might be having an impact on her health.

"I have a great marriage with Bradley, but I still have days where I miss Jamal," Trina went on to say. "I've often wondered how different my life might be right now if he hadn't died. I wonder if JJ's bond with Jamal would be as deep as it is with Bradley. When you lose somebody that intimate and that significant in your life, I don't know if the feeling of loss ever completely goes away, but I'm not still grieving. God gave me a great second chance with Bradley. It's this doggone profession I chose that keeps me sitting in corners, rocking back and forth, and singing old Negro spirituals."

Nadine laughed at the image that formed in her head thanks to Trina's over-exaggeration. She placed her glasses back on her face and diverted her eyes back to the computer screen in front of her. Nadine had an afternoon meeting with the attorney representing Rebecca's abuser, and she had a few things to finalize before the face-off. Trina must have gotten the silent message that her body language sent.

"I'm going to get out of here and let you get ready for your meeting," she said. "Bradley came and picked up my Camry and took it to be detailed. He should be bringing it back to me soon."

Nadine grinned. "He's always so thoughtful."

"He definitely is, but I do need him to get back soon. I've got a client appointment myself, but it probably won't be nearly as interesting as yours. Are you meeting him at his office?"

"No, we're meeting on neutral territory. I told him to meet me at Moe's."

Trina frowned. "Why are you using our relaxing spot for your battleground?"

"I'm hoping that it will be the place where we will call a cease-fire, not a place to pull out the big guns, but if a battle is what he wants, a battle is what he's going to get," Nadine said. "I just want to be at the place where I can have my Homewrecker Burrito no matter what the outcome. It'll either be comfort food or a celebratory meal. Either way, I'm going to enjoy it."

Trina laughed as she made her exit. She paused at the door long enough to say, "By the way, tell Miranda that 'hun's friend' said hello."

"I'll be sure to do that," Nadine promised as the office door closed.

An hour later, she was seated at a table awaiting the arrival of Attorney Charley Bigham, known by most as 'Mr. Big.' The nickname fit him well. At six and a half feet tall, over three hundred pounds, and with snow-white hair and a beard to match, Charley looked like he lived at the North Pole with nine reindeer and a bunch of elves. He had the look and the laugh of a jolly St. Nick, but he was anything but friendly in a courtroom. Charley had far more wins than losses, but two of those losses were in toe-to-toe matches with Nadine. Since she had only played defense to his prosecution twice, Nadine was the one enjoying an undefeated winning streak.

She chose not to stand as Charley was escorted to her booth, but she did offer a friendly smile and accept his handshake. "Glad you could join me," Nadine said. She was being a bit facetious since the invitation to lunch was extended by him, and he was ten minutes late.

Charley caught her verbal jab and chuckled as he wedged his oversized frame in the space across from her. "Sorry about that, Nadine. I left my office in time, but traffic just wasn't my friend this afternoon. I hope I didn't inconvenience you too much."

"Not as long as you already know what you want to eat," Nadine said as she signaled Miranda. "I'm hungry."

"Your usual, hun?" Miranda asked as soon as she approached their booth.

"Yes, of course."

Miranda scoped out Charley and then looked at Nadine again. "You've got a different lunch date today, I see."

"I do," Nadine replied. "And oh, by the way, Trina said hi."

"Who?"

A laugh started in Nadine's belly and escaped through her mouth before she could stop it. She couldn't wait to tell her friend that she'd been right.

"Trina," Nadine repeated. "That's the name of the young lady who is usually with me when I come."

"Oh, okay. Well, tell her I said hello."

"I definitely will." Nadine glanced toward Charley, and then back at their server. "Miranda, this is Attorney Charley Bigham. Attorney Bigham, Miranda is one of the best servers I've encountered in all of Atlanta."

"Nice to meet you," Miranda said with a friendly nod of her head in his direction. "You must be somebody pretty special to share a table with Attorney Nadine Jackson. I might be one of the best waitresses in Atlanta, but she is the absolute best attorney."

Nadine looked up at her and offered an appreciative smile. The waitress knew her name after all. "Thanks, Miranda."

"No, I mean it."

Charley made an uneasy shift in his seat. "You're not the first person I've heard say that," he admitted to Miranda, "but some of us might just disagree."

"Well, I'm sure this won't be the first time some of you have been wrong," Miranda said without missing a beat. "Now, what can I get for you this afternoon?"

Nadine picked up her water and sipped, praying that as she drank the liquid she'd also swallow the new laugh that threatened to break free. She was concentrating so hard on drowning her laughter that she didn't even hear what Charley ordered. Before she knew it, Miranda was gathering both their menus and walking away.

"Folks around here tend to think highly of you," he mentioned as soon as they were alone.

"I'm honored that they do."

"I expect that's why that husband of yours keeps being re-elected," Charley observed. "It doesn't hurt him none to have a popular attorney wife."

Nadine's insides cringed. If Damon had been within earshot of that remark, her head would be throbbing all night from the consequences it would have brought.

"I think the advantage is mutual," she chose to say. "I'm probably as popular as I am as an attorney because I'm married to the mayor of the city."

"I don't think so. As I recall, you were already plenty admired before you married him. It's true that he was already the mayor when y'all got hitched, but if memory serves me correctly his ratings shot up after the wedding. I'd bet you my bank account that his being married to Attorney Nadine Jackson is what gave him the edge here about a month ago. If it weren't for you, the Wynette Corvette would have smoked the Deville Mobile."

Nadine needed to change the subject. Just the thought of how Damon would react to this conversation had jumpstarted a dull throb in the back of her head. She welcomed Miranda's brief interruption when she brought Charley the soft drink he'd ordered.

"I'll be out with your orders shortly," she promised before disappearing again.

"Let's talk about this bogus claim that your client has launched against mine." Nadine figured it was best to get right to the point. She didn't want to leave room for Charley to pick up his conversation from where he'd left off before his Coke arrived.

He leaned back in his seat and scratched his beard before saying, "Well, a gunshot wound and a hospital bill prove that the claim is very much valid, Counselor." He patted the briefcase that he'd placed on the cushioned space beside him. "I've got it all here in black and white."

Nadine slid the folder that had been resting on the table beside her toward him. "Remember all that evidence I told you that I was going to get last time we spoke? Well, my printer prints in color, Counselor, and it's all there. Police reports, hospital bills, affidavits from witnesses who will testify of the abuse; a neighbor even caught your client on his security camera slapping my client around in her backyard just a few weeks before the shooting. Aside from that, I have the results from the investigation—which I'm sure were also sent to you—that substantiate my client's statement for how the shooting happened."

Nadine paused while she watched him flip slowly through her paperwork. "Let's face it, Charley," she continued. "Your client is a piece of scum that uses women as a punching bag. He's a horrible excuse for a human being. He's a violent, serial abuser. Oh … did I forget to mention that I've been in touch with girlfriends from as far back as middle school and high school who have agreed to take the stand and talk about their horrible experiences? Experiences, I might add, that will also raise the suspicion of whether your client is also a rapist?"

Charley's eyebrows shot upward, and he looked up from the paperwork. "A rapist?" He whispered the words like he didn't want those at nearby tables to overhear.

"That's right. Claims of date rape were filed against him when he was sixteen years old. He went to juvenile detention back then. Did he really think I wouldn't find that out? And I'm sure you knew about this. Did you think I wouldn't uncover it?"

"You can't bring up his record as a minor," Charley told her, slamming the cover of the folder closed. "That's privileged information, and it would be inadmissible."

"It's privileged, alright," Nadine said while never breaking eye contact. "If there is even the smallest loophole that will allow me to bring it up, I'll find it. And believe me, it will be my privilege to present it, and the entire courtroom will hear it. And even if that's not brought into evidence, I still have enough to acquit my client while possibly having a new case opened against yours."

"Your client shoots mine, and you think she'll be totally exonerated? Listen, Nadine; I came here with an open mind to discuss the possibility of reducing the charges, but you can't expect us to drop them."

Nadine leaned across the table. "Why not? It was pure self-defense, Charley. You know that. I know that. My client knows that, and so does yours. So, you go back and tell him that he's kicked a lot of women around in his lifetime, but when my client put me on retainer, his luck ran out. This is one woman who will put her foot so far up his butt that he won't be able to find the shoe I was wearing when I did it."

"So, you're not even interested in discussing a reduction of the charges?"

"Charley, you listen to me and listen to me good. If this gets to court, I have enough evidence and testimony to convince the judge and the jury that your client is a repeat offender whose infractions are now escalating to levels that could land him on death row. If he doesn't drop these charges, mark my word, I will prove that he would have likely murdered my client had she not wrestled the gun into the position where he was the one who caught the bullet. Either way this goes, my client is going to walk free. The question is, where will your client end up?"

Miranda's timing couldn't be more perfect. As soon as Nadine finished her spiel, she approached the table balancing her tray.

"Here you go, hun," she said, placing Nadine's plate in front of her. "Be careful now," Miranda added. "That tofu Homewrecker Burrito with extra guac is fresh, so the dish is hot. And here is your iced tea as well." Turning to Charley, she said, "Here are your nachos with sirloin steak and pork." Miranda placed a small stack of napkins in the middle of the table for them to share. "Can I get either one of you anything else?"

"Yes," Charley told her. His face appeared flush, and his countenance now looked more like that of a sick St. Nick instead of a jolly one. "If you don't mind, I'll take that in a to-go container instead. I don't have much of an appetite now, and I need to be on my way."

"Sure," Miranda replied. "What about you, hun? Do you need me to prepare yours to go too?"

"Nope." Nadine flashed her a wide grin. "I'm going to enjoy mine right here."

Miranda reclaimed Charley's dish and said, "I'll be right back with your take-out. And hun ... I'll be back with that second water you're going to want later."

When she walked away, Charley pulled out two twenties from his wallet and dropped them on the table before sliding out of the booth.

"That should take care of both our meals plus a tip," he said. "You can give that takeout to whoever you know will eat it. I'll be in touch."

"Thank you," Nadine said. "Next time, lunch is on me; okay?"

Charley made a grunting sound, and with that, he grabbed his briefcase and excused himself.

As soon as he was out of sight, Nadine picked up her cell phone and dialed quickly.

"Hello?"

"Hi, Rebecca," she greeted her client. "Can you meet me at your house at around four o'clock?"

"Yes, ma'am. I'll be here. Is everything okay?"

"Yes, it's all good. I'll explain it to you more when I get there. In the meantime, if you get any calls from Mr. Big or anyone else; don't talk to them before you talk to me."

"Okay."

Nadine ended the call and took the first bite of her burrito. Victory had never tasted so good.

Chapter 7

When It Rains, It Pours

Nadine arrived home feeling better than she had in a long while. Aside from the fact that every cloud in the sky seemed to burst during her drive, her day could not have gone more perfectly. Today, she was especially thankful for their attached four-car garage that kept her from being personally attacked by the liquid bullets that fell from the sky.

When Nadine saw that Damon's parking space was unoccupied, the tension that she didn't even know she had began draining from her body. Mayoral responsibilities must have held him longer at the office than normal, and for that, she was thankful.

Nadine loved Damon; she had no question about that. But she also couldn't deny that years of discord were taking their toll. If her devotion to her husband wasn't true, she would have walked away a long time ago. Instead, she chose to stay and hold to the hope that things would change, and the marriage she dreamed she'd have with Damon would one day become her reality.

That faith was the main reason she'd kept the whole truth bottled up all these years. She couldn't think of anyone she could tell the fullness of what she'd endured for nine years that wouldn't insist that she leave. She didn't need that kind of stress. Nadine wasn't ready to give up yet. Nothing was too hard for God. Not according to Aunt Pat.

Upon entering the house, the sound of laughter caught Nadine's attention. She turned to see her father-in-law standing in his bedroom's open doorway. He loved watching and re-watching classic comedies from the fifties, and apparently, Lucy was up to her usual shenanigans that would always have the audience cracking up.

"Are you okay?" Nadine asked when she noticed that he was heavily leaning against his walker.

Daddy Deville's smile said it wasn't as bad as it looked. "I'm headed to the kitchen for a bottle of water. I was just trying to get this thing lined up right to get through this doorway."

"I'll get it for you. You don't have any more in your personal fridge?"

"Drank the last bottle a couple of hours ago. I told Damon last night that I was down to my last two, but I guess when you're running a city the size of this one, you don't have time to be nobody's water boy." He laughed at his own statement.

Daddy Deville was always making light of his son's thoughtless behavior. Nadine had asked Damon more than once to keep an inventory of what was inside his dad's refrigerator, so he didn't run out of anything. The last time she brought it up, Damon pointed out that surgery notwithstanding, his father had easy access to any room on their first floor.

It was true that they had an open floor plan, but Nadine always worried that he might lose his footing, and the consequences of falling after the kind of surgery he'd had could be dire.

"You go back to your chair," Nadine told him. "I'll bring you what you need."

"I appreciate it," he replied.

While Daddy Deville maneuvered his way back to his favorite La-Z-Boy, Nadine headed upstairs to put away her business belongings. As soon as she set her attaché case in the corner of her closet, her cell rang. Nadine smiled when she saw the name on her display.

"Well, hey baby girl," her favorite aunt said.

"Hi, Aunt Pat! It's so good to hear your voice. You just crossed my mind a few minutes ago."

"Oh yeah? Well, you know I always say that when somebody crosses your mind, it might be God trying to tell you to check on them. Were you about to call me?"

"Uhmm ..." When Nadine was backed into a corner, she could force herself to lie to a lot of people, but her Aunt Pat wasn't one of them. "Probably not," she admitted with a laugh. "Daddy Deville was struggling to walk to the kitchen when I came in the house, so I promised I'd bring the items he needed to him. I was just about to head down there."

"Well, don't let me hold you up," her aunt said. "I didn't want nothing. I just called because you suddenly crossed my mind too, and I just wanted to check on you. Are you good?"

"Yes ma'am." Nadine was happy to say it truthfully. "Today was a really good day for me. I'm handling a case that could have easily turned ugly, and I was able to get the charges against my client dropped."

"That's a good thing as long as they weren't guilty," Pat said. "Don't be getting charges dropped against people who are out there doing devilish things. They need to stand trial so the Lord can put some love on them."

Nadine frowned. "So He can put some love on them?"

"That's right. When good parents spank their children, it's because they love them too much to let them stand by and watch the devil destroy them. God is a good parent, and the Bible says who the Lord loves, He chastens. When we step out of line, He knows how to spank our behinds and get us back in alignment. Some people get so far out of line that they need to be loved real good by God."

Nadine laughed. "I've never heard it put that way before. But you'll be glad to know my client was innocent; she didn't deserve to be dragged through a trial."

"I hope she knows how blessed she is to have my niece in her corner. I'm so proud of you, baby girl. Have I told you that lately?"

Nadine felt warm all over like her aunt had just somehow reached through the phone and delivered her the biggest hug. "I think you tell me that every time we talk, Auntie," she replied.

Pat chuckled. "Well, I can't say it enough. I'll let you go so you can take care of your father-in-law. How is Damon doing, by the way?" she asked.

Squeezing her eyes shut, Nadine took in a deep breath. She was hoping they could avoid any talk about him. She didn't want her aunt to ask any questions that she didn't want to answer truthfully.

"Damon's fine. He has a late workday today, so he hasn't made it home yet. When I go in the kitchen to get Daddy Deville's things, I'm going to start fixing a quick dinner and try to get it ready before he gets in." As much as she liked talking to her Aunt Pat, Nadine had thrown in that part in hopes that it would help the conversation come to a close.

"Oh yes, do that. Fix your husband something to eat. If he's had a tough day, a good meal will do him good. I love you, and I'll talk to you later."

"I love you too, Aunt Pat. Take care."

As soon as she ended the call, Nadine returned to her closet and stepped out of her pumps and into her bedroom slippers before heading back downstairs and into the kitchen. She immediately went to the refrigerator and grabbed twelve bottles of water from the bottom shelf. That was as many as Daddy Deville's fridge would hold.

"Knock-knock," she said while simultaneously walking through his open door. Nadine allowed Daddy Deville to grab one bottle from the armload she carried, and the rest she took to his refrigerator and stacked them inside. "That should hold you for a while. I'll pick up another case of them on my way home from work tomorrow, and I'll put the entire case in here so you can restock whenever you want.

"I 'preshate that," he said.

"You're welcome. Do you need anything else?"

"No, I'm good. I guess Damon is working late this evening."

"Yes, sir. I guess so," Nadine replied. "And even if he's heading home right now, that rain won't help his commute. It was stop and go for me all the way."

"Well, he's used to it," Daddy Deville remarked as Nadine exited his room.

She was tired and really wanted to just go upstairs, relax, and grab a good book to read from her sitting room. But Nadine had told her aunt that she was going to cook a quick meal for Damon. Although that was nowhere in her original plan, since she had told Aunt Pat that she was going to do it, she had to follow through.

Forty-five minutes later, just as Damon was walking in the door, she was putting the finishing touches on her meal of steamed broccoli, cauliflower spaghetti, and hand-rolled meatless meatballs. Damon's timing was perfect. As soon as the garlic bread was done, they could all eat.

"Something smells good," he said as he made a beeline to the kitchen to peek into the pots.

Nadine and Damon had only started talking to one another again last night. It was good that she had taken the day off to rest, and it was even better that she'd taken advantage of that time to talk to Olivia. The day must have done Damon some good too. He came home from work yesterday as if nothing had happened. No mention of him banishing her from his car and leaving her stranded was ever made.

Despite it all, Nadine couldn't help but smile at the compliment Damon had just made regarding the food she was preparing. "By the time you get comfortable, I'll have everything done, and you can eat," she told him.

As though he couldn't wait that long, Damon lifted the foil from the pan she'd taken from the oven and popped a meatball in his mouth. He held his mouth open and puffed out several heavy blows indicating that his hasty decision may not have been such a smart one.

Nadine laughed at the sight of it. "You want some water?"

"Nah, I'm good," Damon replied while sharing the laughter. With the meatball finally cooled enough to chew, he added, "I didn't expect you to be cooking after you sent me that text earlier today to say you might be late getting out of your client meeting."

"I've only been home for about an hour, so I was late," she explained. "But since I got here ahead of you, I thought I'd throw something fresh together instead of eating leftovers from the weekend.

Chapter 8

Message From God

Nadine looked toward the driver's seat and smiled at her husband's handsome profile. It had been ages since she and Damon had gone on a vacation together. It had been even longer since they'd gone on a road trip. Spontaneity had never been her husband's strong suit, so when Damon awakened early this morning with the idea that they should get away for a couple of days, Nadine couldn't pack quickly enough.

"Where do you want to go?" she'd asked him.

Damon had spread his arms wide and spun in a circle. "Wherever your car takes us."

His excitement had made Nadine giggle. It was as if God had sent an angel to visit her husband during the night, and the divine experience had given him a new lease on life.

"We should take the Bentley and let the top down," she'd suggested. "This weather is so nice. It would be a shame to let it go to waste."

Damon paused as if to give it some thought before he made his reply. "Your BMW gets better gas mileage," he'd pointed out, adding, "and we'll probably need that on a trip where the destination is 'wherever'."

Nadine had felt like a schoolgirl as she got up, showered, got dressed, and began gathering her clothing for the trip. She didn't even know what to pack. Would they be doing anything black-tie? She pulled a garment bag from the closet. In it, she put one of her best little black dresses. In her suitcase, she tucked a shawl just in case it got breezy during the evening hours and deposited her favorite Red Bottom shoes to top off her outfit.

"Is that all you're packing?" she had asked Damon when she saw the few items that he placed in a small duffle bag. He was packing more like they were going on an overnight camping trip than the fabulous getaway that she'd conjured up in her mind.

"All I need are the necessities." He'd winked and added, "You're probably packing too many clothes, if you know what I mean."

Nadine didn't know which angel God had sent during the night, but she wanted to put his or her number on speed dial.

Flirting was something that she'd thought Damon had forgotten how to do. Still, if they were going to get away, she wanted them to have at least one dinner out on the town. They could spend the rest of the time doing "you know what I mean," but she'd love for them to make time for a nice dinner and two glasses of wine at a fine dining restaurant.

"Can you pack just one suit?" Nadine hugged him when she asked and hoped that would butter him up even more.

"Alright, alright." He'd raised his hands in surrender. "One suit. And I plan to wear it only once. Deal?"

"Deal." Nadine's grin was toothy and wide.

While Damon went into his closet to retrieve his formal wear, her next move was to disappear into the ensuite to gather her toiletries. Her excitement almost had her floating. Nothing could bring her down. When she came from the master bathroom, she checked the time on her cell phone. Ava would be in the office by now even if the attorneys hadn't yet arrived. Nadine picked up the phone and made the necessary call. A great perk that came with owning her own business was that she didn't need anybody's permission to skip work if she desired.

"Nadine Jackson & Associates." Ava's voice always sounded adolescent—like that of a young teenage girl instead of a woman on the verge of thirty.

"Good morning, Ava."

"Good morning, Attorney Jackson. How are you?"

"I'm doing great. Is anyone else in the office yet?" Nadine was really just making small talk. It was only eight thirty. The only time any of her attorneys got in the office that early was if they had clients meeting them there.

"No ma'am. Not yet."

"Okay. Can you take a look at my schedule and see if I have anything listed for today?" It was another pointless question. Nadine was well aware that she didn't have anything scheduled except lunch with Trina, and that wasn't on her business calendar. She'd cleared much of the week to go over briefs, evidence, and testimonies just in case Charley Bigham hadn't gotten his client to drop those charges. If they had dragged Nadine into court, she was going to walk in fully loaded, so she'd made sure that nothing would be on her calendar to deter her from being completely prepped for battle.

"Don't tell them you're with me," Damon whispered as he emerged from his closet with a suit he rarely wore. "I don't want my office to get word that I'm shirking my duties. I'll call them when we get where we're going and tell them that I got stuck out of town. I don't want it to look like I planned to be away for two days."

Nadine nodded her understanding before mouthing, "Okay, I won't."

"No ma'am," Ava had said after a lengthy pause. "As a matter of fact, it looks like the first blocked time you have on your schedule is Friday. You just have it marked unavailable. No information is attached, so I'm not sure who that meeting is with."

That was Nadine's meeting with Olivia. She had left it unlabeled for a reason. It was nobody's business but hers. "Okay, thanks for checking," she'd told Ava. "Please let the others know that I'll be out of the office until Friday. I'm taking some personal time. I'll have my cell with me, but please don't call unless it's an emergency. Let Attorney Richards know that I'll shoot her a text message later today. I know she has an appointment this morning, so I'll reach out to her this afternoon to reschedule lunch."

"I'll let everyone know. Have fun."

"Thank you," she'd told Ava. "I'm counting on you to keep those crazy lawyers in line while I'm away."

"I'll do my best," Ava promised with a chuckle.

"Why are you staring at me?" Damon asked.

The sudden sound of his voice snapped Nadine from her introspective reflection of the busy morning. She'd been so deep in thought that she'd not noticed her eyes were still locked on him.

"I can't look at what's mine?" she teased.

His grin was a tell-tale sign that he liked her response. "Sure, you can. But as early as I got you up this morning, I'm surprised you're still awake."

"I'm nosey. I'm trying to see where we're going."

"We've been on the road for an hour. You haven't figured it out yet?"

Nadine looked around. "I think I have some idea, but I'm not sure."

"What's your idea? I'll tell you if you're right or not."

"Well, at first, I thought we might be going to a beach in Florida, but—"

"Real wrong," he chimed in.

"Yeah, I knew I was wrong about that when we hit the interstate going north. So, now I think we might be going to a cottage in the Georgia mountains."

"You're close," Damon told her. "We're staying in Georgia, but we're not going to Helen, Georgia if that's where you're thinking."

That was exactly what she was thinking, and Nadine was a little disappointed to learn that she was wrong. They had spent a three-day weekend there during the first year of their marriage. She remembered them getting out on the walking trail together and enjoying the sights and sounds of nature. Secretly, she had hoped they would revisit one day, and for a while, she relished the thought that today was the day.

"Where are we going then?" Nadine asked.

"Lake Taguloo, near South Carolina," Damon replied. "This will be an adventure for both of us."

Something about the sound of "an adventure" renewed Nadine's excitement. She'd never been to Lake Taguloo, but she liked the sound of spending time near the water. With Damon being a highly demanded mayor and her being a top attorney, the opportunity to leave it all behind and just enjoy the roles of husband and wife didn't come very often.

When Damon took an exit and pulled into the gas lane of a Quik Trip station, she let down her window and breathed in the fresh air. They could not have picked a more beautiful day to flee the stresses of their lives.

Damon opened his car door and then turned to her. "While the gas is pumping, I'll go inside and grab us both something to drink. We'll hold off on snacks so we don't mess up our appetites."

"You want me to run in and get something while you pump the gas?" Nadine offered.

"No, I'll get it. You just sit back and relax."

Nadine was glad to oblige. Everything about today felt like an answer to her prayers. It had been a long time coming, but right now, it felt well worth the wait. This was the Damon she'd fallen in love with a decade ago. Where he'd been all this time, she didn't know, nor did she care. Nadine was just thankful to have him back.

She slipped her sunglasses on her face and watched Damon walk toward the store. He was stopped by a White gentleman who was on his way out. Nadine saw them exchange a few words and then share a handshake. Even this far outside of the boundaries of Damon's mayoral seat, people still recognized and respected him.

Nadine heard the gas nozzle pop, indicating that the tank was full. There was plenty of gas in the tank when they left the house, and they hadn't been on the road that terribly long, so it couldn't have been that low when Damon pulled into the station. Nadine had stopped just short of asking him why he'd decided to stop for gas so soon. She didn't want to say or do anything to disturb the sweet peace that they had been enjoying. Damon didn't like it when she questioned his decision-making skills.

It wasn't long before Nadine saw her husband making his return with a cup in each hand. She figured the larger one was his. When Damon walked, he took long strides, and he exuded charm and confidence. It was a trait that had captured her attention the first time she saw him in person. The shameless double-take that the two redheads did as they passed Damon on their way toward the store was proof that Nadine wasn't the only one who found her husband attractive.

Nadine flashed a smile as he delivered her drink to her window. He had already taken the time to insert her straw in the space at the top.

"Tea for milady," he said in a mock English accent. "Thank you," she said.

Damon bent down and kissed her lips before placing the cup in her hand. "Anything for you, baby."

Her husband was arousing all her senses. As far as Nadine was concerned, they couldn't arrive at their destination quickly enough. She couldn't wait to show him how much she appreciated the affection and attention he was extending to her. She also couldn't wait to call Olivia and cancel that stupid appointment. Clearly, her marriage didn't need a therapist.

Nadine watched while Damon climbed back into the driver's seat and took time to use sanitizer to clean his hands before buckling himself in and cranking the car.

"Ready?" he asked.

"More than you know," she replied.

The way he smiled, Nadine knew he caught the meaning of her response. "Drink up," he said, nudging the hand in which she held her cup. "Drink it real fast because you might need your strength even before we go out to get a bite to eat this evening."

Hurriedly, Nadine put her cup to her mouth and began taking in large gulps of the too-sweet sweet tea that he had given her. Usually, Damon was good at measuring sugar that he added in unsweetened tea. Today, he had overdone it. She could feel undissolved granules lingering on her palate, but she didn't even care.

Laughing at her eagerness, Damon picked up his own cup and took a couple of swallows before setting it back in the cup holder and driving the car off the parking lot.

After digesting several more mouthfuls, Nadine had to take a break. She grimaced. The tea was so cold that it gave her a headache.

"Brain freeze?" Damon asked, laughing as he shot a glance in her direction.

Nadine couldn't help but laugh with him. "Uh-huh. That's what I get for sucking in so much so fast." She swirled the cup in her hand hoping it would help the sugar dissolve. A few more swallows told her that the liquid must have been too cold to melt the sweetener.

She wanted to stay awake for the entire trip, but Nadine's eyelids were starting to get heavy. Damon must have seen her struggle.

"We still have about forty-five minutes to go, baby," he said. "I know you're tired. Get some rest. I'll wake you up when we get there."

Nadine didn't feel like she had a choice in the matter. Her body was demanding sleep. If she just caught a quick fifteen minute nap, she was sure she'd be good for the rest of the ride.

Nadine leaned back in her seat, and just before she dozed off, she felt Damon sliding the cup of tea from her hand.

A horrific smashing sound caused Nadine's eyes to open. She tried to shake herself but couldn't. Her arms and legs felt like they were made of heavy iron. She was clearly awake, but from the neck down, it felt like her body was still asleep. She looked toward the driver's seat only to find that she was sitting in it. A glance at the passenger seat showed that it was empty.

"What's going on?" Her words were slurred as she looked around the car for any signs of her husband. "Damon?" She was clearly alone, but why? And where was she? "Damon?" she said again while still trying to shoo the fog from her head.

Looking straight ahead, Nadine noticed that the car was no longer on the road. As her vision cleared, she saw that her car's front end was badly damaged from the impact. A quick look in the rearview mirror reflected blood trickling down her forehead. She saw water rising around her, and she came to realize that she was in more trouble than she first thought. She was sinking. If she could raise her arms and move her hands, she could free herself, but immobility continued to hold her hostage.

"Damon!" Screaming his name didn't help either. He wasn't with her.

The more Nadine's head cleared, the more frantic she became. She was hyperventilating and every gasp of breath felt smothering. Looking toward her closed driver's side window, she saw a man standing in the distance on the side of the road. And not just any man.

"Damon!" she cried out.

His arms were folded. He was watching her die. Nadine looked at the place where both their cups once sat in adjoining cup holders. There was no sign of Damon's but hers was now floating in the rising water. That stuff she thought was sugar must have been something else. Damon had slipped something in her drink when he made it inside the store. He'd given her something that caused her to fall into a deep sleep, and whatever that was must've also been the thing that was now rendering her paralyzed.

Tears flooded Nadine's eyes and raced each other down her cheeks. How could he be so cruel? Did he hate her this much? What had she ever done to him to deserve this? He'd made her believe he loved her and wanted to spend quality time with her only to get her alone in this God-forsaken place and watch her go to a watery grave.

"Damon! Help! Please help!"

Water was pooling on the inside as her car sank lower into the water. Nadine wasn't a great swimmer, but she could do enough to survive if she could get out of the vehicle before it drifted too far out.

Wasn't anybody else traveling the stretch of road that led to where she was? Did no one see him push her off the road? Is this what he meant by an adventure at Lake Tugaloo?

"Damon! Don't do this! Help me! Damon! Damon!"

As the water quickly elevated, Nadine wondered what it was that he was going to tell people. Damon had moved her into the driver's seat. It would look like she was the one in control of the car. It would look like an accident ... or a suicide.

Nadine's tears were now blinding her. Her dead muscles wouldn't allow her to wipe her face. She could still see her husband's figure standing on the side of the roadway at the top of the hill, but she could no longer make out his face.

"Damon! Please help me! Please! I'll do whatever you want. Please! Please!"

It all made sense now. It made sense that he only packed a few items of clothing and that the suit she'd seen him put in the garment bag wasn't one of his favorites. It made sense that he'd insisted on taking her car. He didn't want to destroy his Bentley. It made sense that he didn't tell her exactly where they were going; nobody would come looking for her here. It would be days, weeks, months, maybe even years before her body would be found. It was possible that she'd never be found at all.

And what was he going to do? Find a way back home and pretend he never left? Damon had told her not to tell Ava that they'd be together, and he hadn't told his office anything at all. He'd said he would call them later and let them know he'd gotten stuck out of town. As the cold water rose around Nadine's neck, she knew it was all a setup. It was too little, too late, but it was all crystal clear. With cold water now touching her chin, fear gripped every part of Nadine's soul.

"Oh God ... help me, please!"

The piercing sound of her alarm clock brought her to an upright seated position. Nadine felt cold and wet; her body shivered. She looked around and realized that she was in her own bed, and the water on her body was sweat—and there was plenty of it.

Nadine raised her arms and was glad to see that they actually worked. It had all been a bad dream. She grabbed her pillow and used the underside of her pillowcase to dry the perspiration from her face. The top side was already drenched. The part of the bed that Damon occupied was empty. He had told her last night that he had an early meeting with city council members today.

For several minutes, all Nadine could do was sit in place. Her racing heartbeats and quickened breaths took some time to calm.

She'd had nightmares before, but this one had to be the worst and the most realistic feeling of all. When she was a little girl, Aunt Pat used to tell her to never discount her dreams because they were often God's way of sending messages.

Nadine felt warm tears trickle down her face. That thought alone was even more frightening than the nightmare.

Chapter 9

What's a Girl to Do?

Becky, your lawyer's here!"

Each time Nadine went to the home that Rebecca Everson now shared with her mother and four teenage brothers, she gained a better understanding of why the girl had made the enormously bad decision to stay with a boyfriend who was far less than ideal.

"Come on in, Your Honor." Ms. Everson's southern twang was twangier than most. With a sweep of her arm, the voluptuous woman opened the door wider for her guest to make an entrance.

"Thank you," Nadine replied while forcing a smile. She had twice told Rebecca's mom that the term she insisted upon using was for judges and not attorneys, but either the woman had a terrible memory, or she was just insisting upon being ignorant.

Nadine looked around the living room. Today, it was a bit cleaner than it had been on her last visit, but not by much. There was still far too much clutter. Clothing items, that she assumed had been laundered, were covering most of the sitting area of the sofa. Wireless joysticks and remote controls for gamers did the same on the non-matching loveseat.

Being offered no direction, Nadine chose to head straight for the round dining table that was positioned in the middle of the kitchen. It was small, but at least it was clean. There was a pretty vase of fresh flowers sitting on top that made the otherwise plain table the most attractive piece of furniture in the home. Nadine placed her attaché case on top of the table beside the vase, all the while wondering how a family of six could share a meal in that space when the table was so small and only two chairs accompanied it.

"Becky Ann!"

The home wasn't large. It was 1,000 square feet, if that. Nadine wanted to ask Ms. Everson to just take the few steps to her daughter's room and get her instead of yelling like they were outside, but she held her tongue. If Rebecca had had her own vehicle, Nadine would have scheduled this meeting in the comfort of her office.

"I'll be there in a second!" Rebecca could be heard saying. Her voice was coming from the vicinity of the only bathroom in the three-bedroom house.

"Can I get you something to eat or drink?" Ms. Everson asked while helping herself to a can of soda that was inside her refrigerator.

It was the most inopportune time to make the kind offer. Before the question could be fully posed, Nadine caught sight of one cockroach chasing another into a space behind the kitchen cabinets.

"No, thank you," she replied. "I have a lunch meeting right after this one."

"Becky!"

Nadine winced at the unexpected sudden yell from Ms. Everson.

"Get on out here, girl!" she continued. "You ain't the only one this lady got to go see today!" Ms. Everson turned her attention back to Nadine. "That girl lives in the bathroom. I appreciate what you did for her but at least when she was living with Danny, I could use my own bathroom."

Nadine opened her mouth to say something but closed it again. Somehow, she knew that whatever she said would be wasted.

"Hi, Attorney Jackson," Rebecca greeted as she joined them in the dining space.

Nadine stood up and received the warm hug she was offered.

They both sat in the only chairs at the table. "How are you feeling?" Nadine asked.

Rebecca was dressed in a floral blouse and matching blue slacks. Her brunette hair was pulled into a sleek ponytail that did nothing to hide the sizeable scar on her forehead. Despite the permanent reminder, she looked very poised and pretty.

Rebecca looked as out of place sitting in the untidy home as the vase of flowers did.

"I'm feeling good," she said. "I'm sorry about all the mess," Rebecca added.

A one-word profanity rolled off her mother's tongue at the sound of the apology. Then she said, "If you're sorry about it, you ought to clean it up. It's messy 'cause of you. I had somewhere to put all this stuff before I had to make room for you to move in."

Rebecca's embarrassment was made obvious when her cheeks turned ruddy. She looked at Nadine as if she wanted her to say something to make it all better, but Nadine was way too smart to get caught in their family drama. Instead, she changed the subject.

"I wanted to meet with you for two reasons. First, to give you a copy of all the paperwork showing the dismissal of the charges." Nadine reached for her attaché and handed Rebecca the folder that she pulled out of it.

"Thank you so much. I'm just glad it's all over," Rebecca responded.

"That leads to the second reason for my visit," Nadine told her. "I don't think you should let it end here. I strongly suggest that you launch your own case and press charges against him for the domestic violence you endured."

"Oh, I don't think—"

"Listen to me, Rebecca," Nadine urged. "You can be the one female that was strong enough to stand against him and make him pay for his crimes. Doing this would help to ensure that he won't be free to do this to any other woman."

"You mean, take Danny to court?" Rebecca's eyes enlarged like quarters.

"Yes, that's what I mean." Nadine reached across the table to place her hand on top of her client's. "Rebecca, this man is cruel and abusive to women. He did it to women before you, and he'll do it to women after you. Someone has to be brave enough to put a stop to his behavior, and you have everything you need to be the one to do it."

"Wait a minute, wait a minute, wait a minute," Ms. Everson interjected. She placed her can of soda on the countertop as if she needed both hands to get her statement across. "She don't need to be taking nobody to court. You see them flowers right there? Danny had them delivered this morning straight from the florist."

Nadine's eyes shot to the floral arrangement, and then back to Rebecca. "Is he trying to get you to come back to him?"

The girl's mother answered before she could. "Yes, he is. He's sorry for what he did, and he said so right on the card that came with them. Now, Danny may not be perfect, but what man is? He wants to set things straight. If she takes him to court and tries to make him pay for the mistakes he made, they'll never get back together."

Nadine didn't even try to hide her disgust. It was written all over her face as she rose from her chair. "Ms. Everson, are you saying that you want your daughter to go back to a man who has repeatedly abused her? She has had to receive medical attention because of him. He tried to shoot her, for God's sake. You want her to go back to that?"

"Listen, Your Honor. You can stand there and talk all high and mighty because you got a man. You live in a big house behind iron gates that protect you from stuff like abuse. You're married to the mayor of Atlanta, so you can't even come close to knowing what it's like to be in our shoes. Becky is a whole lot like me. She's strong-willed and she always wants to try to speak up for herself. You see what that got me, don't you?"

Ms. Everson paused long enough to extend an arm and gesture toward the clutter inside her home. She tossed her bleached-blonde hair over her shoulder, rolled her neck, and continued.

"All that got me was five children and no man. Becky is my only daughter, and I don't want her to end up like this. Danny got his faults, but at least she had a good-looking man with a house, a good job, and a nice car. That's way more than I got. She don't need to be coming up in here and kicking two of her brothers out of their room where now all four of them got to sleep in the same bedroom. Danny done apologized, and now she needs to swallow her pride, put on her big girl panties, and get on back to him before it's too late. While she's over here playing hard to get, some other woman will come along and take her place."

Nadine had heard a whole lot of malarkey in her years as an attorney, but what Rebecca's mother had just unloaded was about the worst. Nadine knew that she had to keep her professionalism despite a strong desire to match Ms. Everson's attitude. Instead of addressing the woman directly, Nadine decided to turn to the only one whose opinion and actions truly mattered.

"Please tell me that we didn't go through all of this for nothing," she said to Rebecca. "Don't forget that if Danny's had had his way, you would be the one serving time. He didn't drop these charges because he wanted to; he dropped them because we had evidence to prove that he lied and was trying to frame you for a crime you didn't even commit. This is a man that tried to shoot you. You can't forget that."

"We don't know that he was trying to shoot her—that's just what she said," her mother charged while pointing at her daughter. "He might have just been trying to scare her. All we know is that the gun went off when they were struggling over it. Are you going to take care of Becky if she ends up all by herself for the rest of her life?"

Nadine knew the question was posed to her, but she refused to lose eye contact with her client. "Rebecca, I don't know what his motives are for trying to get back with you, because just a few days ago when he was trying to get you locked up, that clearly isn't what he wanted."

"I don't know what to do," the girl whispered. "He really did sound like he was sorry, and he sounded like he meant it when he said he would never do it again."

"That's right," Ms. Everson said. "I talked to him myself and I believe him."

"How many times has he said that to you?" Nadine asked, still focusing on Rebecca. "This is not the first, second, or third time that he has promised not to hit you again. Am I right?"

"Yes. That's true," Rebecca mumbled.

"Of course it is. You've believed him in the past. You've dropped charges against him several times and gone back to him several times. At the end of the day, he always does it again, and instead of getting better, the abuse is getting worse. Now, weapons are being brought in. Whether it's to scare you or to harm you, him pulling a gun on you should be a no-brainer for you to cut ties."

"Becky Ann, when you have a man that loves you, you don't just throw that away. You better take it from somebody who knows."

"This is not love, Rebecca," Nadine said. "If he loved you, he wouldn't keep hurting you like this."

"But take him to court?" Rebecca looked completely conflicted. "I don't know if I can do that. That would really make him angry. And Mama's right; I wouldn't want him to get with anybody else. I know a lot of girls who … all they'd need to know is I'm not getting back with Danny. They would be on him like buzzards on roadkill."

"You better believe they would," her mother said. "And you'll be sitting around this house looking sick while some other woman is enjoying the same house, car, and man that you threw away all because he made one little bad decision."

"One?" Nadine finally turned to face Ms. Everson. The frown lines on her face deepened when she added, "Little?" Nadine took a few steps toward the woman as if being closer would make her understand better. "Ms. Everson, don't you think your daughter deserves better than this? Do you really think a good car and a nice house is worth Rebecca's safety?"

"No," she replied. "But then again, I ain't the one who thinks she's in any danger."

Nadine couldn't believe her ears. "Really? Look at her forehead. You can't deny the evidence that she's in danger."

"That little scar? That ain't nothing!" Ms. Everson shot back. "Your Honor, look at me. Am I crippled? Am I dead? No, I ain't. I can't tell you how many times I done came to blows with a man. My mama told me that I deserved better too, and I believed her. That's why I'm forty years old, single, and ain't got no man. That's why I'm in this neighborhood living like white trailer trash. I want better for Becky, and you ain't helping by trying to get her to put Danny in prison."

"But—"

"Have you ever been abused, Your Honor?"

"No, I haven't," Nadine said, "but as an attorney, I see it every day in the women that we represent. Women just like Rebecca who men use for punching bags, but can't seem to make the decision to completely cut ties."

"I'm cutting ties," Rebecca suddenly blurted. "I've made the decision. I'm not going to go back to him. Attorney Jackson is right. I don't need to be with Danny."

Nadine sighed in relief, but as Rebecca continued talking, it was a breath Nadine soon discovered she'd released too soon.

"I'm not going back to him, but I'm not going to press any charges either," Rebecca clarified. "I just want to live my life and let him live his."

"And where do you plan to live that life?" her mother challenged. "Becky, I love you, but you can't stay here. When I moved into this house, you were already living with Danny, and I was just trying to get a place where me and the boys could be comfortable. Eric and Nolan need their room back. Your four brothers are way too big to be forced to share one room."

"I'll sleep out here until I save enough money to get my own place, Mama. They can have their room back. I'll sleep on the sofa or make a pallet on the floor."

Nadine shook her head at the conversation she was witnessing. She wondered whether Rebecca's father would allow her to come and live with him. Nadine didn't know the man personally, but he'd sent a check all the way from Texas to retain her legal services, and her fees weren't cheap. He had to be more financially stable than Ms. Everson for sure.

"Could you stay with your father until you get on your feet?" The words jumped from Nadine's mouth without her permission. She hadn't meant to make her thoughts vocal, and as soon as she said them, she knew she'd made a mistake.

The swear words that Ms. Everson released were so fierce they would have caused a drunken sailor to blush.

Nadine held her hands up in surrender to stop the verbal lashing. "I'm sorry. I'm sorry. I was just trying to help by making a suggestion."

"Well, with all due respect, Your Honor, this ain't none of your business."

"You're right," Nadine told Ms. Everson. "Like I said, I'm sorry I overstepped my bounds, but you've sacrificed enough. You've been the primary caretaker of Rebecca all her life. I just think that it should be her dad's turn to carry some of the load."

Nadine's well-constructed words softened Ms. Everson's attitude, as she knew they would. She hadn't spent all these years in court without learning how to skillfully use words in a manner that buttered up a hard-nosed judge or an irate witness.

"Well, now, you're right about that," Ms. Everson agreed. "He should have to step in and do his part. But all he good for is sending a check. That wife of his ain't gonna let Becky come stay with them, and even if she would, I wouldn't want her to. I don't like her, and she don't like me. I gave Aiden his first child, and his wife hates me for that. He wasn't the best man in the world, but I should have just put up with it. All that stuff that she got with him, would be mine if I had. She's living the life I should be living. That's why I ain't against Becky taking Danny back. I believe she's gonna live to regret that she didn't, just like me."

"I'm twenty-two years old, Mama," Rebecca said. "It's not like my best years are behind me. I still have plenty of time to find a good man."

"Umph! I was about your age when I broke up with your daddy, thinking the same thing," Ms. Everson told her. "You were just about ready to start kindergarten. It would be two more years before I got a new man, and even then, I kept that same stupid holier-than-thou attitude. I thought I was better than what I was getting. And look where it got me. It ought to scare you to know that when you look at me, you're looking in a mirror that's showing you your future."

Rebecca walked over and hugged her mom. "I'll be fine," she assured her. "I don't want to see Danny with anyone else, but maybe somebody else would be better for him than me."

She turned to look at Nadine. "And, maybe what we already did is enough to change him. You say I can be the first woman to take him to court and get him locked up, but I'm already a first. I'm the first one to scare him with a lawyer good enough to see through his fake charges and dig up all the stuff he's done. I think we shook him up enough. He did wrong, yes. But I still love him, and I don't want him locked up even though we're not getting back together. When he sent me the flowers, he promised to change."

"As he promised many times before," Nadine reminded her once again.

"I know, but this time, he also promised that he was going to get counseling. That was new. He's never promised that before." Rebecca turned back to her mother. "After he's gone through counseling, if he still wants me, then maybe we can talk."

Ms. Everson sucked her teeth. "If you don't stick with him now when he gets better, he ain't coming back to you because he's going to see you as the one who wasn't woman enough to stick with him through the thick and the thin. Why do you think me and Aiden ain't together? What you're going to do is mess around and let him get better for somebody else, not you. Take my word for it; you're going to live to regret this."

Nadine couldn't stomach any more. "Call me if you change your mind and want to press charges," she told Rebecca while retrieving her attaché. "We have prosecuting attorneys in the office that will be glad to handle the case."

"Thank you for what you did, but she won't be needing anybody's prosecuting services," Ms. Everson said.

Nadine walked out without another word and heard the door slam behind her. After getting in her car and locking the doors, she shook her head. No wonder Rebecca had been in the situation as long as she had. Instead of her mother helping to open her eyes to the fact that she was an abused woman, Ms. Everson's blinders were just as thick. Nadine's greatest concern was that with the only voice in Rebecca's ear being her mother's, she would find herself in the same situation again—if not with Danny, it would be with someone else just as awful.

Chapter 10

Malicious Intent

It had been a long week, yet Friday arrived far more quickly than Nadine wanted it to. She'd thought she was ready to face her demons, but as she sat at her desk staring at her computer screen, what Nadine wanted more than anything in the world was for time to stand still. But, it wouldn't. The countdown on the timer she'd set for her meeting with Olivia Fields was speaking loud and clear, and what it was telling her was that she had less than five minutes before she'd have to click a Zoom link that would bring her face-to-face with a woman that, up until now, she had only spoken to over the phone.

Ever since the troubling dream Nadine had about Damon the other night, she had been dreading Friday. Her hope had been that by the time her session came around, she'd be able to tell the therapist that God had worked a miracle and her mental health services were no longer needed. Her real-life wish had been just as strong—and just as wrong—as the one in her dream. It was plain to see that asleep or awake, her marriage needed help.

Five minutes, two seconds. That's how long she had until she would cross the line of no return. All day long, even as Nadine carried out her legal responsibilities, her mind would somehow find its way back to thoughts of today's pending meeting.

How much should I tell Olivia? How much can I truly trust her? Should I tell Olivia everything, or would it be best to only share a little? Damon is the mayor. If his behavior leaks out, it could destroy him. It could destroy our marriage. I love him. I don't want to hurt him; I just want to help me. How do I handle this?

The thoughts had been bombarding Nadine's mind for over eight hours, and they hadn't stopped yet. She had all the questions. What she needed were the answers. Three minutes and forty-six seconds. That's all she had left, and the decision she made between now and then could change everything.

Nadine jolted back to reality at the sound of a soft knock on her office door. She swiftly closed her laptop just before seeing the doorknob turn and her uninvited guest peek in.

"Hey, girl. You okay?"

It was Trina, and Nadine released a soft sigh of relief. "I thought I'd locked the door," she replied.

"You don't have to," Trina told her as she stepped all the way inside. "I'm the last one here. I knew about the time of your call, so I shooed everyone out of the building. I told them to take care of any overtime work at home because we had a company coming in to clean our carpets."

Nadine's eyebrows raised. "We do?"

"No. But it got them all out, didn't it?"

"What are you going to do on Monday when they don't catch that familiar clean and crisp scent that we always enjoy after our carpets have been freshly shampooed?"

"I'll rant and rave about how sorry and incompetent the new carpet cleaners were and how it'll be a cold day in hell before I ever use a traveling mobile service again. Then I'll get on the phone and talk real loud to the dial tone on the other end, demanding a refund of my money. I mean, I'm going to want all my money back, and I'm going to want it right now." Trina stressed that last part with her teeth clenched together. When she looked at Nadine's laughing face, she added, "Oh, girl … it's going to be a great show. You need to be sure to be here at nine o'clock Monday morning to see it. I'll deserve an Oscar. I promise you."

Nadine was still laughing when she opened and repositioned her laptop in preparation for her meeting. Trina wasn't the only one fabricating stories to mask what was really taking place this evening. When Nadine saw that after-hours was the only time she could clear to meet with Olivia, she'd told Damon that she had a late virtual meeting with one of her clients who had contracted COVID-19. She'd led Damon to believe the client had been sick and needed all day to rest before having the meeting, which is why it had been set for five o'clock. Her tale wasn't as dramatic as Trina's, but it was enough to convince Damon, and that's all that mattered.

"I've got forty-five seconds," Nadine observed aloud.

"And that's my cue," Trina replied while throwing up two fingers to form a peace sign. "I'm out," she added. "Call me afterward if you need to. Bradley and I are going out to dinner tonight, but my cell will be with me. Don't you give a second thought about disturbing me."

"Okay."

"I mean it, Nadine." Trina pointed a finger at her for dramatic effect. "If you need me, call me."

"I will. I promise."

Nadine felt a lump rise in her throat as the door closed behind Trina. She swallowed hard and then took a few deep breaths before hovering her computer mouse over the link Olivia had sent her. Another even deeper breath was taken before Nadine clicked on it.

"Good evening, Attorney Jackson. How are you?"

"Hi, Ms. Fields. It's been a busy week but I'm doing well. How are you?"

"Oh, I know about that long week," Olivia said with a pleasant smile. "I have those all the time, but I'm doing well too. And please, call me Olivia."

"I will if you call me Nadine."

"Fair enough," the therapist said. "Do you mind if we pray together first?"

Nadine had played out in her mind how today's meeting would go, but this was an action she hadn't anticipated. Trina had told her that Olivia was a believer, but praying before a meeting wasn't something her friend had ever mentioned. Immediately, Nadine felt the tenseness in her body ease.

"No. I don't mind at all."

"Lord, our week has been full of appointments and demands, but we thank you that it's also been filled with your goodness and mercy. Thank you for allowing Nadine and me to meet this evening. I ask that you rest with us. Give her the peace of mind that comes with the assurance that she is safe in this space with me, and give me the wisdom, knowledge, and understanding to share what is needed to provide clarity for her as she moves forward. In Jesus' name. Amen."

It was a simple and softly spoken prayer, but Nadine found herself using her fingers to quickly wipe away tears that were beginning to build around her bottom lids. She got them erased just in time for Olivia's "Amen." But to be sure that any evidence of them was hidden, the first thing Nadine did at the close of the prayer was reach for her designer eyewear and place the frames on her face.

"Let's jump right in," Olivia directed. "When we spoke earlier this week, you mentioned the pressures that came with being our city's mayor and how those things are now beginning to have some adverse effects on your marriage. What we didn't go into are the intricate details of those hurtful impacts and what leads up to them."

"It's not hurtful," Nadine quickly defended. "He's not hitting me or anything. It's not hurtful," she repeated.

"I didn't mean that in a manner of physical pain. Hurt can come in many forms; physical injury is just one of them. Let's just talk about one of your more recent experiences—the incident where you found yourself being left on the curb last Sunday. Can we talk a little more about that one?"

Nadine sat back in her chair. Why was Olivia using phrases like "one of your more recent experiences" and "talk a little more about that one?" What did she mean by "one of" and "that one?" The side-of-the-road incident was the only experience that Nadine mentioned to her in their phone call. What made Olivia think there were others? Had Trina been talking to the therapist behind her back?

Nadine fell just shy of asking Olivia that question straight out. As soon as she opened her mouth, though, she remembered that Trina couldn't have divulged any information to Olivia. Nadine hadn't told Trina about any of the other incidents she'd had with Damon.

"Are you comfortable with talking more about it?" Olivia asked when Nadine's silence lengthened.

"Yes. Yes, I'm sorry," Nadine said. "What is it exactly that you want to know?

"Let's talk about the moments that happened prior to the climax of your being asked to vacate the car."

"I wasn't asked; I was ordered." The words slipped out before Nadine could stop them.

"Okay." Olivia nodded as though she understood. "Tell me what transpired beforehand that made him feel it was necessary to make such a demand."

The tenseness was making a return. Nadine felt like her body was on the verge of a hot flash. Her insides were warming as though someone had set a match in her ribcage and the heat was slowly rising toward her neck and face. She reached up and touched her brow, but there was no moisture to wipe away.

Over the years, Nadine had repeatedly said that it wasn't possible for her to ever become more nervous than she had been on the day of her first trial hearing. It felt as though the eyes of every juror and every courtroom attendee were trained on her every move. As a new defense attorney standing before one of the city's most stern judges and working in opposition to one of its winningest prosecutors, she felt like a frightened toddler on the brink of wetting her pants. Aunt Pat had prayed for her that morning over the phone, and God must have heard it because some way, somehow, Nadine beat the immeasurable odds and came out victorious. Her court case had been a win! It gave her a reputation at the very start of her career and set the tone for the years to come.

Nadine wished she'd thought to call her favorite aunt before this meeting with Olivia because the anxiety she felt now superseded that of her memorable day more than twenty years ago. She took a sip of water from the cup on her desk and then proceeded.

"We had just left the church," Nadine said. "If I recall correctly, the conversation started with him pointing out that I hadn't complimented him on his sermon delivery. And, when I did tell him that he spoke well, I think he had a problem with how calmly I said it. Like, I didn't sound believable, or I didn't sound excited enough."

"Are you typically enthusiastic when you make comments about his speaking?"

Nadine took a moment to mull over that. When she spoke, her reply was, "I don't feel that my tone was any different this time than any other. Damon's a good speaker. He's good at expressing himself whether he's at a podium in front of the press or at a podium in front of a congregation."

Olivia nodded her head and smiled. "I can attest to the press part. I've seen many interviews on television." She paused to write something on her notepad and then continued. "Do you recall what happened next?"

Flashes of that day popped in and out of Nadine's mind as she fished for the details that she'd rather forget. "Damon tends to overexaggerate," she prefaced. "He said something about me just sitting there with a stone face while he preached, but in reality, I was responding to his message, just not as energetically as some of the other church people were. From there, the conversation just spiraled out of control. Before I knew it, he threw water in my face, pulled the car to the curb and told me to get out."

"I'm sorry," Olivia said. "Did you say he threw water in your face?"

From the surprised look on Olivia's face, Nadine could see that was a detail her therapist wasn't expecting.

"It wasn't hot water or anything," Nadine explained. "He was drinking from a bottle of water he brought out of the church, and he squeezed the bottle, which made the water squirt out."

"When he squeezed the bottle, making the water come out and squirt on you, was it intentional, or was it an accident?"

"Intentional."

"And, was it done as a joke or did he do it out of anger."

"He was upset at the time."

"Okay." Olivia set her pen and pad aside. "Let me take a moment to explain to you why I asked those particular questions. I asked because the answers to those questions are the only ones that determine the definition of what took place in your husband's car last Sunday. The temperature of the water doesn't play a role at all. If he was holding the bottle and, let's say, the vehicle hit a bump in the road causing the water to splash out of the bottle and dash into your face; that would have made a difference. Or, had the two of you been laughing, playing, and kidding around with each other, and he squeezed the bottle to squirt water in your face, that would have made a difference. But the temperature of the water—whether it was hot, cold, or lukewarm—isn't a determining factor in whether there was malicious intent."

Nadine's eyes blinked several times in succession. Malicious intent? Did she just say malicious intent? That's a term I use in court when defending clients who suffered harm at the hands of a perpetrator who had carried out an intended evil.

"I think 'malicious intent' is way too strong of a phrase," Nadine emphasized. "It's like I said before, my husband sometimes overexaggerates. He can go from zero to one hundred without stopping or slowing down in between. That's what the stress of his office causes. I just need to understand how I can better function in an environment that comes with that kind of stress."

"How you can better function? So, you're blaming yourself for this?"

"I'm not blaming anyone." Nadine was beginning to feel trapped. These weren't the questions she'd predicted. "If there is blame to be placed, it's on the world that he works in. Being the mayor of Atlanta comes with major stress points that can't be avoided. So, since they're unavoidable, and I'm the mayor's wife, I just need to understand how to navigate so that these types of results don't keep coming up."

Olivia tilted her head slightly to the right. "Yes, it's true that he can't avoid the stress. However, he can and must handle it differently. If, indeed, his behavior is something that rises out of the weight of his governmental responsibilities, then Mayor Deville must find a different avenue in which to channel that.

From what I'm hearing, this isn't about you needing to make a change, it's about him shifting from the way he handles his stress so that you don't continue to be the target." Olivia paused, and then asked, "May I be completely honest with you?"

Nadine braced herself. "Sure."

"I don't necessarily think—from the information you shared with me previously and what you've shared with me so far today—that the mayor's job can be blamed for his conduct. I'm not saying the job isn't stressful, it most certainly is. But, how many instances of this type can you recall ever having any underlying tone of what went on that day at his office? How many times have matters of the city come up in your heated discussions? Can you even name one time?"

"Well, if I can't it's because Damon doesn't really bring work home with him," Nadine answered. "He really doesn't talk much about it unless I ask directly."

"Okay, then tell me exactly what it is that your husband deals with on a daily basis that you believe can possibly justify this. In those times that you've asked directly, has he ever aggressively unloaded a mountain of stress points on you? Anything that made you say to yourself, 'No wonder he acts this way sometimes.' Has that ever happened?"

Nadine had never thought of it that way before, but even as she jumbled through her memory bank now, she could not readily think of a time that mirrored Olivia's example. Most times, even when Damon spoke negatively of things or people involving his job, he never did so out of anger. There were times when he sounded frustrated. There were times he sounded exhausted. But in all the nine years they had been married, Damon had not once yelled or thrown anything when he referred to his job. Not once had he called his female colleagues the "B word." Not once had he described his constituents by using vulgarities. Not once had he ever voiced the desire to brutally beat a citizen of the city. All those things seemed to be reserved for Nadine, and the realization of it was a hard pill for her to swallow.

When Nadine didn't offer a verbal response, Olivia leaned forward in her seat, which, even with a computer screen separating them, brought her face closer to Nadine's. "It's important that we first clarify that abuse can present itself in many ways," she started. "Sometimes—"

"Abuse?" Nadine cut Olivia's sentence short. "Who mentioned anything about abuse? That's just what you said. I never said that. I would never tolerate abuse."

"Nadine, abuse is not one-dimensional. It can—"

"I know what abuse is. I'm not ignorant," Nadine cut in again, this time using a tone that was far more rigid. "I'm a defense attorney, and over half of my clientele is made up of abused women. I know what it is, and I know what it looks like. I could strip naked, and you wouldn't find one bruise on my body. I came to you to talk about how I can become a better wife to a husband who is carrying the weight of an entire metropolitan city on his shoulders, and you're calling me an abused woman. Frankly, it's not your business what my husband deals with on a daily basis. But one thing is for sure; Damon has never—and I mean never—laid a hand on me. I'm not bruised, crippled, or dead, so you can stop talking to me about abuse. As a matter of fact, I'm done talking period. Goodbye!"

As soon as the final word came from Nadine's mouth, she clicked the button to end the call. Her hands were shaking, her brows were sweating, and her heart raced like it was trying to run right out of her chest. She forcefully closed her laptop, and simultaneously with the sound of it slamming shut, a recent memory hit Nadine's brain so hard it caused tears to run from her eyes.

The end of her high-spirited spiel to Olivia sounded a lot like the one she had received from Rebecca's mother. Nadine had shaken her head at the woman's insanity, but as she removed her eyeglasses and looked at her own reflection in the mirror hanging on the wall across from her desk, Nadine came to a frightening realization. All she needed were bigger boobs, a change in ethnicity, and bleached blonde hair, and she and Ms. Everson would practically be twins. The harsh but undeniable truth turned Nadine's quiet weeping into a full-on blubbering sob.

Chapter 11

I'll Kill You

Nadine sat in her reading room staring at the bookshelf in front of her. There were hundreds of titles to choose from on this lazy Sunday evening, but none of them said what she wanted to hear. Even her fictional novels were scolding her for her behavior two days ago. Every book had an action scene, love scene, dramatic scene, or suspenseful scene that included somebody making some fool-hearted rash decision that they'd later regret.

The only person who had admonished her more than the characters in the books on her shelf was Trina. Nadine was sure that the only reason her best friend wasn't screaming at her at the top of her lungs was that they were on the grounds of the church today when Trina was finally able to corner her. Of all the days that Damon could have had a Sunday business meeting, it had to be today. He was always in a rush to leave after service, but without him, she had no excuse for a quick escape.

"I can't believe you. I truly cannot believe you," Trina had said to her as they stood together in the church parking lot. Her voice was at a level that secured their privacy, but her clenched teeth told Nadine that she had really ticked off her bestie.

"Well, I felt like she was crossing the line," she'd replied. "Look, I don't know what she said to you, but I know Olivia. She didn't say anything that didn't need to be said. If a line was crossed, it needed to be crossed to give you a wake-up call or something to think about. I know this because she's done it to me many times. But guess what? I didn't slam a phone in her face. I can't believe you, Nadine," Trina had reiterated for the third time.

"I didn't slam a phone in her face. I just ended the Zoom meeting."

"Same thing," Trina had pointed out. "Either way, it's disrespectful. How can she help you if you won't let her."

"Maybe I don't need any help." Nadine remembered feeling the back of her neck heating up at that point. "Just because my husband has one bad day doesn't mean I need help. I should have just walked home that day or called a cab. If I'd never called you, I wouldn't be in this unnecessary situation now. Maybe my problem isn't with Damon. Maybe my problem is with you. I told you about Damon leaving me on the side of the road and look what happened. I told you that I ended my call early with Olivia and look what happened. I think I see a pattern here."

Trina had snatched her shades from her face at that moment.

JJ had been approaching them from a distance, but when he saw his mom's sudden movement, he took a few steps backward and then turned around to walk in the other direction.

"Oh, that's real cute, Nadine." The volume of Trina's voice had increased a little, but thankfully, no one was nearby to overhear. "So, I'm the problem now? Okay, fine. Blame me if that makes you feel better, but both of us know the truth. The problem isn't me, and right now, it ain't Damon either. It's you. Your need to keep pretending that there is no problem is the problem. Every tumultuous situation begins with one bad day. You don't wait until that one bad day turns into a bad month or a bad year. You catch problems early so you can stop them from getting worse. The purpose for you calling Olivia was to get direction on how to nip it in the bud."

Trina had slipped her shades back on her face, but she wasn't finished talking. "I wasn't on the call with you, but I'd almost be willing to bet my life on the fact that you got offended because Olivia got too close to the truth."

Nadine had rolled her eyes, smacked her lips, and then pointed her key fob toward her vehicle to disarm and unlock it. "I'm going home. I'll see you tomorrow in the office."

"Fine. But you do know that ending a conversation with me doesn't change the truth any more than ending the conversation with Olivia did, right? What is, still is. And until you face it, it will always be."

Nadine had nothing to say in response. Her choice had been to walk away and seek refuge inside her car. On the drive home, tears found their way down her cheeks. Her sunglasses hid her eyes and the tint on her windows was enough to mask everything else. At least, she hoped so.

Exchanges like today's were very rare. Nadine and Trina would have their disagreements as all friends did from time to time, but those times rarely escalated to the point of today's dispute.

When Nadine finally arrived home, she had been able to avoid Daddy Deville long enough to change out of her Sunday best and clean up any residual water from her eyes. Damon still hadn't made it home when she finished dinner, so Nadine prepared a plate for her father-in-law and set it on a tray that she placed in front of his chair in his room. She knew Damon would not have allowed her to if he had been home, but he wasn't, so she did.

Now, as she sat in her office staring at the spines of books, Nadine wanted little more than to take back the entire after-church confrontation with Trina. With Damon conducting business today, it would have been the perfect Sunday for them to escape to dinner or enjoy a little Sunday shopping. She never should have told Trina about the call with Olivia.

A familiar ringtone required that she walk back to the master bedroom where her cell phone still rested on the vanity beside her purse. Nadine took a moment to compose herself before picking it up. She couldn't allow any trace of sadness to be heard in her voice.

"Hi, Aunt Pat," she said in as cheery a voice as she could muster. "Happy Sunday to you."

"Happy Lord's Day to you too, baby girl. How are y'all doing today?"

Nadine's mind raced for an honest answer, but avoiding a straight answer seemed like the best way to go. "We had a great service today at church, and I fixed a good meal when we got home. I made my homemade mashed potatoes that you like so much."

"Well, I'm sure sorry I missed that one," Aunt Pat replied with a chuckle. She paused and then asked, "How's the mayor doing?"

"I haven't seen much of him today, but when he gets back, I'll tell him you asked about him," Nadine responded.

"So, he's not at home right now?"

"No ma'am. He had some kind of downtown meeting to attend today, so he had to miss church. I'm sure he'll be getting home anytime now."

"Okay, then let me talk fast so I can be done before he walks in," Aunt Pat said.

Her tone had taken a turn, and it made Nadine tense.

"I had another dream about you, baby girl," her aunt went on to say. "You seemed lost like you didn't know which way to go. You had a phone in your hand, but you wouldn't call nobody. It was like you had too much pride, or maybe it was too much fear, to ask for directions. Are you sure you're all right, baby girl? You know that if you need help or somebody to talk to, you can always come to me."

Nadine took a deep breath and steadied her voice. "Yes, ma'am; I know, and if I ever need you, I'll cash in on that invitation."

"Don't lie to your Aunt Pat."

"I'm not, Auntie," Nadine said. "I promise. I think you worry about me because of the line of work I'm in, and you know that Damon's job is stressful too. We always manage to handle all the responsibilities and balance work and home life. I'm okay, but I'm glad you're just a phone call away if I ever need to talk to you."

"Or a few hours' drive away if you ever need to come for a visit. You don't even have to call ahead. You're always welcome here."

Nadine smiled at the words. "I know, Aunt Pat. I've always been welcome at your house. Yours felt more like home than the one I grew up in."

"That's 'cause you really my baby—I done told you that before," she said with a laugh. "I just made Rose go through them nine months of pregnancy and them long hours of labor; that's all."

Nadine couldn't count the number of times, as a child, that she wished that were really true.

"By the way, I talked to your mama the other day," Aunt Pat suddenly said. "She told me you ain't called her in a while."

"It has been a while, but I've called her twice since the last time she called me," Nadine pointed out. "That phone works both ways. If she wants to talk to me, she knows the number."

"She's still your mama."

"I know, Aunt Pat, but I'm a little bit offended that she would tell you I haven't called her in a long time when she hasn't called me in an even longer time."

"I understand that, baby girl. But just because she hasn't called you doesn't mean she don't care."

"Well, that's what it feels like."

"So, should I feel that way?"

"If she hasn't called you and you're always calling her, then yes, you should."

"I don't mean Rose. I mean you."

Nadine walked toward the large bay window that she loved. It allowed so much natural light into their bedroom. She said nothing as she looked out onto their massive property. Nadine knew where her aunt was headed with this conversation, and she didn't have a leg to stand on in her own defense.

"I've called you two or three times since the last time you picked up the phone to call me. Does that mean you don't care about me?"

"Of course not. I love you, Aunt Pat. You know that."

"Yes, I do know that. And I don't let not getting a phone call change that knowledge. Maybe you shouldn't let something as little as a cell phone tell you who cares about you and who doesn't. Don't get love mixed up with convenience," Aunt Pat went on to say. "Sometimes the people you don't see and hear from every day love you more than the ones that live right in the house with you."

Nadine didn't like the way that sounded. She didn't know if Aunt Pat was hinting at something or not. Nadine felt her defenses rising, but she remained quiet. The one thing she had never done was speak out of turn to her favorite aunt. She and her mom had exchanged a few cross words in the past, but that wasn't an experience Nadine had ever shared with Aunt Pat.

"I'll give her a call this week," she conceded. "I promise."

"That's two promises you done made me today," her aunt reminded.

"I know."

"I love you, baby girl. I'll talk to you later."

"I love you too, Auntie."

Just as the call disconnected, Nadine spotted Damon's Bentley coming through the security gates. He appeared to be driving faster than normal, so she rushed into the restroom to wash her hands in order to get downstairs to prepare Damon's dinner plate.

In the kitchen, she pulled a plate from the cabinet, then began filling it with rice, baked salmon, and spinach. Nadine was setting it on the dinner table, along with a glass of lemonade, as her husband walked in the door.

"Your dinner is ready for you, honey. As soon as you get comfortable, you can eat. Your dad and I have already eaten."

Damon made a beeline for the formal dining room where Nadine was placing napkins beside his dinner fork. "What did you tell Charley Bigham about me?" he demanded.

Nadine stepped back. "What?"

"Don't play stupid with me, Nadine," Damon charged. "You know I hate it when you play stupid."

"I'm not playing stupid. I don't know what you're talking about. I didn't tell Charley anything about you."

"I also hate when you lie to my face!" he said, swearing in the process.

"Damon, please calm down." Nadine's eyes shot toward his father's room.

"And I hate when you tell me to calm down too!" he said. "You're always doing stuff to upset me, and then telling me to calm down so you look like the angel, and I look like some out-of-control madman."

Nadine saw Daddy Deville using his walker, limp to the door, and use one hand to close it. She guessed by closing himself in the room, he could make it seem believable that he had no knowledge of his son's behavior.

"Damon, as God is my witness, I don't know what you're talking about. I haven't seen Charley since our meeting when I convinced him to drop the falsified claim against my client."

"And on that day, what did you tell him about me?"

"Nothing. Our conversation wasn't about you; we were discussing the case."

"So, he's just lying to you then."

"If he told you that I said something bad about you, then yes, he's lying."

"You didn't tell him that my popularity shot up after I married you? You didn't tell him that you are the reason I keep winning re-election?"

Nadine's head felt as though it was spinning. Mentally, she traveled back to her meeting with Charley at Moe's. She replayed their conversation in her mind. When she got to those statements in her review, those weren't words that had come out of her mouth.

"Charley is the one that said that," Nadine blurted. "He's the one who kept insisting that—"

"Shut up!"

With one sweep of his arm, Damon sent his dinner plate and everything on it crashing to the floor. Bits of porcelain flew everywhere as the dish hit the hardwood floor and shattered into what seemed like a hundred pieces. Nadine let out a yelp and jumped backward to avoid the scattering debris.

"I get so sick of you lying," he added. "I knew it! I knew that when you get behind my back with your uppity lawyer friends, you talk about me like you did me some favor by marrying me."

"That's not true. I promise I didn't say any of that to Charley."

"What reason that man got to lie, Nadine?"

"What reason do I have to lie?

"Because you're just a liar," Damon told her.

Nadine held up her right hand like she was about to take a stand in a court of law. "I swear I didn't tell Charley that. May God strike me dead right now if I did."

Damon slammed his briefcase on the top of the table, popped it open, and pulled out a handgun. He pointed it directly at Nadine. "God might not strike you dead, but I got a bullet that will."

Nadine tried to show no terror, but she could feel her knees weakening beneath her weight. "Damon, please put that away. Guns are nothing to play with."

Some days, curse words rolled off Damon's tongue like they were his second language. Today was one of those days.

"You think I'm playing?" he said, walking closer. "Is that what you think? You think I won't pull this trigger and send your brains splattering all over these walls?"

When he took a step closer, Nadine took a step back. "Damon, please," she repeated.

"You actually think you made me?" He burst out in a laugh and then sobered as if the laugh never happened. "Do you know what it feels like to go to a meeting and have some fat White buffalo have everybody at the table laughing at you because your spouse thinks they're all that and a bag of chips?"

"Damon, I—" Nadine froze and came to complete silence when she heard a cocking sound and saw the chamber rotate.

"Say one more word, and I swear, I'll kill you," he threatened. "Go ahead, if you think I'm playing." As she remained silent, he added, "You don't talk until I tell you to talk."

While there was a big part of Nadine that didn't think Damon truly had it in him to pull the trigger, as she was now looking into the barrel of the handgun, she wasn't about to test him. Nadine had often wondered what it felt like to have a gun aimed at one's face. She'd seen enough courtroom dramas to know that this kind of thing happened to lawyers in big cities all the time. There were times she wondered if it would be something she'd have to experience. But in all her speculating, not once did she imagine the person on the other end would be her husband.

They had only been standing there for minutes, but to Nadine, it felt like hours. When Damon finally stepped back and lowered the gun, Nadine felt overwhelmed with relief. Then, just as quickly as he lowered it, he brought it back to her face and pulled the trigger three times in succession. When Nadine screamed, he laughed just before dropping the gun back in his briefcase.

"You're about the stupidest woman I've ever met," he muttered. "You really thought I would shoot you in this house with my dad on the other end." He grabbed the case from the table and began walking toward the staircase. He didn't even bother to look back when he added, "And clean up that mess off my floor."

Nadine felt as though she had been holding her breath the whole while. She felt lightheaded, her eyesight was blurred and the exhale she released felt labored and constricting. As full reality set in, she couldn't stop the shaking of her body and had to hold on to the back of one of the dining room chairs to keep herself from crashing to the floor along with the bits of porcelain.

Nadine knew that she had to talk to somebody about this, but she also knew it couldn't be Trina. Not yet. She just wasn't ready to divulge the dirty details. She couldn't talk to Sophia either. Her sister would never understand. There was Aunt Pat, who, deep down inside, Nadine knew she could share anything with. But she also knew that if she called Aunt Pat regarding what had just happened, law officers would be taking Damon out in handcuffs before their phone call ended.

No, she couldn't reach out to any of them and bare her soul. There was only one person she could call, and that was the one she insulted on Friday. Nadine could only hope that Olivia would still be open to talking to her.

Chapter 12

Answer
The Question

N adine looked at the countdown timer on her computer screen and watched the seconds tick away. It was a moment of déjà vu. She had definitely been here before.

Her plan for the day had been to keep clear of the office, and she had done that for the most part. Nadine checked in with Ava throughout the day to see if there were any phone calls or unscheduled visitors for her. There were a few of both. She returned the calls from her car while driving around the city or parked in whatever secluded place she could find. The visitors had been instructed to make an appointment. Ava had taken care of that.

Yesterday's turn of events still had shaken up Nadine. Tears had flowed from her eyes uncontrollably for most of the day, which was the reason she kept her distance from Nadine Jackson & Associates. Her sunglasses had been working overtime to keep her emotions hidden today, and when she was finally ready to come into the office, an hour ago, Visine became her best friend. It helped to remove the tell-tale redness that would have been a dead giveaway.

She and Trina still hadn't cleared the air between them. They hadn't spoken since yesterday's fiasco in the parking lot. Nadine had every intention of talking to her friend today and offering an apology for her behavior, but she'd forgotten that Trina had taken a vacation day. She hadn't bothered to remind Nadine of that when she walked away from Trina yesterday saying that she'd see her at the office tomorrow. Nadine couldn't remember the last time she and Trina were so upset with each other that they went a full twenty-four hours without conversation. Probably not since college.

With everyone gone from the building, the sounds Nadine heard in the quietness were almost eerie: the hum of the personal fridge in the corner, the echo of seconds ticking away on her office's oversized wall clock, even the airy sounds of the cool air that flowed through the vents in the ceiling. All of them were subtle noises that she didn't pay attention to on an average workday, yet today, they were practically deafening.

At the three-minute mark, Nadine got up from her desk to retrieve a bottle of water from the refrigerator. She grabbed a small Tupperware container full of seedless grapes while she was at it. Nadine had gone all day having consumed nothing but a banana and a cup of Daddy Deville's coffee, both of which she grabbed on her way out the door this morning. She needed the coffee because last night she hadn't slept a wink. Every time Nadine closed her eyes she saw images of the gun that Damon pointed at her face. It's true that the gun wasn't loaded, but still, why would he do such a thing? Why would he even want his wife to have any kind of notion he would threaten her at gunpoint? As she sat up in bed last night watching him sleep, Nadine couldn't figure out how Damon could carry out the shocking act he'd done just a few short hours earlier and find the peace of mind to sleep so soundly.

She turned and walked toward her desk. What has become of my life? The question in Nadine's head begged to be answered, but she didn't have one to give it. She couldn't figure out how or why things had gone so awry. On the day of her storybook wedding, no one could have told her that as she continued to turn the pages, her tale of romance would turn into some kind of twisted comedy.

With only twelve seconds to go, Nadine threw two grapes in her mouth, and then got situated in her chair. The rotating seat came to a standstill just as Olivia was admitting her into their virtual conference room.

"Good evening, Nadine." Her smile was bright and welcoming like she wasn't greeting a person who had, with no advance notice, exited a meeting with her just three days prior.

"Good evening." Nadine found it hard to look into Olivia's eyes as she spoke. "Again, I'm sorry about—"

"Your apology has already been accepted," Olivia assured. "I know you think I was offended, but I wasn't. Nadine, you're not the first person to storm out of a session with me, and you won't be the last. As a matter of fact, you're already not the last," Olivia added with a laugh. "I had a couple's session this morning, and the husband got angry and left. And they were here physically, so the dramatics were real. He slammed the door and everything."

"Still," Nadine said. "That's not how I normally do things. I don't accept that from people I'm trying to help, so I shouldn't do it to people who are trying to help me."

"Listen, Nadine. You're an attorney. We're in different lines of business. In my profession, what you did with me is not only accepted, but also expected. If you'd slapped me, thrown something at me, spit on me, or attacked me in any way physically, believe me when I tell you that we would be having a very different conversation. Ending sessions prematurely happens more times than I care to count. So, before we move forward, I'm going to need you to do me a favor."

Nadine looked her squarely in the eyes for the first time. "Okay," she said cautiously. "What's that?"

"I need you to forget last Friday and agree to move forward with a fresh slate starting today, forgetting the things that are behind us and pressing forward to those things that are ahead."

Nadine smiled. "That's Galatians, right?"

"Close. It's from Philippians, chapter 3." Olivia clasped her hands on the desk in front of her and asked, "Can you make that promise?"

"Sure." In truth, Nadine was more than happy to accept the challenge, and knowing that Olivia wanted her to would make it that much easier to talk freely today. "Great. Let's pray."

Nadine nodded in agreement and bowed her head. She could hear Olivia praying, but her words sounded off in the distance. What remained at the forefront of Nadine's mind was whether she should reveal all the skeletons in her closet to her therapist.

"Amen," Oliva said signifying the prayer had come to an end.

"Amen," Nadine endorsed.

"Now, let's dive in," Olivia suggested. "Over the past couple of days, have you given any attention to the things we talked about on Friday, particularly the things I said?"

Nadine pondered a moment. If she were honest, she'd have to admit that she hadn't given much thought at all to the conversation they'd had. The thing that kept playing in Nadine's memory was how she'd left the session. The conversation between Olivia and her had gotten lost due to the scolding Nadine had given herself and the scolding she'd received from her best friend.

"I remember words you used, like abuse and malicious intent," Nadine recalled. "They were terms that made me feel like you were calling me an abused wife."

"Are you ready to revisit that conversation now?"

Subconsciously, Nadine saw herself cleaning the dining room, sweeping up porcelain chips that she had not broken and chunks of food she had not wasted. She saw herself mopping residue left behind by the salmon she'd taken such care to cook just the way her husband liked it and wiping sticky scum off the wall that had been delivered when the lemonade splattered there under Damon's rage.

"Yes, I'm ready," she replied.

"Good." Olivia sounded relieved, like she wasn't sure that was the reply she would receive. "In our last conversation, you mentioned being forced to get out of the car at the roadside after a Sunday service. Another Sunday has passed since that time. How did things go yesterday? Were there any arguments on the car ride to or from church?"

"No," Nadine was glad to report. "Actually, Damon had a meeting with some other officials and Atlanta businesspersons yesterday, so he wasn't at church."

"What about Saturday? How did that go?"

"It went fine. It was a pretty quiet day around the house." Nadine thought back as she spoke. Saturday had been more than a good day; it had been a great day. Damon had no work obligations and neither had she. They were able to relax and watch a midday movie together in the theatre room. Nadine hadn't even had to cook; they'd gone out to their favorite restaurant.

After dining at STK Steakhouse, Damon said he didn't want to leave the downtown area. He wanted to spend the entire night there. They hadn't packed an overnight bag, but as it turned out, clothing was the last thing they needed. On a whim, Damon had Nadine call and book a room at the Four Seasons Hotel. They had experienced a magical evening in the presidential suite.

"That sounds absolutely amazing," Olivia said.

Until Olivia's comment broke into her thoughts, Nadine barely realized she was making her reflections verbal. "Yes, it was," she agreed.

"The presidential suite there doesn't come cheap. That cost you a pretty penny, for sure."

"Yeah, it did." Nadine nodded. "He promised to pay me back when the charges show up on my card, but after yesterday…" Nadine allowed her voice to trail.

Olivia leaned forward at her desk. "After yesterday?"

"After yesterday, I'm not counting on him making good on his word to pay for our overnight date."

"So, something did happen yesterday? You said he had a business meeting. Did something happen there?"

Nadine pushed her glasses up on her nose. She felt the onset of tears. "We both left the hotel early Sunday morning and went home to prepare for the day. He went to his appointment, and I went to church. When I got home, I cooked one of Damon's favorite meals so it would be ready when he arrived. In my mind, I'd hoped that we'd have a continuation of Saturday."

"But you didn't?"

"No. At his meeting, someone told him I said something about him, and it made him angry. I couldn't convince him that it wasn't true. I told him, but he thought I was the one lying." Nadine reached for a tissue from her Kleenex box. "I'm sorry," she said as she began wiping away the tears that fell.

"Don't dare to apologize," Olivia said. "You cry as much as you need to in order to keep going, okay?"

Nadine's answer was a quiet nod, and Olivia continued to talk.

"So, you're saying that what was told to him was never said?"

"It was said, but it wasn't said by me. A colleague of mine was at the business-slash-government gathering that was going on. This is the same colleague that recently had to go back to his client and convince him to drop the charges he'd launched against my client because I'd gathered evidence to prove he was misrepresenting the facts."

"So, you think that this colleague did this as a means of getting back at you?"

"I can't think of any other reason for it," Nadine replied. "He knew I didn't say those things. In fact, as he was saying them, I was correcting him. He was basically accusing Damon of having low popularity until he married me. He said that I was the reason my husband was enjoying such success as a mayor. I told him that it wasn't true, that Damon and I equally complemented each other. We've been opposing counsels in court on a few occasions, and although I know he's not very fond of me, I couldn't believe he'd stoop so low as to blatantly lie to Damon, telling him that I bragged about how he was nothing before he married me."

Nadine's tears were falling heavier now, and she grabbed another tissue to help with their absorption. In the extended pause, Olivia spoke.

"Mayor Deville believed your constituent instead of you, and his belief that you'd said these things made him angry. How did he handle his heated emotions? Did an argument ensue?"

Nadine nodded while still trying to dry her eyes. The waterworks just wouldn't stop. Her bottom lip trembled as she struggled to talk legibly. "He called me a liar. He called me a ... well, you know."

"The 'B' word?"

Another nod and more tissues followed. Then Nadine said, "He got so angry that he took the plate of food that I had fixed for him and knocked it to the floor. He didn't eat any of it; he just knocked it on the floor. Food went everywhere. Drink went everywhere. The drinking glass broke, so glass went everywhere. The plate the food had been on was smashed, and the broken pieces went everywhere. It was just a mess!"

Nadine buried her face in her hands, ashamed that she was so emotional that she was barely understanding her own words.

"It's okay to take a moment to gather yourself," Olivia told her.

Nadine hadn't joined today's meeting with the intent to expose it all, but once she started, it was as if she couldn't stop. Things she had kept from those closest to her, she was pouring in the ears of a perfect stranger. She felt embarrassed. She felt vulnerable. But, she also felt the need to keep talking.

"He pulled a gun on me."

Olivia stopped writing and stared at the computer screen. "I'm sorry. What?"

"It wasn't loaded," Nadine quickly added. "But when he pulled it, I didn't know that."

"What made him think threatening you with a gun was necessary? Had you first threatened him, and he felt the need to protect himself?"

Nadine shook her head while she wadded new sheets of Kleenex in her hands. "I said God could strike me dead if I was lying to him about not saying what he thought I said. Then, when I made that comment, he pulled his handgun and said God wouldn't have to do it because he was going to."

For the first time in the short time they'd been in communication with each other, Nadine thought Olivia was going to lose her composure. She watched as the woman closed her eyes and took what appeared to be a few cleansing breaths. Olivia's lips moved rapidly but no sound accompanied it. It literally looked like she was silently speaking in tongues. Nadine wondered if the therapist was praying for God to give her the strength to remain professional.

"I think I already know the answer to my next question," Olivia said ultimately, breaking her silence, "but I'll ask it for the record anyway. Did you call the police?"

"No. Like I said, the gun wasn't loaded. He never laid a hand on me. I wasn't hurt or anything. I was just a little frightened."

"A little frightened?" Olivia cocked her head to the side, clearly questioning Nadine's choice of words. "Let me ask you something, Nadine, and I really want you to feel free to give me an honest answer. Are you still of the mindset that you're not an abused wife?"

"Deep inside, I knew he wouldn't shoot me," Nadine immediately responded while wiping away the last traces of her tearful meltdown. "Him taking out the gun startled me because the only time I'd ever seen him holding it was when he was locking it away in the house. I knew Damon couldn't shoot me. He was just so angry because when he was confronted with this lie, the conversation wasn't a private one. Damon said people at the function were laughing at him."

"So, taking all that into consideration, do you believe his reaction was warranted? Do you think him believing what was told to him, and his being laughed at by others, made for a good reason for him to threaten your life at gunpoint?"

Nadine hesitated but finally said, "No."

"Good. I'm certainly glad that you realize that. Now, let me go back to my previous question, which you cleverly dodged instead of answering. "Do you still hold to the claim that you're not an abused wife?"

"I don't know anymore." Nadine's voice was little more than a whisper. "I don't want to be an abused woman. I see them all the time, and I don't want to be one of them." New tears were making an introduction. "If Damon would get some help with his temper—maybe take some anger management classes—I believe he could become the model husband. Back when our troubles first started, I used to try to convince him to agree to couple's therapy, but he never would. He said he was fine and didn't need any help discovering his problem. He said he already knew what his problem was. It was me."

"Which is why you became so upset when we spoke last Friday," Olivia interjected as she flipped through her notepad. "When I indicated that you might be in an abusive relationship, you said, and I quote, 'I came to you to talk about how I can become a better wife to a husband who is carrying the weight of an entire metropolitan city on his shoulders, and you're calling me an abused woman'."

Olivia looked up from her notes and back into the camera at Nadine. "You've been told that you're the blame for so long that you've started to believe it. Nadine, how long has this been going on? You've been married nine years. When did all this start?"

Nadine took a moment to think it over. The first time Damon called her stupid during a heated conversation, they had only been married a few months. Nadine couldn't remember what that argument was about, but she would never forget how shocked she was when Damon called her stupid. The "B word" shocked her even more. They'd probably been married two years by the time he defined her as that. Nowadays, very little that came out of Damon's mouth took her by surprise.

"Nadine, when did it all start?" Olivia repeated her question.

"I can't exactly recall as far as dates go," she told Olivia, but what I do know is that it has gotten worse over the years. Damon and I used to have more good days than bad days, and if the truth be told, we probably still do. But lately, the bad days have been so bad that they have been outweighing the good ones."

"Does he ever apologize? Does he ever admit that he's wrong?"

Nadine shook her head slowly. "Not in words, but I guess he does in his actions. For example, we can have a huge blow-up like the one we had Sunday, and then a day or two later, I'll get flowers or jewelry, or we'll have an amazing night like the one we just had Saturday."

"That's typical abuser behavior, Nadine." Olivia repositioned herself in her chair before speaking again. "Look, you have expressed your desire to see your marriage survive, but please know that if your husband doesn't see a problem and he is unwilling to seek or accept sound counsel, things will only continue to worsen. You've said these episodes are happening more often than they used to; that means it's getting worse. You're probably also noticing that they last longer than they used to, or they are becoming more intense or even more dangerous than they used to be. This is what happens when we pretend problems don't exist. When it comes to things like this, we can't just hope they will magically go away.

"Nadine," Olivia continued, "if you want your marriage to survive, you're going to have to convince the mayor to seek counseling with you. And guess what? If Mayor Deville truly wants your marriage to survive, he will do everything within his power to see that it does. He won't let his pride kill his marriage; not if he genuinely wants to find healing for what ails it. If your husband isn't willing to recognize that there is a problem and that he, too, plays a role in it, this can't get any better, Nadine; it can only get worse. You must ask yourself, 'what's worse than him pointing an empty gun at me and pulling the trigger?'"

Chapter 13

Oh My God

A gentle knock at Nadine's bedroom door pulled her attention from her journal. She looked at the clock on her cell phone and smiled before tucking her pen between the pages, closing the book, and slipping it all beneath her covers.

"Come in," she said in the strongest voice she could rally.

It really had been Nadine's intention to be the first to extend the olive branch and bridge the gap between she and Trina, but life happened, and for the past three days, Nadine had barely been able to get out of bed. It all started Tuesday morning when she woke up with a headache like none she'd ever had. It wasn't what she'd describe as a pounding one; it was more like a consistent dull, aching throb. The drumming started at her temples, and then radiated nonstop across her forehead. Just the act of moving around to get dressed for work that morning felt like too much for her to handle. Even the hot shower she took didn't ease her misery.

Nadine had already spent Monday going everywhere else and doing anything else to avoid the office, so, despite her agony on Tuesday morning, she willed her body to respond to her every command. Her initial thought was that the stubborn headache was the penalty she was being forced to pay for the hard crying spell she'd had on Monday while speaking to Olivia. However, even with extra-strength over-the-counter pain medication, Nadine's headache persisted.

With her alarm set to wake her early and a planned agenda to get a head start on catching up on what hadn't finished on Monday, she had been the first to arrive at the office Tuesday. But after being there an hour and feeling too miserable to make any progress on her paperwork, Nadine realized that mind over matter wasn't going to work this time. Ava was the only one who had arrived before Nadine left, and the legal assistant didn't hold back when she told her boss how bad she looked.

An emergency doctor's visit confirmed what Ava had guessed and what Nadine had feared. During the height of the pandemic, when many people contracted the virus—including two of her own attorneys—Nadine had been one of the lucky ones. When vaccines were ultimately approved, too much conflicting information about the new drugs had aided in her decision not to get them. Yet, she still managed to stay COVID-free. Now that the threat of the virus had considerably lessened and mask-wearing and social distancing were no longer mandated in most places, her body decided to make her a statistic.

At her doctor's order, Nadine had gone straight home. By the afternoon, she was experiencing fever and chills, and by that night, she could hardly breathe due to nasal congestion. She had barely seen her husband or her father-in-law since then. Upon hearing of Nadine's infection, Damon immediately began avoiding her as if she had the bubonic plague. It was Trina that had come by every day, twice a day, to make sure that she had everything she needed. It was Trina who was walking in her room now, making her second visit for the day.

"Your eyes look much better today," Trina remarked as she set a fresh bowl of soup on Nadine's bedside table. "They don't look nearly as droopy as they did on Tuesday, and your voice is clearer than it was yesterday, for sure."

"Thanks." Nadine adjusted her mask. The days were starting to run together for her, but she knew today was Thursday because she had watched a new episode of *Abbott Elementary* on television last night. "I feel much better," she went on to report. "It took a minute for those meds to get in my system, but I started feeling better yesterday, and I can breathe better today. I'm still a little hoarse and have a bit of a nagging cough, but other than that, I feel okay." Nadine said a quick grace and immediately took in a spoonful of the chicken soup Trina set in front of her. The warm liquid felt good going down her throat. "I'm sure glad I didn't lose my sense of taste," she commented.

Trina chuckled. "Girl, your Aunt Pat swears it's her prayers and this homemade soup recipe of hers that's raising you from the dead. As far as she's concerned, that medicine had much less to do with your recovery than her soup did."

Nadine nodded knowingly. She'd had a brief telephone conversation with her aunt earlier today. "Yeah, that Aunt Pat believes in the power of prayer; that's for sure."

"I guess that's something your grandparents instilled in all their kids," Trina commented as she used a can of Lysol to spray the space then removed the gloves from her hands. "Ms. Rose is the same way."

Nadine shook her head slowly from side to side. "Please don't compare Aunt Pat to Mama. They have two totally different viewpoints on this matter. When I talked to Aunt Pat, she was encouraging me to follow the doctor's orders but to also keep in mind that my healing came from God. If I had been talking to my mother, she would have crucified me for going to the doctor in the first place." Nadine paused to cough and clear her throat before continuing. "Then she would have gone into this whole sermonette about how, if I had faith like I should, I would have just trusted God."

"That's Ms. Rose for you," Trina said with a laugh. "Gotta love her."

"Maybe you should get out of here while I eat," Nadine said. "I can't eat with my mask on, and I'd feel horrible if you caught this."

"Don't you worry about me. I've been vaccinated, got my booster, and I'm double-masked."

"None of that guarantees you won't get sick."

"True," Trina said. "But leaving won't guarantee that either." Nadine looked at her friend and smiled in appreciation.

She was glad she wasn't leaving. Nadine was happy to have company. She didn't know what she would have done over the past few days if Trina hadn't stepped up. When Ava notified the office of Nadine's diagnosis, it was as though last Sunday's strife never happened. Trina immediately jumped into action. She sent Ava to the store to buy additional sanitizing products so that she could disinfect Nadine's office, and she'd called Aunt Pat to fill her in so she could get the prayer chain going. Aunt Pat shared her chicken soup recipe with Trina and told her exactly how to make it. It was all Nadine had eaten since being ordered into quarantine by her doctor.

"This soup is so good," Nadine remarked.

"I know, right?" Trina replied. I made extra to keep at home. Bradley and JJ have been tearing it up. I have to make a bunch so that I'll have enough for us and you," she added with a laugh. "I don't usually do soup except in the wintertime, but I could do this all year long."

Nadine leaned back against her pillows and took a moment to rest. She couldn't help wondering what she'd be eating if Trina had decided to hold a grudge against her. She literally had not seen Damon since he came in to get some of his belongings in order to move to one of the guest bedrooms on Tuesday. He had texted her a couple of times to ask how she felt, but not once had he put on a mask and peeked in her door, let alone come into the room or offer her a meal.

"Mr. Deville is getting around better now," Trina said, breaking into Nadine's thoughts. "When I saw him downstairs, he told me that he starts physical therapy tomorrow."

"Oh, does he?"

Trina looked at her. "You didn't know?"

Nadine shook her head from side to side. "I knew it was in the works and that he and Damon had been talking about it, but I wasn't aware that therapy had been scheduled."

"You're going to be having strange people—maybe even strange men—coming in your house to work with your father-in-law." Trina's face morphed into a frown. "Seems like Damon would have told you that so you wouldn't be blindsided."

Nadine shrugged uncomfortably. She avoided eye contact with Trina as she blew on another spoonful of soup. "I guess my getting sick threw everybody off. I'm sure he meant to mention it," she said before filling her mouth.

While Trina sat quietly on the edge of her mattress, Nadine kept her eyes trained on her bowl. She could feel the threat of a question arising that she wasn't ready to answer, so she jumped in first to change the subject.

"I didn't tell you that I rescheduled my meeting with Olivia, did I?" She finally looked at Trina as she asked.

Her friend's raised eyebrows gave away the fact that this news made for a pleasant surprise. "Did you? I'm so glad. When will you meet with her?"

"I already did. We met on Monday."

"Oh, wow. I'm shocked that she was able to get you in so quickly on such short notice."

"So was I. She had a cancellation, so the timing of my request was perfect, I guess."

"Did you have an in-person meeting?"

"Ah-uh. I didn't want to go in."

"Okay, I knew you'd said you only wanted virtual sessions. I was just asking because I'm wondering where you picked up this virus," Trina commented.

Nadine ate more soup before replying. "I did a lot of running around outside of the office Monday, so there's no telling."

"So, how did your session go?" "Well?"

"I don't mean for you to give me details," Trina said, interrupting Nadine's response. "I know all that is confidential. I just meant, did everything go well?"

"Yes, it did." Nadine's mind drifted back to the emotional conversation she'd had with Olivia, but she didn't dwell there long before returning her full attention to Trina. "She's easy to talk to, and she really seems to have a special way of hearing the words behind the words that you say. You know what I mean? Like, even when you can't figure out how to say everything, she hears what you're trying to say."

"Oh, you don't have to convince me. Now that you've had the chance to experience her, maybe you can better understand why I've been going to her all these years," Trina said.

Nadine readjusted herself against the stack of pillows that supported her back. "I guess so. I don't intend for it to be a regular thing with me though. I can handle the stress of the office. I just needed an ear for this specific situation."

Trina stood and rolled back the tray that had been positioned in front of Nadine. "I guess you've had enough since you've stopped eating and put your mask back on. I'll take your leftovers and place them in the fridge on my way out."

"Thank you, Trina. I know I've said it before, but—"

"Only like one million, three hundred and sixty-five thousand, eight hundred and twenty-four times," Trina said.

Nadine laughed until she coughed. "You're so over-dramatic," she told Trina.

"No, really. I've been keeping count. That's an accurate number."

"Lies," Nadine said with more laughter.

"The point is, you don't have to keep thanking me," Trina stated. "I'm glad to do it. You would do the same for me, or at least you'd try. Bradley would be all in the way though. You'd probably have to fight him to try to take care of …"

Trina's voice drifted, and the expression on her face was one that reflected regret—like she wished she could snatch back the words she'd just put in the atmosphere. "I'm sorry, Nadine," she finally said. "That didn't come out right. I wasn't trying to throw off on Damon."

"Oh, girl, please. The thought never crossed my mind." Nadine hoped she sounded believable. "Damon and Bradley are just two different kinds of men, that's all. For some husbands, taking care of their wives when they're sick comes naturally. Damon's not one of those men."

Trina proceeded with caution. "So, it doesn't bother you?"

"What do you mean?"

"I mean, does it bother you that Damon's not taking care of you? If I mentally put myself in your place, I must admit that I would be ticked off. I really wasn't going to say anything about it, but when I came in early this morning to bring you your soup, the bowl from yesterday was still here, and tissue that you'd used to blow your nose into was still on the floor from where you missed the garbage can. You were out of juice and water. When I brought you those bottled waters this morning, you drank one bottle without taking a break to breathe. It was as if you were totally dehydrated. And when I came in this evening to bring you this fresh bowl of soup, I looked over here on your nightstand and saw the bowl of soup I brought you this morning. Nadine, he's not even doing the minimum."

"He can't chance getting sick, Trina. He's the mayor of the city of Atlanta."

"And you're his wife. Bump Atlanta. If he drops dead tomorrow, you can bet your bottom dollar Atlanta will have his seat filled by an interim mayor before his body can get cold. You should be his first priority, not the citizens of Atlanta."

Nadine knew her friend was right, and she wished to God that Damon was that kind of husband, but he wasn't, and there was nothing she could do to change that. "I'll be fine, Trina. Really, I will."

"Oh, I know you'll be fine; I'm not worried about that. I know you'll be fine because I'm going to make sure you're fine. But the truth is, I shouldn't be the one saying this, Nadine. Me and Damon ought to be fighting over those bragging rights. Don't you see that?"

Nadine reached toward the nightstand. It was time to take her medication, and she decided to also use this time to try and think of a response. She shook one of the tablets out of the bottle into her hand, then grabbed the water bottle that was already open and ready to help her wash down the pill. The entire task took less than thirty seconds. It wasn't nearly enough time for Nadine to come up with an excuse, and quite frankly, she was tired of trying to justify Damon's behavior.

"I do see that, Trina," she decided to say. "But what am I supposed to do, demand that he take care of me? If it's not an instinct, then it's not a natural instinct. I don't want to feel like I twisted his arm and made him do something. That's not going to make him happy and it's not going to make me happy either."

Trina sighed and put on a fresh pair of gloves to begin gathering the trash and leftovers. "Okay, I hear you," she said.

"I'm going to go to the restroom. I'll be right back," Nadine announced.

"Here, let me help you."

"I'm not an invalid, Trina." Nadine playfully swatted away her friend's extended hand. "You might have missed your calling. Maybe you should have been a nurse. You're really good at this."

Trina grunted. "That was actually my second choice of career paths, but when I saw what RNs earned versus what lawyers had the capacity to earn, I thought, 'I'll take Courtroom Etiquette for one hundred, Alex.'"

Nadine laughed out loud and then coughed out loud as she closed herself behind the door of her master ensuite. Trina had always been the one who could keep her laughing even during the worst of circumstances.

After quickly emptying her bladder, Nadine flushed the commode and made her way to the sink to wash her hands. It felt good to be up and moving around. While the water warmed, Nadine looked at her reflection in the mirror. She looked like she'd been in bed for three weeks instead of three days. She was surprised Trina hadn't told her how bad her hair looked.

"While you're in there, tighten up that ponytail, girl," her friend suddenly called out from the bedroom. "Just because you feel like a mess don't mean you got to look like a mess."

The timing of Trina's words drew more laughing—and coughing—from Nadine. She allowed the faucet to continue to run while she retrieved her comb and brush from the drawer. While her main hair products were hidden in the drawer of her vanity that was set up in the bedroom, there were always extras in the bathroom.

Nadine removed the bow that had been failing in its attempt to hold her hair in place, then used the comb to rake together all the stray hairs that were sticking from her head in all directions. She pulled a bottle of leave-in conditioner from under the cabinet and used it to add moisture and sheen before picking up her brush and bringing it all together.

"That looks much better." She whispered her approval to the reflection in the mirror as though the reflection was another person.

Nadine washed her hands, then used them to splash warm water on her face. Feeling the liquid on her skin felt so good that she decided to take it to the next level. After using the hand towel to dry her face, Nadine slid open the stall door and turned on the water. She hadn't had the strength to take a full shower since Tuesday. It was past time.

Opening the bathroom door, Nadine stepped back into her master bedroom to let Trina know what she was about to do and to grab fresh clothes. She found her friend sitting on the mattress with one hand over her mouth. In the other hand, Trina held Nadine's open journal. In her time tidying up the room, she must have discovered it under the covers where Nadine had tucked it earlier.

Nadine had no words. She didn't know how much Trina had read, but the expression on her face as she slowly looked up from the pages was a dead giveaway that Trina had read more than enough.

"Nadine." Trina's hand slid from her lips in slow motion and her eyes were beginning to fill with tears. "Nadine," she repeated. "Oh my God…"

Chapter 14

Spiraling Out of Control

Nadine couldn't remember a time when her life had been so chaotic. A person's life would have to be in a mess for them to think having COVID-19 was a blessing in disguise, and that's exactly the way Nadine felt. As far as she was concerned, COVID's visit couldn't have been more perfectly timed. Stubborn traces of her cough and nasal congestion lingered, and her body couldn't seem to get enough sleep, but for the most part, she felt fine. Still, the virus gave her the excuse she needed to remain barricaded from everybody in her life. If this week had taught her only one thing, it was that she had no one she could trust.

Her husband definitely hadn't been showing the concern that he should, but the one person who had been checking on her had turned out to be the world's biggest snoop who made a living sticking her nose where it didn't belong.

The week was ending a lot worse than it had begun. At the beginning of the week, Nadine had good friends and good food. Now, she had neither. Three long days had passed since she walked out of her bathroom to find Trina reading her personal writings, but the passing days had done nothing to fade the memories that still played in high definition in her mind. It was as fresh as if it had happened just an hour ago.

"What are you doing?" Nadine had demanded upon seeing her friend holding her private journal. "Who told you you could read my stuff?"

"I—I—I was straightening your covers." Trina was visibly caught off guard by Nadine's stiff reprimand. "I was fixing the bed, and it fell on the floor." Her voice reduced to a terrified whisper. "Oh my God, Nadine. Why haven't you told me about all of this?"

"Because it's not your business!" The virus still had Nadine sounding a bit hoarse, but the level of her response was in vast contrast to Trina's. Nadine yelled the words as best she could. "If I wanted you to see it, I would have shown it to you. I can't believe you thought it was okay for you to invade my privacy!"

Trina looked down at the book, then back at Nadine. "How is this not my business? Since when do we keep secrets like this from each other? We've always been able to trust each other, haven't we?"

Nadine had released a dry laugh that turned into a dry cough. When she got her wind back, she'd said, "I thought so too, but apparently, I was wrong! It's evident that I can't trust you. I turn my back for one second, and you're all up in my private journal!"

Rising from the bed, Trina had given Nadine a look of disbelief. "How are you trying to make this about me? How have I become a bad person in this situation? Nadine, your husband has been throwing things at you and calling you the most disrespectful names imaginable." Trina flipped to one of Nadine's most recent writings and pointed her finger at the page, as if Nadine needed to be reminded. "Look at this, girl. Damon pointed a gun at you! He aimed a pistol in your face, and you've got the nerves to be mad at me?"

Nadine had hoped that Trina hadn't gotten that far, but her words proved she had. She reached forward and snatched her book from Trina's hand. "Give me this! You had no right! How much of my journal did you read?

"I read enough to know that your husband should be locked in jail somewhere for assault."

"The gun wasn't loaded, and I wasn't hurt. Did you read that part too, Ms. Nosey McNosey?" Tears had begun to spill from Nadine's eyes. Her name-calling even sounded childish to her own ears, but she didn't care. "If anyone should be in jail, it's you for breaking and entering!"

"Breaking and entering? Breaking and entering what?"

"Into my private property; that's what. I didn't give you permission, did I?"

"What law book are you pulling that from? That wouldn't even hold up in the stupid court shows on TV, let alone a real court of law. You're just trying to get out of talking about this. You're grasping at straws."

"How 'bout you grasp for that doorknob and get out of my house?"

"Nadine!"

"Don't 'Nadine' me. You heard what I said. Get out!"

"Girl, what is wrong with you? How are you going to stand there and defend this monstrosity? Listen, I'm sorry for reading your diary, okay? Maybe I shouldn't have, but I didn't go looking for it, and I certainly didn't break into it. It was right there. When it dropped from under the covers, it fell in an open position, and once I got a glimpse of that sentence you wrote about him grabbing your shirt one day and ripping it while it was still on your body, all because you wouldn't do something he'd demanded, I couldn't stop reading. I didn't mean to invade your privacy, but I couldn't pretend I didn't see what I saw. Nadine, Damon needs help and so do you."

"No, you're the one who needs help, and apparently the first thing you need help with is your hearing. I said for you to get out of my house, and I meant it." Nadine had stomped to the bedroom door and opened it before continuing her verbal attack. "You will not stand in my face and talk about my husband. Just because yours is a wimp who lets you run all over him doesn't mean mine is a monster because he doesn't."

"Are you freakin' kidding me with this?" Trina's eyes were bulging. "Bradley ain't nobody's wimp, and you know that just as well as I do. Bradley is confident in who he is. His manhood is not so flimsy that he's threatened when his wife has an opinion, so he has no need to flex his muscles against me when I disagree with him. You really think it makes Damon a man because he cusses at you, humiliates you, and threatens you? Nadine, you are way smarter than this. How can you—"

"Oh, so now I'm stupid? Because I'm keeping the vows that I made before God, to stay married for better or for worse, I'm stupid. Is that what you're trying to say?"

"On the contrary, Nadine. You're one of the smartest women I know, and that's why this ain't making no kind of sense to me. You know full well that God doesn't mean for you to stay in an abusive marriage where you're being terrorized by your husband. You can't be thinking rationally here. I did not, nor would I ever call you stupid."

"You might not have said the word, but from where I stand, calling me stupid is what you're doing."

"Well, maybe you're getting me mixed up with your husband, because from what I read, calling you stupid is his job!"

It was at that moment that Nadine lost total control. Before she knew it, she had reached forward and slapped Trina across the cheek. Even with vision that was blurred by her own tears, Nadine's strike landed perfectly, and the intensity of it had caused Trina to take a step back. This was way worse than the conflict that brewed in the church parking lot last Sunday. In all their years of knowing each other, Nadine and Trina had never come close to blows. They'd had plenty of disagreements that resulted in raised voices, but prior to Tuesday, raised hands had never been introduced.

For a few seconds, Trina seemed dazed by the fierce contact. It was as if she couldn't quite process what had just taken place.

Nadine was dazed by her own reaction. She was sure that a scene from an episode of one of those really wretched Black cinema flicks was about to play itself out in her bedroom. In the first moments after the slap, she had envisioned the next scene being one where earrings would be removed, shoes would be kicked off, and hair would be pulled. Nadine found herself bracing for the worst. She felt anxious and a little fearful, because truthfully she wasn't at all sure that she'd win this fight.

For what seemed like a lifetime, Trina didn't say a word. When her lips finally parted, her tone of voice was nearly unrecognizable. It was an unnerving mix of fury and anguish.

"Yeah, I'm leaving, but not because I'm wrong. I'm leaving because if I stay another minute, I'll have to call the police on myself for snatching you by the throat and dragging your stupid you-know-what down the steps of your own house. And yes, I called you stupid," Trina added, "because there ain't no other way to describe you after what you just did. I'm leaving because if I don't, I'm gonna put my foot in the same place that your sorry-excuse-for-a-husband threatened to put his in the entry you wrote the day before your birthday last year."

"Get out of my house!" Nadine yelled.

Grabbing her handbag, Trina had replied, "Gladly!" She took two steps, and then turned to look back at Nadine. "At first, I was feeling bad for you, but now I think you and your low-down wife-beater deserve each other after all. The people of Atlanta have no idea that they have their very own version of Ike and Tina Turner running the city."

The door slammed behind her exit, and although Trina had already left the room, Nadine picked up the container that held the leftover soup and flung it at the closed door. The top popped off the storage container upon impact, and she watched her favorite aunt's recipe splatter and ooze down to the floor.

Now, three days later, Nadine realized that she was the only one suffering the consequences from her unrestrained angry outburst. The soup had not only been delicious on those days that Trina had brought it to her; it had also been filling and comforting. She would gladly pay a hundred dollars to be able to have just one bowl of it right now. Nadine had never thought to ask Aunt Pat for the recipe, so she couldn't recreate the dish now even if she wanted to—and she really, really wanted to.

Nadine had not cooked since being ordered into quarantine by her doctor, but Damon wasn't going hungry. Every day, he stopped somewhere to get himself something on his way home from work. Yesterday, he called for a restaurant delivery. Damon would apparently get food for his dad too, but not once had he brought Nadine even a morsel of anything. He probably thought Trina was still making her daily rounds. At least that was what Nadine had convinced herself to believe. It was very probable since she hadn't told Damon about the awful fight. Nadine was sure Daddy Deville had overheard the upstairs commotion that had played out on Tuesday, but evidently he hadn't shared it with his son.

The battle with COVID-19 had been no fun, but being quarantined with the potentially deadly virus had saved her from having to come up with a reason for not going to work. And not going to work had saved her from having to face her former best friend. How she was going to handle things after her time of isolation, Nadine didn't know. She hadn't thought that far into the future yet, but she still had a few days to come up with a plan.

Right now, her stomach was talking so loudly that it was drowning out any hope of her thoughts being heard. It was after four 'o clock, and Nadine hadn't eaten anything all day. Fatigue was now her biggest enemy. She'd slept later than noon, and when she did wake up, Daddy Deville's therapists had already arrived; she could hear them downstairs attending to his needs. They left while she was deep into watching reruns of *The Good Doctor* on Hulu. Since then, it had been Tuesday's haunting memories that had held her hostage in the room. Now, Nadine needed to get something in her stomach.

Her session with Olivia was less than an hour away. The virtual follow-up with the therapist had been set at the close of their first session. After what happened on Tuesday, Nadine had contemplated canceling it, but she'd decided not to.

Wearing a mask and gloves while armed with a can of Lysol, Nadine made her way downstairs where she quickly prepared two veggie sandwiches. The tomatoes and cucumbers were already sliced, and the lettuce and spinach leaves had already been rinsed and prepared for use. Before returning upstairs, Nadine grabbed a can of unsalted cashews and a box of raisins from the cabinet just in case she wanted something to snack on later. For good measure, she sprayed disinfectant throughout the downstairs space as she walked back to the stairwell.

Most days, Damon didn't get home until around six, and she prayed that he would stick to that schedule today. He hadn't been coming to their bedroom all week, but it would be just like him to make today—of all days—the one where he did. Damon wouldn't be happy to discover she was seeking professional help, and he would be downright incensed to know that the therapist was someone who knew he was her husband.

Once inside her bedroom, Nadine tried to get as comfortable as possible while she ate her meal. Somehow, knowing she was about to talk to Olivia was making her anxious. The therapist had a way of getting Nadine to let down her guard, so much so that Nadine would end up telling her things unintentionally. Like during that other session. She hadn't intended to tell Olivia about the incident with the gun. On the contrary, she had emphatically promised herself that she wouldn't bring up the horrible experience. However, as determined as Nadine had been, she found herself freely offering the information.

Nadine finished her sandwiches, washing them and her medication down with a bottle of water. The clock on her cell phone reminded her that she now only had six minutes before her session would begin. Nadine proceeded to the sitting area near the bay window of the master bedroom and set her laptop on the table that rested between the two chairs. From this position, she would be able to see Damon's car enter the security gate of their courtyard if he showed up earlier than expected. If necessary, she would alert Olivia and end the session early.

With less than a minute to spare, Nadine ducked into the bathroom to freshen up her ponytail, put some pressed powder on her face, and moisten her lips with a cocoa butter-based gloss. By the time she got settled in her seat, Olivia was giving her access into their private meeting.

"Hi." Nadine's greeting was accompanied by a wave when she saw her therapist's face on the screen.

"Hi, Nadine. It's good to see your smile. How are you feeling today? I was so sorry to get your text about the COVID infection. I hope you're feeling better."

"I'm feeling okay, but I have to stay in quarantine for a few more days."

"It's been cut back to ten days now, right?"

"Yes and no," Nadine said with a slight chuckle. "Yes, for people who get the virus despite being vaccinated, and no, for those of us who never took the shot. I was advised to take the full fourteen days, but I didn't get a lot of the more severe symptoms, so I really think ten days will be enough for me. I'll take another home test at that time, and if I get a negative result, I'm going to get back to life."

"I'm glad to hear that your symptoms have remained on the milder end of things. That's a blessing." After a very brief pause, Olivia added, "Speaking of getting back to life, how has yours been this week? You were very emotional during our session last Friday. How have things been this week?"

"Well, I've been in quarantine, so I haven't had much interaction with anyone this week." Nadine hoped her response would satisfy Olivia's inquisitiveness.

"I wouldn't expect you to have much face-to-face interaction, but I'm sure you've spoken with your husband since you've been in quarantine—even if it's just been through the closed door. Have the two of you talked at all about the unfortunate situations that happened prior to your developing COVID?"

Nadine shrugged her shoulders and repositioned herself in her chair.

"You know, I picked up on your body language in our initial consultation as well as in our first session," Olivia revealed. "You squirm when I ask a question you don't particularly want to answer. From your reaction, am I right to suppose that you and the mayor have not talked about this at all? There have been no apologies, no admission of wrongdoing, no discussion of any type?"

Nadine shook her head slowly. "No. We really haven't spoken about that or anything else. He's texted a couple of times, but we haven't talked." Nadine sighed and shook her head again. "He hasn't even bothered to set a tray of food outside my door."

"You haven't been eating this week?"

"My best …" Nadine stopped and started over. "Trina … you know Trina."

"I do," Olivia said with a smile. "She's great."

"Well, she brought me something to eat at the beginning of the week, but ever since she stopped coming, I've been waiting until I felt strong enough to go downstairs and make a meal out of whatever food we've had here in the house."

"Trina stopped? I can't believe she stopped; especially if she knew Mayor Deville wasn't doing it and that you're battling fatigue."

"Well, believe it or not, she did. She stopped, so I've been getting my own. But that's just fine by me." Nadine could feel her emotions rising. "I don't need her to wait on me, and I don't need Damon to wait on me either. I've been eating with or without their help."

"Uh-huh." It was all Olivia said for a moment. After writing in her notepad, she looked back at the camera. "Let's talk about it, Nadine. I know that you and Trina are close friends, and I know her well enough to say with confidence that she's too loyal not to help you if you're in need. So, let's start from there."

"You think I don't know that Trina has already talked to you?" Nadine blurted. "I know she's been seeing you for years and she tells you everything in her sessions. You think I'm naïve enough to believe she hasn't already filled your ears with bad stuff about me? That's why you started out talking about how great she is and why you made it your business to point out how loyal she is." Each time Nadine emphasized a word, she made quotation marks in the air with her fingers.

"You think I don't know that she's told you about our fight? And I'm sure she made me out to be some kind of crazy woman when she told you I slapped her." Nadine reached up to remove her glasses and wipe her eyes. She hated it when her tears made appearances without her consent. It seemed that the closer she got to her fiftieth birthday the more emotional she became, and she hated that too. "I know she's already got you on her side because y'all have known each other forever," Nadine went on to say. "So, go ahead and tell me how wrong I am and how right she was. Go ahead and say it."

"Are you done?" Olivia asked after Nadine finally quieted.

Without responding, Nadine turned her face away from the computer screen and looked out the window.

"First of all, it doesn't seem that I have to say much of anything," Olivia said. "I think you already know what's right and wrong here. Secondly, despite what you believe, Trina hasn't told me a thing."

Nadine faced the screen again, but her silence remained. Her only response came in the form of more tears that she struggled to wipe away.

"You're right when you say I've known Trina for a long time," Olivia continued. "But you're very wrong if you believe she ran to me to say anything about whatever transpired between the two of you this week. I didn't know anything about a disagreement or you physically attacking her until you just disclosed it."

With her tears falling heavier now, Nadine buried her face in her hands and wept. Her hands prevented her from looking at the screen, but she could hear Olivia loud and clear. The therapist's signature soothing tone was there, but her words were straightforward.

"We're going to take about a five-minute break," Olivia instructed. "Take that time to get yourself together. Go grab some tissues, wash your face, get some water. Whatever you need to do, you have five minutes to do it. When you come back, bring a pen and paper with you, and get as comfortable as you can, because we've got some work to do today. The first thing we're going to do is pray together, and then we're going to have a real heart-to-heart talk. Your life is spiraling out of control, Nadine, and God and I aren't going to just sit by and let the enemy take you out like this."

Chapter 15

Regrets

It felt a bit strange not to go to church on a Sunday, but at the same time, Nadine was glad she wasn't there. Rev. Proctor was out of town fulfilling a ministry assignment today, and he had handpicked the congregation's favorite to substitute for him. Damon was always the pastor's first choice; probably because his speaking meant that the sanctuary would be as full as—or maybe even fuller than—it would be if Rev. Proctor was there.

Whether he lived by the Word of God or not, Damon's knowledge of Scripture couldn't be denied. When he preached, his delivery was always charismatic. Mayor Damon Deville's magnetism didn't end when he walked out of city hall. He knew how to win amens just as well as he knew how to win votes.

No doubt they were having a good time at Gate City Christian Center today, but Nadine was relieved not to be there feeling the pressure to overcompensate in order to stoke her husband's ego.

The house was almost too quiet today. For the first time since his knee replacement surgery, Daddy Deville had gone to church. When he heard that his son was preaching today, he insisted. He had already missed hearing Damon preach once since the surgery, but on Friday, his physical therapists said if Daddy Deville was careful and used his wheelchair more than his walker, he was cleared to go where he wanted.

In one sense, the quiet house was a great thing, but in another, the silence meant that there was nothing to distract Nadine from her own thoughts. Memories of the past week were consuming her more than ever. The fight with Trina and the session with Olivia were double-teaming Nadine today— and they were winning. A new record had been set. This was the longest that she and Trina had ever gone without speaking to one another, but then again, they'd never had a fight like that one either.

When Nadine thought about the mean things she'd said to Trina, the things she'd said about her, and the things she had said about Bradley … she couldn't help but shudder. Nadine knew this was a feeling that she might as well get used to. Forgiveness was never going to be extended for this one. When they'd argued in the parking lot that Sunday, Trina had let her off the hook quickly. She had even been the one to reach out first, rushing to Nadine's side upon hearing about her COVID diagnosis. But not a peep from Trina had been heard since she stormed out of Nadine's bedroom last week. There was no coming back from this one. Nadine could feel it in her gut.

Her spirits lifted momentarily at the sound of her ringtone, but one glance at her cell phone dashed those misplaced hopes. She tried to shake her disappointment before swiping the screen to answer.

"Hi, Sophia."

"Well, dang," her sister replied. "I called hoping that you were feeling better, but as dry as you sound, I almost hope you're sick. Otherwise, I'm going to have to take it personally."

"Sorry. I guess I'm feeling some kind of way about missing church today," Nadine responded. "Speaking of which, why aren't you at church?"

"I needed to help a friend take care of some time-sensitive business," Sophia told her. "It could be viewed as ministry, so I think God was okay with it," she added with a laugh. "I was thinking of coming there to see you, but I think I'll wait until you're totally over the cooties. I don't want to catch what you've got."

Nadine laughed before responding. "I don't have the cooties, for your information. And I feel pretty good; I just have this annoying cough that's insisting upon hanging around."

"Nobody else in the house got it, did they?" Sophia asked.

"No. But how could they? Nobody in the house has been around me. I'm isolating."

"I know. But all it takes is for someone to touch a dish after you've touched it. Like if Damon picks up a fork that you've been using, and then he fails to wash or sanitize his hands, that would be enough to pass it along right there. All he'd have to do is touch his nose or his lips after not washing his hands. That's how one of my coworkers got it. Her husband was isolating too, but she caught it just by handling dishes that he was eating off of."

Nadine shook her head knowing full well that this was a mishap that certainly wouldn't happen with Damon. "We've been extra careful," she told Sophia. "Nobody here is going to catch it."

"Well, my coworker said she was glad to get it. For her, it meant that she was there for her husband." Sophia giggled, and then added, "She quoted Fred, from Sanford and Son, when he said, 'A family that sicks together sticks together.'"

Nadine remembered seeing that scene play out on an old rerun of the popular seventies television show. She had laughed back then. But right now, it was hitting home a little too hard to be amusing. "Well, that's a pretty thoughtless remark for her to make," Nadine tried to smooth the edginess from her tone, but she knew she wasn't doing a good job. "Personally, I'm glad I haven't infected anybody else. I wouldn't want any of my family to be sick on because of me."

"It's a TV show, Nadine," Sophia said. "It's entertainment; not real life."

"Well, it just sounds like you're trying to throw shade. As if you're hinting that Damon should risk his health to come in and see about me, and since he doesn't have COVID like I do, he doesn't really care like a husband should."

The conversation went dead for a period of time. Several seconds passed with Nadine hearing nothing from the other end, not even breathing.

"Hello?" she probed, thinking the call had dropped.

"How did this get to be about you and Damon?" Sophia's question was framed in suspicion. "I'm telling you about something that Fred Sanford said on television, and you're hearing me accuse your husband of not caring for you. Seriously?"

"It wasn't what you said about Fred Sanford. It was more what you said about your coworker."

"Nadine, what's going on with you? Are you and Damon having problems that you're not telling me about. He's not checking on you?"

"I'm fine, Sophia. Nothing is wrong. I'm sorry. I guess being caged in this room and not being able to go to work, church, or even the store, is making me stir crazy. Damon and I are doing fine. He makes sure I have everything I need; he just sets my food and anything else I need outside the door instead of coming in. But that's fine; that's what I want him to do. If I wanted him to come inside, he would. I asked him not to." Nadine's stomach felt nauseous. She was beginning to get sick of her own lies.

Another span of silence hovered before Sophia spoke again. "Okay." She sounded doubtful that her attorney-sister was telling the truth, the whole truth, and nothing but the truth, but she didn't challenge her on it. "And I'm sure Trina steps in wherever she's needed," Sophia added.

Nadine swallowed before responding. "Yeah, she's been here. She made some of Aunt Pat's soup and brought it in the early part of last week."

"Aunt Pat's soup? You got any left? That, all by itself, might be worth me taking a trip to Atlanta to come see you!"

"There's no more. It's been gone since Tuesday."

"You know, Aunt Pat swears that soup is anointed and has the healing power of Jesus Christ. If you'd been eating it every day, I'll bet you would've been able to go to church today. You need to get Trina to make some more."

"I don't want to be a bother. I have plenty of other stuff to eat."

"But that other stuff ain't anointed. I'll call Trina right now, and–"

"No," Nadine abruptly interrupted. She softened her tone, and added, "Thanks for the offer, but that's okay."

"Girl, you know Trina won't mind one bit."

"It's not that," Nadine said. She felt another lie coming on, but as far as she was concerned, it was the only way she could get out of this conversation. "I ate it all day for two days in a row. Aunt Pat's soup is good, but I was starting to get tired of it." Sophia made a grunting noise before saying, "I remember a time when you could eat Aunt Pat's soup every day for two weeks straight and not get tired of it. You get tired after two days now?"

"COVID probably affected my appetite in ways that I just didn't recognize right away." Nadine released a soft sigh, and then asked, "How's Mom doing these days? Have you talked to her lately?"

"Wow, you must really want to change the subject," Sophia remarked under her breath.

Nadine pretended not to hear her. "I've been promising Aunt Pat that I would call her, and I haven't gotten around to it yet."

"You've been locked in a room for a week. What do you mean you have gotten around to it yet? It's not like you've had anything else to do."

"For your information, yes I have," Nadine said. "Just because I haven't gone to the office doesn't mean I haven't done any work. I had a virtual meeting yesterday, and tomorrow I have some contracts that must be returned with an electronic signature." She paused to cough. "I'll text Damon and ask him to pick up a home test for me on his way from church. As soon as I get a negative result, I'll get back to my normal schedule."

"You should probably wait until that cough is gone," Sophia advised. "No sense in wasting a test by taking it too early."

"I'm going to probably wait until the end of the week, but whether my cough is completely gone by then or not, I'm going to take the test. I've heard people say they still had a lingering cough with a negative test."

"Well, it's almost noon. Mom's church starts at nine, so most Sundays, she's home before noon. You should go ahead and give her a call before you get distracted with anything else."

"I'll probably wait and call her tomorrow."

"Nadine …"

"No, really," Nadine said. "First of all, there is an hour's difference between her time in Texas and mine here, so it's an hour earlier there. She's probably still in church. I'll call her tomorrow. I hate to call her on a Sunday anyway. You know how she's always inviting some of the sisters over after church for dinner, or she'll accept a dinner invitation from one of them and go to their house. Sunday is Mom's day to chill and spend time with her church friends. Calling her tomorrow would be better for her and for me."

"How is it better for you?" Sophia challenged.

"Because I'm hungry, that's how. I didn't eat any breakfast, and I need to eat so I can take my medication. After I eat, I can spend the day reading over those contracts to be sure they are ready for my signature. Tomorrow will just be a better day all the way around."

"Okay, well, I was mainly reaching out to check on you," Sophia said. "I'm glad you're feeling better. I'll let you go so that you can get something to eat and take your meds."

"Thanks for calling," Nadine told her. "When I get over this virus and catch up on my work, you and I have to plan a girls' day out—like a shopping trip or a spa day."

"Sounds good. You need to get well real soon so we can do that."

"Okay. Love you. Talk to you soon."

"Love you too," Sophia replied. "And don't forget to call your mama," she added just before ending the call.

Nadine knew her sister was right. Aunt Pat had been right too. She really did need to give Rose Jackson a call and check on her. Nadine still didn't understand why her mother wouldn't just pick up the phone and call her, but she would be the bigger person. Nadine would make the call tomorrow, as she'd promised.

Sliding her feet into her bedroom slippers, she walked into the master bath and started running the water for a bath. By the time she finished eating a quick lunch, the water level in her jet tub should be perfect. While the water ran, she went downstairs to put together another veggie sandwich. Nadine was far more tired of eating veggie sandwiches than she ever could have been of eating the soup, but they were easy to prepare and healthy to eat.

While she was in the refrigerator getting the tomatoes, her eyes fell to two containers—one filled with fresh strawberries and the other with fresh blueberries. She was in the middle of pouring some of both in a bowl to go with her meal when she heard the whimsical tone of their security system alerting her that someone was entering the home. In the distance she could hear Damon talking. He and his father had gotten there earlier than Nadine expected, but she was glad to have the opportunity to see them.

"Hey, handsome," Nadine said, breaking into a smile as they rounded the corner into the shared spaces of the home. Damon looked great in the charcoal grey suit he wore. "How was church? I know you preached the house down today." Nadine was intentional in adding that last part so her husband would see that she was taking interest in his ministry assignment.

"What are you doing down here?" Damon demanded while peering at her through narrowed eyes. "And why are you touching my stuff? Where are your gloves?"

Nadine looked at her bare hands. She had not even thought to put on her gloves, and by "my stuff," Damon must have been referring to the fruit she still held in her hands. Nadine watched Daddy Deville immediately turn his electric wheelchair and head straight to his bedroom. He was notorious for pulling a disappearing act when he suspected that his son was about to misbehave.

"I-I'm sorry. I forgot to grab my gloves before leaving the room," Nadine said. "But I really don't think I'm contagious anymore. I feel much—"

"I don't want to hear about how you feel. Have you taken another test to be sure?"

"No. I meant to text you and ask you to stop by the pharmacy and pick up one for me on the way home, but I was on the phone with Sophia, and I forgot." Nadine eyed the bag in Damon's hand while she spoke. He had stopped and picked up food. "Church must have ended earlier than normal today," she said. "I wasn't expecting you to get home while I was still down here."

"Well, I'm glad we did come home early because if we hadn't, I wouldn't even know you had been down here contaminating everything. You would have gone right back upstairs like nothing ever happened, and I would have walked in breathing the same air you coughed in and touching the same stuff you touched."

"I haven't coughed once since I've been down here," Nadine defended.

"That's what you say, but you can tell me anything." Damon shook his head in disgust. "I can't believe you came down here with no gloves, no mask, nothing. How stupid can you get? Are you trying to make us sick? Daddy's an old man with underlying conditions. You have no business down here!"

"'Down here' is where the food is, Damon. I didn't expect you to get home this early, and I didn't know you were picking up dinner, otherwise, I would have waited. I was hungry. I haven't had anything to eat all day. I came down to fix lunch so I could take my medication." While she spoke, Nadine could feel a cough coming on, and while she fought hard to suppress it, the cough won. The timing of it couldn't have been worse.

Damon pointed an accusing finger at her. "See there! See how you lie? Look at you. You're spreading germs right now. Get back upstairs!" He pointed at the stairwell like he was sending a misbehaving child to their room.

"That was my first time coughing since I came down, Damon."

He walked toward the front door and grabbed the can of Lysol that sat on the table near it and began spraying. "Go back upstairs!" he repeated.

Without a word, Nadine began to walk toward the staircase. "Take your food with you," Damon told her. "And that includes all the fruit. I don't want that mess after you've touched it."

Nadine looked at the bag in his hand again. "Well, since your brought food, I can just eat the sandwich later."

"This ain't for you," Damon said as he tossed a glance toward his bag, and then looked back at Nadine. "This is for me and Dad. Take your sandwich and my fruit that you've tainted with you. That's your meal."

Nadine stared at him in disbelief. "You mean you didn't get anything for me?"

"Did you ask me to get you anything for you?"

"No, but since you stopped and got yourself and your dad something, it just seems like you would have gotten me something too. I would have gotten you something if I'd stopped for food and you were at home sick."

"Yeah, right." Damon released a short laugh as though what Nadine said was the most ridiculous thing he'd ever heard. "Well, look at it like this: I did get you something—my fruit that you touched without my permission. It's all yours now. Bon appetit! Now, go upstairs and take your germs with you so I can sterilize everything before bringing Dad out here to eat."

Nadine gathered the food from the counter and made her way up the stairs. Once she was closed inside the bedroom, she placed the food on the dresser and went into the ensuite to turn off the bath water. She sat on the edge of the tub and buried her face in her hands. Olivia was right in what she had told her Friday during their session. Her life really was spiraling out of control, and it was up to Nadine to find a way to stop it before it was too late.

Chapter 16

Denial Runs Deep

I know my marriage is a mess. I don't need anybody to tell me that; okay? Nobody knows it better than I do. I know I don't deserve to be treated like this. I know that my life is falling apart, and I know that a lot of the reasons for that point back to my marriage." Nadine wiped tears from her cheeks as she spoke.

From the dresser beside her, she picked up a beautifully framed picture of her and Damon that was taken on their wedding day and stared at the image. The couple in that photo were barely recognizable. They had stopped being the people in that photo a long time ago. Nadine placed the frame back on the dresser and continued. "As crazy as it may sound, I love Damon, and I really want my marriage to work. After all that has happened, I know that makes me look foolish, but it's the truth."

Today's session wasn't on the schedule. In fact, it wasn't even a forethought. Nadine picked up the phone and called Olivia's office without prior notice of any kind. It must have been the favor of God that the therapist was between appointments. When Olivia's receptionist informed her that Nadine was on the phone, she didn't hesitate to take the call.

"That doesn't make you foolish at all, Nadine. Every wife should want to do all she can to keep her marriage intact. But guess what? So should every husband. One spouse—whether it's the husband or the wife—cannot make a marriage work. Marriage is a joint venture. It's a collaborated undertaking, and it takes both people wanting it to be a success for it to be a success. No matter how much you talk to me or anyone else, substantial and lasting healing to your marriage can't take place without Mayor Deville being a willing participant."

"Well, I can tell you right now, that's not going to happen. Damon doesn't see where any healing needs to be done, at least, not on his part."

"Are you assuming this because of kickback that he gave you in the past, or is this something the two of you have discussed recently?"

"As recently as yesterday," Nadine said emphatically. "I let the rest of Sunday slide without saying anything further to him after the exchange we had when he got home from church. And between reading contracts, signing contracts, and finally talking to my mom, I kept myself busy on Monday until he got home from work."

Nadine walked to the chairs beside her bedroom window and sat in one of them. "I waited until he had eaten, showered, and settled in the guest room for the evening; so, it was around nine o'clock last night when I sent him a text and asked if he would be willing to go to a marriage counselor with me. I told him we didn't have to go to Rev. Proctor. I know how important it is for him to keep up his image with the people who know him well. I even told him we could find a therapist clear on the other end of the country who wouldn't know who he was. Everybody is doing Zoom sessions since the pandemic, so we could do that with a therapist in Utah if he wanted. He could pick whomever he wanted and was comfortable with."

"And his response?"

"Oh, I got an eye full."

"I gather that means he didn't respond favorably."

"That's putting it mildly," Nadine said as she scrolled through the text messages on her phone for the evidence. "His first message was just full of a bunch of laughing emojis—like I'd just told the best joke he'd ever heard. And I'd read you the second text he sent, but it's so full of profanity that even a drunk sailor would be embarrassed. I'm sending it to you now." Nadine paused long enough to cough and to take a quick screenshot of the message for her therapist. "In a nutshell, he told me he didn't need help; I'm the one who needs it."

"Well, from what I see, it looks like a whole lot more than that was said," Olivia remarked. "His opening line is very disconcerting. He starts his response off with, 'Why are you even still here?' What does he mean by that?"

"Oh, he says that every now and then, especially when we have disagreements. I think it's his way of acknowledging that he knows being married to him can be a challenge. When he asks, 'Why are you even still here,' I think that's his way of complimenting me for being resilient and sticking by him."

"Hmmm," Olivia responded. "Okay, we're going to put that one on the backburner for now. He goes on to say that you need to learn how to be submissive and how to just say, 'Okay' when he says something to you instead of always giving him lip and having an explanation."

"Yeah. He's told me that many times," Nadine said. She opened her mouth to say more, but Olivia spoke again first.

"And I see that the 'B-word' is his favorite nickname for you."

"With 'stupid' running a close second. I know," Nadine disclosed. "I've gotten so used to it that it really doesn't bother me as it once did."

"You know that's not healthy, right? You should never get so accustomed to being degraded that it becomes comfortable. You should never be okay with abuse of any kind."

Nadine sighed. "I hate the word 'abuse' being used here. I just don't think—"

"Most women in denial feel the same way," Olivia interrupted.

Nadine opened her mouth to speak again, but before she could form her words, her therapist cut in again as though she could see Nadine through the phone line.

"Before you say anything," Olivia uttered, "let me finish. There are many forms of abuse, and as a legal professional, I'm sure you know this. Indulge me for just a moment." Continuing, she said, "All abuse isn't acted out in physical violence, as in someone slapping you around. Abuse can come in the form of coercion and threats, such as when your husband threatens to harm you or threatens to get someone else to harm you. Abuse can come in the form of intimidation. That's what happened when he pulled the gun on you. Loaded or not, that was abuse.

"Isolation is another form of abuse," Olivia maintained. "In your determination to try and cover and even defend his volatile behavior, you have allowed it to damage a tried-and-true friendship with a woman who you know would give you her kidney without a second thought, if you needed it. She's your dearest and closest friend, and now there's a bridge the size of Alaska between you and her because of how you've chosen to handle this abuse from Mayor Deville."

Nadine wiped away fresh tears that suddenly arose out of nowhere and spilled down her cheeks. She missed Trina more than she had been willing to admit to herself or anyone else. She could talk to her mom, she could talk to Sophia, she could talk to Olivia. She could even talk to Aunt Pat, but it wasn't the same thing. There was no one who could fill the role that Trina played in her life. As her tears got heavier, Nadine placed her phone on mute so that Olivia couldn't hear her weeping.

"When he calls you stupid and the 'B-word,'" Olivia further stated, "that's not only verbal abuse; it's emotional abuse. It's a way to make you feel bad about yourself and to strip you of self- esteem, self-worth, self-image, self-confidence, self-respect. It's a means to strip you of self. Before long, you lose your identity, and you start to think of yourself not as who you are but what you are called."

"But let's be fair," Nadine said, sniffing before continuing. "I can't lay all the blame on Damon as if I'm an angel in all of this. I may not say the stuff he says out loud, but there have been plenty of times that I've called him an ugly thing or two in my mind."

"This text is brutal." Olivia picked up where she left off as if she hadn't heard what Nadine just said. "And it's interesting how, after all his tongue-lashing, he ended it by reminding you of just how fortunate you are. He says, 'God made me the head. I'm the man of this house. You don't tell me that we need a counselor. I'll tell you if a counselor is needed! You're too blankety-blank stupid to even know how blessed you are. I wish I would go to a blankety-blank, blankety-blank, blankety-blank-blank-blank counselor! Don't you know that there are a ton of other B-words who would love to be married to me and have the notoriety that comes with being the wife of Atlanta's mayor?'"

"He's told me that many times too," Nadine stated. "Olivia, are you still there?"

It was at that moment that Nadine realized that she'd never taken her phone off mute. No wonder Olivia didn't respond to her earlier comment. Nadine pressed the icon to release the silence. "Yes, I'm still here."

"I know this isn't what you want to hear, Nadine, but all of what he said in this part of the text makes for a form of abuse as well," Olivia informed her. "In relationships, this is sometimes referred to as 'male privilege.' It's when a husband or boyfriend builds himself up by making his wife feel subservient. When a husband resorts to saying stuff like, 'I'm the man of this house,' or when he says things that are intended to make you feel as though he did you a favor by marrying you, or if he's always trying to define the roles of what you, as the wife are supposed to do—all these things are forms of abuse."

When Olivia finished her spiel, the quiet lingered, but this time it had nothing to do with Nadine's phone being placed on mute.

After a moment, Olivia released a sigh, and then said, "Nadine, in our conversations, you have often mentioned your love for Mayor Deville, and I truly believe you do love him. Strong love will propel you to give someone chance after chance after chance. The power of love has the potential to be quite mind-blowing. It's mind-blowing to think that a mother would jump in the deep end of a swimming pool to save her drowning child when she, herself, can't even swim. It's mind-blowing to know that a son would run back into a burning house to save his wheelchair-bound mother when even the trained firemen won't go back. It's mind-blowing to know that God sent His only begotten Son to die as a sacrificial offering so that a world of sinners like us can be saved. When you really think about it, that's crazy. I mean, who does that? That's the power of love."

"But," Olivia emphasized, "if we don't accept His love, repent of our sins, and live as we love Him, that God who sent His Son to die for us is the same one who going to say, 'Depart from me, you worker of iniquity; I don't even know you.' How do we live like we love God?" Olivia posed. "By loving Him right back; that's how. And not with our words only, but with our deeds. You love Mayor Deville, Nadine. But when was the last time Mayor Deville loved you back?"

The question socked Nadine in the middle of her chest. It hit so hard that she had to take a moment to catch her breath. It was true that Damon didn't say it often, but it wasn't like he never said it at all. "Probably the last time we were intimate," she finally answered. "He always says it when we make love, but it's been two or three weeks since we've done that."

"I didn't ask when was the last time he said he loved you. I asked, when was the last time he loved you."

Nadine didn't have a ready reply, so this time, she didn't answer at all. It was Olivia's voice that would end the silence.

"Have you spoken to anyone, other than me, about what's going on in your marriage? You mentioned that you talked to your mother yesterday. Does she know?"

"Goodness, no," Nadine stressed. "My mother would probably be the last person I'd tell. We don't have that kind of relationship. She's way too critical for me to tell her something like this. I haven't told anyone. Well, I mean, Trina knows about some of it, but not because I told her."

"She only knows whatever she was able to read in your journal, right?

Nadine's eyes widened. "She told you about that?"

"No. You did during our last session when you thought I already knew. Remember?"

"Oh yeah." Nadine rested her back against her chair. "Trina thinks I should leave Damon. From the things she said during our fight, it was made clear that she thinks I'm crazy for still being here."

"What do you think?" Olivia asked. "Don't worry about what Trina thinks, don't worry about what I think; don't even worry about what the mayor thinks. What does Nadine think Nadine should do? In your heart of hearts, what do you think should happen?"

Nadine stood from her chair, crossed her arms in front of her chest, and stared out her bedroom window. The workers from the landscaping company they used were outside taking care of the lawn and sprucing the flowerbeds. Their diligence kept the massive property looking blue-ribbon good all year 'round.

From where Nadine stood, she could also see her own image reflected in the window. It was a good thing that she was talking to Olivia on the phone today instead of being on camera. The reflection in her windows was that of a woman who hadn't taken the time to groom her hair or wash her face. It was already afternoon, and she hadn't even changed out of her pajamas.

"Is that a hard question for you to answer?" Olivia said, breaking Nadine's drifting thoughts.

"To be honest, yes." Nadine took a moment to adjust her earbud for a more secure fit. "I really don't know what I think I should do. I have been praying for God to send me a sign or something so that I'll know which direction He wants me to go. I've even been writing those prayers down like you advised in our last session. I've started a whole new journal that consists of nothing but my prayers to God. I'm writing in it two, sometimes three times a day because that's how often I'm praying. Whatever I do, I want to be in His will."

"Of course you do, as a woman of faith; that's how it should be. But let me ask you this. If God did show you a sign, would you recognize it?"

"What do you mean?"

"I mean, what if He's been showing you signs all along? What if you're praying for an answer that has already been provided? Would you be able to identify God's answer if it didn't look like what you were hoping for?" Olivia asked.

"I-I don't know."

"Nadine, I wouldn't dare tell you what to do. That's not my job. But it is my job to raise your awareness and give you a few things to consider based on the insight you've given me in the last few sessions we've had. Are you open to listening to what I have to say?"

Taking a breath and bracing herself, Nadine replied, "Yes. I'm open."

"Okay. Consider this. You've probably read countless text messages like the ones he sent you last night," Olivia began. "You've endured years of crude yelling and demeaning name-calling. Whether you've been hit by objects or not, you've had food thrown at you, books thrown at you, clothing, and other foreign objects thrown at you. You've had water dashed in your face and clothes furiously ripped while you wore them. You've been banished from the car and stranded by the side of the road. You've been threatened to be spit on, and you've had a gun pointed at your face while a threat was made to shoot you. You've been sick in your room for a week, and not once has he brought you food or water. Think about all of this, Nadine, and then ask yourself: Could any of these things possibly be a sign from God?"

Nadine's knees felt weak. She walked back to her chair and sat. Every memory that Olivia rehashed with her words left a sting like Nadine was being whipped with a switch plucked from a plum tree. The chair she sat on gave her stability, but it didn't provide any comfort. Nadine changed positions, but it still felt like she was sitting on a concrete block.

"You're fidgeting, aren't you?" Olivia stated. "I can't see you, but I know you are, because that's what you do when you're challenged with questions that you'd rather not answer."

"Are you saying I should leave my husband?"

"No, Nadine. As I said earlier, I wouldn't dare tell you what to do. Every decision is yours to make, but you're asking God for a sign. And if that's what you want, I'm sure He'll give it to you. But, when we choose to ignore the—quote-unquote—little signs, we have to be sent a billboard, and that can be devastating. All I'm saying is you shouldn't minimize the evidence you've seen or the dreams you've had. We can't pray for things and then pretend to be blind and deaf. Amid your prayers, be willing to listen. You can pray with your eyes closed, but you have to open them to see the answer. Am I making sense?"

"Yes." Nadine's reply was barely above a whisper, but it was comprehensible enough for Olivia to hear.

"My next client has arrived, so I'll need to end our call now," the therapist said. "But here is what I need for you to do this week. I need you to trust someone enough to let them know what's going on inside your marriage. Someone other than me needs to know, and it does need to be someone that you can trust wholeheartedly."

"You're talking about Trina, aren't you?"

"Only if she fits the description," Olivia stated. "And since her name is the one that popped out of your mouth, I'm going to guess that she does. But this is a decision that you have to make. I feel that it's important that someone who you trust to hold the details of your life in confidence is made fully aware of what's going on. Every woman in an abusive relationship should have a confidant. Finding yours and being transparent with that person is your assignment for the week. Do you think you can do that?"

Nadine looked at the bedroom ceiling and rubbed the palms of her hands back and forth against her thighs.

"Stop fidgeting and answer me," Olivia said.

The therapist's comment triggered a much-needed laugh from Nadine. "Yes," she finally said. "Yes, I think I can do that."

Chapter 17

Give Me A Sign

A negative test result on Wednesday had Nadine sitting at Moe's on Thursday for the first time in a while. Anxiety and uncertainty engulfed her. Nadine's stomach felt tied up in knots. She had no clue how this meeting would play out.

It came as a surprise when Trina answered her text this morning to request the lunchtime meeting. If Nadine were totally honest, she'd have to admit that there was a part of her that hoped Trina wouldn't respond. At least, then, she could report to Olivia that she had tried, and at the same time, avoid what could turn out to be a very unpleasant situation.

That was a big part of the reason Nadine had chosen to meet at the restaurant. Hers was the most private booth in the establishment, but other people were still within view. She figured that even if Trina wanted to scream at her, she wouldn't do it in a public place.

As Nadine sat in the booth that Miranda had given her, she readjusted the mask on her face. She hated these things, but even with a clear test, she'd decided to wear it.

"Hey, hun. Are you sure what's-her-name is still coming? You've been sitting here for a minute. I can go ahead and give them your order in the back, so you won't have to wait so long before eating if she doesn't show."

Nadine checked the time. Trina was late, and that was rare. They were supposed to meet at eleven o'clock, and Nadine had been waiting since ten fifty. She had arranged the meeting for eleven in hopes that they would be in and out before the bulk of the midday rush. It was already thirteen minutes after. Another thirty or forty-five minutes, and Moe's would be slammed with lunchtime patrons.

"She would have called if she wasn't going to be able to make it," Nadine told Miranda, all the while trying to also convince herself of the same.

The old Trina, the one who was her dearest friend, wouldn't dare stand her up. But, Nadine wasn't certain what the Trina that she had literally evicted out of her house—not before slapping her face and calling her husband a wimp—was capable of. The last time she had seen that Trina, she was threatening to drag her down the staircase and to lose her size nine shoe somewhere up in Nadine's butt.

"Well, here are two glasses of sweet tea and some chips and salsa for you to snack on until she gets here or until you're ready to order your Homewrecker."

Nadine offered Miranda a smile although her mask hid it. "Thank you."

Nadine looked around the room. There were a few other mask-wearers sprinkled throughout the establishment, so she didn't look out of place.

It seemed like ages since she had been there. Nadine had skipped breakfast this morning, so she was more than ready to sink her teeth into her favorite burrito. Other thoughts that flooded her mind, however, didn't leave much room for her to dwell on hunger pangs.

The last time she was at Moe's, Nadine had sat in the very same booth she now occupied. That day, it was with Charley Bigham, and the recollection of it ruffled her all over again.

Her thoughts deepening, Nadine took a chip and swirled it around in the salsa before putting it in her mouth and chewing slowly. If she never saw Charley again for the rest of her life, it would still be too soon. And if they ever did meet again, she hoped it was in a courtroom, as his opposing counsel. Nadine was already imagining all the ways she could put a whipping on Charley that would embarrass him so much that he'd want to close the doors of his practice. She would welcome the opportunity to bring "Mr. Big" down to size.

"Here you are, ma'am."

"Huh?" Nadine looked up at the sound of Miranda's voice and found that the waitress wasn't talking to her, but to Trina. She was showing her to the booth where Nadine was waiting.

"Thanks." Trina's tone was dry.

"I'll be right back to get your orders," Miranda said just before walking away.

For a while, Trina continued to stand. Her blank stare felt like it would burn a hole in Nadine's flesh.

"Hi. Thanks for coming," Nadine said.

Trina made no reply. Instead, she continued to stand… and to stare.

Nadine made a sweeping motion with her hand and pointed to the space across from her in the booth. She swallowed to try and moisten her parched throat, and then said, "Please sit."

Trina dropped her handbag on the seat first, and then she plopped down beside it. Silence was still her only contribution, and Nadine knew that if they were going to get anywhere, Trina wasn't going to make it easy.

"Thanks for coming." Nadine coughed and cleared her throat before continuing. "I wasn't sure you would want to be here."

"I didn't, and I don't." Trina ended her longstanding silence with words that cut deep. "Best believe that the only reason I'm here is because Bradley insisted that I come." Her tone turned cynical when she added, "You remember Bradley, right? You might know him better as 'the wimp.'"

"Trina, I'm sorry."

Slamming her hand on the table, Trina replied, "Good, because you ought to be!"

"Uh … Are you ladies ready to order now?"

Nadine had never in her life been so happy to see Miranda. The waitress's appearance owas probably all that saved the exchange between her and Trina from turning ugly.

"Do you want your regular, hun?"

Nadine nodded before quietly saying, "Yes, please. Thank you."

Miranda turned her attention to the other side of the booth. Her demeanor hinted that she didn't particularly like the way that Trina had been speaking to her favorite attorney. "And for you?"

"I'm not hungry," Trina replied. "I don't want anything."

"Bring her a Homewrecker Bowl, and put it all on my ticket," Nadine told Miranda.

"I said, I don't want anything." Trina held her voice at a normal level, but her clenched teeth indicated that she was a far cry from calm.

Rolling her eyes at Trina, Miranda looked at Nadine and said, "One Homewrecker Burrito with tofu and guac, and one Homewrecker Bowl coming up. And I'll make sure you get those waters after having your sweet teas." She tossed one more disapproving look at Trina before walking away.

Quiet blanketed the table for several moments after Miranda left them alone. Nadine found herself praying inwardly that God would take control of the atmosphere because as it currently was, the resentment that hovered around their booth was so thick that it would take a steak knife to cut through it.

The words Olivia had spoken to Nadine two days ago filtered through her mind. "I feel that it's important that someone who you trust to hold the details of your life in confidence is made fully aware of what's going on. Every woman in an abusive relationship should have a confidant."

There was no one else that Nadine could trust more than Trina. She was the only person Nadine could tell the sordid details of her life. As she stared down at the table, Nadine could feel that Trina's eyes were trained on her. This was the hardest thing that Nadine had needed to do in a long time. Not since burying her dad had she faced a more difficult task.

"Are you crying?" Trina asked.

Nadine looked up, and then used her hand to touch her eyes. She hadn't even noticed that tears were there until Trina spoke the words. The mask was catching most of the moisture as it tried to make its way down her cheeks, but Nadine retrieved a napkin from the table and wiped away the rest.

"Okay, you've said you're sorry," Trina said. "I believe you. I just need a minute to get over all this. Don't start crying."

"It's not that," Nadine said while shaking her head from side to side. She removed her mask and used the napkin to soak up the rest of the water on her face. "I mean, I am sorry. I truly, truly am. But that's not it."

"Then what is it?"

Nadine slowly released a lungful of air. She held it together somehow. She had chosen the restaurant in hopes that it would keep Trina's emotions at bay, but now it was her own that she was concerned about. Nadine took a moment to moisten her throat with a few sips of tea before she spoke again.

"That thing you said to me the other day was true."

"Which thing?" Trina asked.

"Everything," Nadine reiterated. "All the stuff you said about Damon after reading what was in my journal." Nadine watched Trina sit up straight, and then rest heavily against the back of the seat.

"Oh my God," she whispered. "How far back does it go, Nadine?"

Wiping her eyes again, Nadine said, "It's been going on for almost the entire time we've been married."

"Oh, Nadine."

"But it hasn't always been as bad as it is now, and it wasn't happening as frequently as it is now," Nadine quickly added. "I've been praying that things will get better, but it's been getting worse."

"And all this time, you didn't tell me because...?"

"Because I'm still with him. Trina, I knew that if you knew all of this, you would be trying to talk me into leaving."

Trina leaned forward in her seat. "You're da..." She let her words trail, and then started over. "You're doggone right, I would have. And waiting almost nine years to tell me doesn't change that. I'm still telling you that you should leave."

"I don't want to end my marriage over this."

"What marriage, Nadine? You don't have a marriage; you have a crisis."

"Trina, I love Damon."

"There are several male celebrities who have shown up in news headlines when they were accused of being abusive. I'm not ashamed to say that I still love to listen to their music or watch them play sports. But just because I love them doesn't mean I have to let them in my house and let them put their hands on me."

"Damon has never hit me, Trina."

Trina sighed and sat back in her seat again. "I know your daddy is turning over in his grave right now."

Nadine winced at the vision of it that suddenly popped up in her mind.

"I know he raised you better than this," Trina continued. "I know for a fact that he was a good example to you of how a man is supposed to treat a woman. I love Bradley with everything in me, but I wish a nigga would. Girl, if Bradley ever rips my clothes, it had better be because he's about to throw me across the bed and make wild passionate love to me. And if he ever draws a gun on me, he'd better pull the trigger and not miss the target because I'll mess him up so bad that he'd wish he was dead."

"It's always easy to say what you would and wouldn't do when you're not in the situation," Nadine pointed out.

Trina sprang into a forward sitting position. "Nadine Jackson Deville, you have known me for almost half of my life. Is there any part about me that would make you think I won't do what I say I'll do?"

Nadine couldn't hold back the giggle that escaped her lips. "Actually, no."

"Exactly," Trina said. "Now, we've got to figure out how to get you out of this."

"No, Trina. Stop." Nadine held her hands out in front of her. "I didn't tell you this for you to help me leave Damon. I'm telling you so that you can help me pray."

"Pray?" The scowl on Trina's face was deep.

"Yes, pray," Nadine stressed. "I mean, doesn't the Bible say where two or three are gathered in God's name, He will be in the midst of them? Doesn't the Bible say one person can chase away one thousand people, but two can put ten thousand to flight?"

"Yes, but the Bible also says for us to put on the whole armor of God so that we can fight against the devil. And it says that God has given us the authority over all the power of the enemy and that we can walk on snakes and scorpions and crush them."

Nadine's jaw dropped. "Come on now, Trina. Do you really believe Damon is a snake or a scorpion?"

"Yes, and the worst kind because he's also your husband. You're sleeping with the enemy, Nadine. You must get out before you end up hurt or worse."

"Well, I believe prayer is more powerful than anything that the devil might try to throw at me."

"Amen to that," Miranda said as she approached with their meals in hand. "I remember praying for my son, and the Good Lord answered by bringing Attorney Jackson in my life." Miranda set their meals in front of them, and then placed her right hand on her hip. "That proved to me that prayer works. I had lost all hope. And then I prayed, and God sent this woman to talk sense into me." Miranda placed her left hand on Nadine's shoulder.

"Amen," Nadine said in agreement.

"Yes, amen," Trina chimed in. "And you prayed, and God sent this woman," she stressed while pointed at herself, "to talk some sense into you."

"Anything else I can get for you ladies?" Miranda placed napkins on the table while she made the offer.

"I think we're good," Nadine told her.

"I'll be back with your fresh waters a little later." She smiled at both before walking away.

"You think she heard what we were talking about?" Nadine whispered. The last thing she needed was for an outsider—especially one who knew her and Damon—to find out what was going on.

"No," Trina assured. "I saw her approaching, and I would have warned you if there was a threat of that happening. She didn't hear anything other than what you said at the end."

Nadine looked across the booth at Trina and smiled. Even after everything that had happened between them, she was still a friend, and still looking out for her best interest. The women graced their food together, and Nadine took her first bite of solid food for the day.

"Do you really want to remain in this marriage?"

After swallowing and wiping her mouth with her napkin, Nadine answered, "Yes, I do. If a divorce was what I wanted, I would have gone for that years ago. I'm not ready to give up. Is there anything too hard for the Lord? That's from the book of Jeremiah, chapter 32."

"Why sit we here until we die?" Trina responded. "That's the second book of Kings." She gave Nadine a side-eye. "I'll match you verse for verse chick. You will never convince me it's God's will for you to stay in an abusive marriage."

"I don't think He wants me to do that either. That's why I'm praying for things to change," Nadine reasoned. "I think even Olivia sensed the need for a prayer partner in this, and that's why she advised me to find someone I could fully trust and tell them about what's going on."

"Olivia told you to do that?"

"Yes."

"And you chose me?"

"I couldn't have told anyone else. If you hadn't agreed to come here today, I don't know what I would have done, really. I don't trust anyone else like this."

A smile crept across Trina's face. It was the first full one that Nadine had seen since their meeting began. The table was quiet for a few moments while the women made headway on eating their meals. It was Trina who first spoke again.

"I'm glad you told me about this, but I'm going to tell you something," she said. "I'm almost sure that Olivia didn't tell you to share this so I could help you pray. I would bet my entire savings that she wanted you to do it so that if something crazy happened, like you suddenly went missing or you died in some type of freak accident, there would be someone who would be able to tell the authorities about this so that they could investigate possible foul play."

"Trina!"

"I'd bet my whole savings," she restated. "It almost scares me that you're waiting for a sign when you've already seen plenty of them. What more do you need to see?"

"I don't know. But God knows what it would take, and He knows that all these past things that you and Olivia are defining as signs are not it. So, until He shows me differently, I'm going to keep the faith that things will change. Damon is a good man.

He has faults, yes. But underneath it all, my husband is a good, God-fearing man."

"So, Olivia told you the same thing I did, and you still can't see it." Nadine shook her head slowly. "Maybe my confirmation of what she said is the sign God is giving you."

"Here are your waters, and here is the receipt," Miranda said while sliding the slip of paper in Nadine's direction and patting her on the shoulder. "Is there anything else I can do for you?"

"I think I'm good," Nadine told her. "Thank you."

"Always a pleasure," she said as she walked away.

"I'm good too," Trina called after her. "Like you care," she added under her breath.

Nadine laughed and reached for her phone that vibrated on the table beside her. "It's Ms. Everson," she said. "I wonder what she wants."

"Who's Ms. Everson?"

"Rebecca's mother. You know, the girl that struggled over the gun with her boyfriend several weeks ago, and it went off?"

"Oh yeah. Aren't you going to answer it?"

"Ms. Everson and I don't see eye-to-eye. She typically works my nerves. I'll let her talk to my voicemail," Nadine replied. Changing the subject, she added, "I know you have to get back to the office, but I just want to really thank you for coming to meet me. And thanks for not holding all this against me. Our friendship means the world to me, and I promise you, it'll never happen again. I need you to believe that."

"If I didn't, I'd get up and walk away right now. I'm glad I came too."

Nadine's phone beeped signifying that a message had been left. She drank a few swallows of water, and then put the phone to her ear to listen. She could barely make out what Ms. Everson was saying through her frantic screams, but she understood enough.

"What's the matter?" Trina asked when she saw Nadine's enlarged eyes.

"Rebecca's dead," Nadine whispered through pants of breath. "Her mom said she went back to Danny. They got into a fight, and he killed her."

"Oh my God!" Trina gasped.

Nadine lowered the phone from her ear and placed it on the table. She felt numb. "Ms. Everson said Danny strangled Rebecca," she told Trina. "They found her body this morning, and Danny has been arrested.

"Well," Trina said. "Is that a big enough sign for you, Nadine? Is it?"

Chapter 18

The Master Plan

Nadine regretted sharing the results of her COVID test with Damon. She didn't realize how much she didn't mind sleeping alone until he moved back into the bedroom two nights ago. Not once had he so much as slid a note under the bedroom door expressing his concern for her while she was in quarantine, but upon hearing that the test was negative, he wasted no time making his return to the master bedroom, with the full expectation for Nadine to resume her "wifely duties."

His move back into the bedroom complicated things on more than one level. Nadine had made the hard choice to leave. And while keeping her decision hush-hush seemed unfair, it was really the only sensible choice. Nadine had lived with Damon long enough to know that this wasn't a decision she could share with him. A divorce from the great Mayor Damon Deville had no chance of being amicable. As much as he obsessed over his public image, she shuddered at the thought of how he might react if told she wanted to end their marriage.

In Nadine's heart of hearts, she couldn't think of a more disrespectful way to end a ten-year relationship and a nine-year marriage. Even to her, it seemed cold and heartless to just walk out without the courtesy of at least issuing a warning. But the findings of the investigation into Rebecca's murder had solidified Nadine's decision to plan a secret escape.

According to Ms. Everson, it was only after Rebecca told Danny she was leaving that he beat her to a pulp, and then took his bare hands, wrapped them around her throat, and squeezed the life out of her. Rebecca gave him one chance too many. Had she just stayed away as Nadine had advised, she would still be alive today. Ms. Everson said Danny won her back with his constant wooing and empty promises that things would be better. Based on Mrs. Everson's version of the story, Danny had told Rebecca to just give him thirty days to prove himself.

When Nadine spoke with the grieving mother on Thursday evening, Ms. Everson said things were good between the two for a few days, but it wasn't long at all before Danny and Rebecca were at odds again. And when the girl decided to take him up on his guarantee that she could leave if he didn't keep his word, Danny decided that if Rebecca wouldn't live with him, she wouldn't live at all.

Nadine had no real heart connection with Rebecca or her mom—they were just clients just like the hundreds that she'd served over the years—but she found herself choking back tears while Ms. Everson shared the gory details. Nobody should have to experience the terror that Rebecca must have endured in those last moments before death put her out of her misery.

"Becky should have listened to us, Your Honor. She never should've taken him back," Ms. Everson had said between sobs during their twenty minute call.

Us??

At the sound of the word, Nadine pulled her cell phone from her ear and looked at it in utter disbelief. She could only guess that it somehow made Ms. Everson feel less guilt-ridden by including herself as one who had tried to talk Rebecca out of reconciling with Danny. Nadine knew firsthand that the woman had clearly been in favor of her daughter rekindling the unhealthy romance with her abuser. Howerver she also knew that to jog Ms. Everson's memory during her time of anguish wasn't the proper thing to do.

Because of the violent nature of the crime, all the local news stations were covering it, and one of the attorneys at Nadine Jackson & Associates had been retained to prosecute. The family had first requested the services of Trina, who was just as fierce in her role as a prosecutor as Nadine was as a defense attorney. But, Trina passed the case to one of the others. She had a more pressing assignment.

After hearing Ms. Everson's initial voicemail, Nadine and Trina ended up spending an extra hour at Moe's on Thursday trying to come to an agreement on an exit strategy for Nadine. The first half hour was spent with Trina trying to get a firm commitment from Nadine that she would abandon her marriage. Even with what she knew, she was still apprehensive.

Trina's plan was simple, yet nothing was going to be easy. The mere fact that Damon had moved back into the bedroom with Nadine complicated matters. His knowledge that she was COVID-negative didn't help either. He was the first person that Nadine told about her negative result. It seemed like the right thing to do at the time. She had sent him a text message with a picture of the negative reading before she reached out to Trina to request their meeting.

The details of Trina's plan required immediate action. Things had to be done in increments so as not to create any misgivings. Nadine had to be able to shift personal belongings out of her house a little at a time. Everything had to appear normal to her husband. Damon could not suspect anything if the plan was to be orchestrated successfully, without a hitch.

Nadine's heartbeat quickened at the very thought of it all. Damon had constantly reminded her throughout their marriage that just because he didn't have the same level of education as she had, he was not to be taken for anybody's fool. And Nadine believed it. She knew that nothing could be assumed. Her every step had to be a well-planned one. There was no room for error.

Today was Saturday, but Damon had nothing on his calendar to get him out of the house. Trina had sent a text that she would be calling at nine forty-five a.m. to go over some details. Nadine looked toward the left side of the bed where Damon still lay. He appeared to be sound asleep, but it was just eighteen minutes away from ten, and he never slept past ten on weekends, even when he had nothing on his schedule.

Nadine eased out of bed. She wanted to head straight to the showers to wash away Damon's scent. He had been all over her last night. By now, she shouldn't be surprised by his bipolar behavior, being hostile one moment and horny the next. But, it was something that, even after all these years, she still couldn't understand. Taking a shower was out of the question though. Not only would the sounds coming from the bathroom awaken him prematurely, but there wasn't time.

Nadine grabbed her robe from the back of her vanity chair where she had draped it last night and put it on. She needed to be able to talk to Trina before Damon started stirring. If he woke up while she was on the phone and found her in some private place talking quietly, that might create a red flag. It was not usual behavior for her.

Nadine moved quietly when she walked out of the room and down the stairwell. She could hear Daddy Deville shifting around in his bedroom when she passed his closed door. Yesterday, his therapists said he was making good progress and could walk around more using just his cane for support.

Daddy Deville had already been out and made his special coffee blend. The aroma had hit Nadine's nostrils as soon as she stepped out of the master bedroom. She was pouring a cup of it for herself as Trina's phone call came through.

"Hey. You don't be late by a second, do you?" Nadine said with a soft laugh as she spoke through her earpiece.

"Am I ever?" Trina responded.

It was true. She was rarely ever late for anything. That was why Nadine had been worried that Trina might have decided not to show up for their lunch date two days ago.

"Listen," Nadine told Trina. "We've got to talk fast. I have a feeling that Damon is going to wake up soon. If he doesn't wake up on his own, his alarm isn't going to let him sleep past ten."

"I'll talk fast, but I need you to hear me out and not get mad or jump to any conclusions."

Nadine stiffened. "Oh, my God. What crazy thing have you done?"

"I said, don't jump to conclusions. I haven't done anything crazy. I've done something necessary."

"Which is?"

"I called your sister."

"Sophia?" Nadine gasped. "You called Sophia? You didn't tell her about what's going on here, did you?"

"Yes, I did. I need her."

"Trina, I can't believe you!" Nadine struggled to keep her voice level low. "You were supposed to be my confidant. Do you even know what that means?"

"I also said for you not to get mad," Trina reminded her. "What do you expect? You know I'm going to get mad that you told my sister."

"Listen to me, Nadine. This is a big job that has to be carried out by this time next week. We have seven days—count them…seven—to get everything done and get you out of that house. I can't do this by myself, and with Damon knowing that you're over COVID, he's going to expect you to return to work Monday, so your time is limited for getting stuff done too. We have to work smart, and if I had to get help from any one person, I figured that Sophia would be the one you would want me to pick."

Nadine released a heavy sigh. "I just didn't want my family knowing about this. Not yet anyway."

"Well, I can tell you right now that it was no real shock to Sophia. She had already detected a problem. She said the last time y'all talked, she knew something wasn't right, and she knew it had something to do with Damon."

"The last thing I need is for this to get back to Mama."

"It won't, Nadine," Trina vowed. "She knows not to tell your mom, Aunt Pat, or anyone else for that matter. You don't have to be concerned about that. Sophia will make a few trips from Tallahassee over the next week to help me get things done. And of course, Bradley is going to help as much as he can, but his company is building that whole shopping strip in McDonough right now and that's keeping him pretty busy. He knows what's going on though, and if we need him, he's prepared to help us do whatever we need done."

Listening to Trina talk was beginning to put Nadine's nerves on edge. She blew into her coffee cup and then took a sip as her mind flooded with thoughts. Was it worth all this? Rebecca's plight had clearly driven Trina over the edge. Had she allowed it to drive her over the edge too? The only thing that Damon and Danny had in common was that both their first names began with the same letter. Just because Danny had gone off the deep end and killed Rebecca didn't mean that Damon might do the same. Danny had been slapping Rebecca around for years. It wasn't like her murder had come out of nowhere. Meanwhile, Damon had never struck Nadine, so why was she letting her former client's outcome weigh into her own situation? "Nadine, are you listening to me?" Trina's voice broke

Nadine's deep thoughts. "Yes, I'm listening."

"Lies," Trina said. "You're not listening; otherwise, you would have answered my question."

"I'm sorry. What question?"

"Have you started pulling any of your small items together yet? If you can bring some of your smaller belongings with you to the office, I can get them from you there."

"Trina, this is crazy."

"What's crazy?"

"Everything," Nadine said. "I need to take more time and think things over. This is just too much. I feel like I'm losing my mind."

"You are definitely losing your mind if you're thinking of backing out of this," Trina responded. "Nadine, a woman has died because of her decision to stay."

"I'm not Rebecca, and Damon is not Danny. Just because—"

"Nadine Jackson-Deville, you listen to me, and listen to me good." Trina's tone sounded like that of a mother scolding a hard-headed child. "You are getting out of there, you hear me? If I have to hog tie you and have you dragged out of that house against your will, you're getting out of there. I refuse to live my life in fear of you losing yours."

Although she wasn't near her bedroom or her father-in-law's, Nadine lowered her voice to just above a whisper. "Losing my life? Let's be reasonable. Do you really think Damon is capable of..."

"Anything," Trina stressed. "I think he's capable of absolutely anything."

Nadine rested her back against the wall of their home's formal dining room, where she had been standing since answering the call. She felt helpless. She felt torn. She felt tears rising.

When Trina spoke again, her voice was a mixture of soothing and haunting. The tempo of her words was slow as if she wanted to ensure that her friend would capture every word. "You asked God for a clear sign, Nadine," she said, "and it don't get no clearer than this. I'm not saying that Damon will kill you if you remain in this marriage, but you've already admitted that his treatment of you has gotten worse and worse over the years. What happens when the stuff he throws at you it starts hitting you? What happens when he starts tearing at your skin instead of tearing at your clothes? What happens when the chamber of the gun is no longer empty? What happens when…,"

"Okay, you've made your point. I swear, you sound just like Olivia," Nadine said, placing her still full cup of coffee on the table and wiping away a tear from her cheek. "Are you sure the two of you haven't talked?"

"As God is my witness, we have not. But I did tell you she was the best, and she is."

After another heavy sigh, Nadine said, "Damon's alarm is going to go off in just a few minutes. Tell me what I need to do."

"First of all, you need to know that Sophia is securing a storage unit today. It will be a space right here in Atlanta so we can get to it anytime we need to, but it will be under the name of Sophia Jackson Kendrick; that way, it can't be directly connected to you. Like I said before, she will be making quick trips here to help take care of things, when necessary, but every time she comes, it will be in the late afternoon after she has completed her responsibilities as a professor there at Florida A&M University."

"This is just inconveniencing everybody," Nadine said. "This is awful."

"Be quiet. Sophia insisted on being hands-on with this. And to honor your wishes regarding not letting people know about what's going on with you, she agreed to withhold the details of all of this from your brother-in-law, nieces, and nephew, for now. They will just assume that she's coming here to check on you. They know you had COVID, and as far as they're concerned, you still do."

As she listened to Trina talk, Nadine couldn't help but be a little impressed that her friend had been so skillfully detailed in her planning. She also couldn't help but wonder how much of the skill had been learned from the records Trina had read while prosecuting criminals.

"As soon as you can," Trina continued. "I need you to get to the Department of Motor Vehicles and get your hands on a new driver's license."

"What? A new driver's license? Why?"

"For the just-in-case," Trina said. "If Damon gets even the slightest notion that you're leaving him, he could take your license and hide it to stop you from driving. You never know, so you need to prepare for anything. It's better to have it and not need it than to need it and not have it," she pointed out. "Just tell the people at the driver's license place that you lost yours and need a new one."

"Great. Now you've got me lying," Nadine mumbled.

"It won't be your first time, and it won't be your last. Now shut up and listen. It's almost ten o'clock," Trina reminded her. "You also need to get yourself a duplicate social security card. Don't keep the new license or the new social security card in your wallet, in the house, or in your car. Have both items mailed to the office, not to your home. When you receive them, we'll lock them away in the storage unit."

"My head is starting to hurt," Nadine remarked.

"Both these things need to be done as early as possible on Monday," Trina instructed. "I'll be in court, so I won't be in the office until later in the afternoon, but I need you to get these done, Nadine. Promise me. And remember, God is listening."

"Get a license, order a new social security card. Got it."

"Promise me."

"I promise, I promise."

"Two more things," Trina said. "Get a new cell phone that only people who know what's going on will have the number to. None of the ladies at the office should have it, nor should your clients. Last thing: pull most of the money out of your personal account. That cash will go in a safety deposit box that we will put in your storage space too."

"What do I need to do that for?"

"Remember when you handed me your journals at the end of last week's lunch meeting?" Trina asked. "Well, over the past two days, I've read all three of them. Some areas of those books—especially the latest one you've written in—were like reading the notes that would be used to build chapters in a horror novel. Nadine, your husband forced you to go to the bank, and using threats and intimidation, he made you withdraw money out of your account and put it in his."

Nadine closed her eyes at the recollection. She had suppressed some of her particularly sensitive experiences so much that sometimes she genuinely forgot about them.

"Once again, I need you to promise me," Trina said. "Promise me that you're going to get a new phone, and that you'll withdraw most of your money on Monday."

"I promise." Nadine's words were soft but audible enough. Faint sounds from Damon's alarm could be heard downstairs.

Nadine wasn't sure whether it was her heart or her footsteps that she heard as she took quick steps toward the kitchen and opened the refrigerator door to retrieve what she needed to make breakfast omelets.

"I have to go," she whispered to Trina. "Damon is getting up. I hear his alarm."

"Okay," Trina said. "Remember, Nadine. Just act normal. I got you, and God's got both of us. All I need is for you to act normal."

Nadine ended the call without saying goodbye. She could hear the master bedroom door open. Acting normal sounded easy, but Nadine anticipated the next seven days being the most unnerving ones of her life.

Chapter 19

Second Thoughts

Nadine felt as though she was having some type of out of body experience. It seemed something like a nightmare, but she knew it wasn't. Over recent months, Nadine had had enough nightmares to know that eventually she could wake herself from those. What she had been dealing with today was different. No matter how hard she pinched herself, waking up from this horrible reality wasn't an option.

Today, Nadine had spent far more time outside the office than in her workspace. It was already one o'clock, and the banana she was currently eating as she sat behind her desk was her first meal of the day. This was also the first time today that she didn't feel as if she was being watched.

As soon as Damon left the house for work this morning, Nadine pulled together a to-do list, making sure she crossed all the T's and dotted all the I's in the directives that Trina had given her yesterday. Standing by her promise to her best friend to follow through with getting her priority list done turned out to be more difficult that Nadine imagined. Damon had been especially sweet to her all weekend.

Saturday afternoon, he suggested that they go bowling with Trina and Bradley. It had been a long time since the two couples had double dated. After Damon's cruel remark some weeks ago about them being Nadine's friends but not his, and then his indication that Bradley was less than a man for not putting Trina in her place, Nadine had decided not to ever suggest they pair up on dates again. When Damon recommended it Saturday, she was shocked.

Now that Trina and Bradley were aware of Damon's mistreatment of her, it took some serious convincing for Nadine to get them to agree to the outing, but they finally consented, and managed to pull it off without raising any suspicions. Overall, the night went well, but somehow, Nadine doubted that it was really an innocent mistake when Bradley dropped his bowling ball on Damon's foot.

Yesterday was just as calm. No arguments or disagreements took place between Nadine and her husband. They went to church and enjoyed the full fellowship. Daddy Deville had gone with them, but Friday's session with his physical therapists had been a little more intense than normal. He said he felt residual soreness and wanted to get some rest. Damon swung by Longhorn and picked a Cowboy Pork Chops meal for his dad before taking him back to the house to relax for the rest of the afternoon.

For Nadine, he went the extra mile. Damon took her to "their place." It seemed that every time they went to STK Steakhouse, a flame for romance was sparked. The atmosphere there somehow was able to erase whatever strain may have been between them and ignite feelings that seemed to be nonexistent in the moments before they arrived at the eatery. Yesterday was no different. Conversation between Nadine and Damon flowed effortlessly, their laughter was genuine, and when they returned home, passions exploded. All those things worked together to make her Monday morning errands extremely difficult.

As Nadine dropped the peel from her banana in the trashcan beside her desk, she had never felt so perplexed. The only thing she was certain about at the moment was that she wasn't certain about anything. The events of the weekend were starting to renew her belief that her marriage could be saved. Even though Nadine kept her promises and followed through on getting the backup license, ordering the new social security card, getting the secret cell phone, and making the cash withdrawal from her account, she was having major second thoughts.

Nadine's own coughing was the noise that shook her back to reality. COVID-19 was long gone, but it seemed to want to leave her a souvenir. She'd stopped by her doctor's office while she was running errands this morning, as a precaution. Nadine was told that the cough would eventually subside.

A knock on her office door captured her full attention. Nadine wasn't expecting anyone, and Ava hadn't buzzed her before letting whomever it was come through. The only person she generally let in without telling Nadine was Damon. Could it be him? Had he heard or seen something? Was he here to confront her about her plans?

Nadine took a breath, straightened her slumped back, took another breath, and said, "Come on in."

Relief hugged her like a blanket when she saw her sister walk in. Nadine stood up. She hadn't seen Sophia in a while, and the two of them hadn't talked since Trina had shared with her the bad news about Nadine's marriage.

"Sophia. Hi," Nadine said while accepting the warm embrace that her sister offered.

"Hey, big sis. Ava told me that you got in not too long ago but that you didn't have anybody in the office with you. She said it would be fine for me to come on back."

"Of course, it is."

"Are you okay?" Sophia looked Nadine directly in the eyes. "Tell me the truth. Are you okay?"

Nadine forced a smile, sat in her chair, and motioned for her sister to sit in the one directly across from her. "I'm about as okay as I can be under the circumstances," she told her. "Listen, Sophia. I know you already know this, but I can't tell you how important it is to me for all this mess not to get back to anybody right now."

"Nadine, I promised Trina that I would not tell anyone, and I won't. Please let that be the very last thing you worry about. We need your total focus to be on getting out, and I'm going to do everything I can to help you do it."

"Oh, Sophia," Nadine whined. "I just don't know."

"Okay, see … what we're not going to do is that right there," Sophia emphasized. "We are getting you out of here, Nadine.

You deserve better than this. You are worth more than this. If Daddy was still here, he would literally kill Damon, and then ask God to forgive him for the murder he just committed."

"No, he wouldn't. Daddy was a man of God."

"I know," Sophia said. "That's where the asking-God-for-forgiveness part comes in. Nadine, this is not a situation that you need to remain in. You've already been in it nine years too long. You can't really want this for yourself."

"What I want is to believe he can change," Nadine said.

"Oh, he can, but he's not going to, so you can stop holding out for that," Sophia responded. "Damon has shown you who he is over and over again. He's not even trying to change. He's a master manipulator, Nadine. Trina read those diary entries to me, so I know what's been going on. There's a pattern there. He treats you like crap, and then he comes back and does something nice to try to make you forget his actions. What was it this time? Did he get your car detailed? Did he buy you flowers? Did he take you on a trip? Did he buy you a cute outfit or an expensive meal? What was it this time?" she repeated.

Nadine's only response was a sigh.

Sophia leaned forward and put her elbows on Nadine's desk. "Please tell me that you did the things Trina asked you to do this morning."

"Yes, I did them," Nadine said dryly.

"Good." Sophia reached into her purse while continuing to speak. "I wish I could hang around a little longer, but I've got a class to teach in a couple of hours, so I need to get back. Here you go," she added while handing Nadine a small envelope.

"What's this?"

"There are two keys to your storage unit in here. I was supposed to meet up with Trina and give them to her, but she was unable to break away from her court case. She texted me and said she should be out of court by two o'clock, so my guess is that she'll be here in a little bit. Trina told me to just bring the keys to you."

Sophia was talking fast now. It was obvious that she was pressed for time. "Extra Space Storage… the one on Lenox Road; that's where your unit is. The unit number is written inside the flap of the envelope. It's a ten-by-fifteen space, which should be plenty of room for your needs since you're not taking any furniture or other oversized items."

Nadine stared at the envelope in her hand. It was all becoming too real now. Reality had already hit her in a major way this morning when she found herself sneaking a few personal items to her car so that they could be taken to the storage unit later today. Reality hit even harder when she came into the office and saw the locked box sitting on her desk, the one that Trina had placed there for her to put the withdrawn cash inside. Now, with the storage keys in her hand, reality was delivering another commanding blow.

"One of those keys needs to go to Trina, and the other one is yours," Sophia continued. "Don't lose it, and make sure you don't place it where Damon might find it." She stood from her chair and walked around Nadine's desk to give her another hug.

It took every ounce of willpower that Nadine had inside her not to break down and weep on Sophia's shoulder. She could feel tears threatening, but she blinked hard to hold them back.

It wouldn't be a good thing for her baby sister to see her falling apart right now. Nadine needed to be the image of a strong woman even if she wasn't feeling like one at the moment.

"I love you," Sophia said. "We'll talk later, okay?"

Nadine nodded. "I love you too, and thanks for everything."

When Sophia closed the office door as she exited, Nadine sank back into her office chair. Her eyes fell to her desk calendar and the tears she'd been able to hold back just moments ago were now flowing. A yellow highlight on Nadine's calendar reminded her that her birthday was less than two weeks away. Making such a drastic life change was certainly not the way she planned to observe it.

Monday's experience marked what would become the norm for the days that followed. Every day was intense, and with Trina scheduled to be in court every morning this week, Nadine had to take care of much of the groundwork herself.

Tuesday morning, after Damon left for work, Nadine rummaged through her closet, removing shoes out of shoeboxes and putting them in bags that could be hidden in the trunk of her car. With the boxes still on the shelf, nothing looked different. Her husband would never suspect that shoes weren't still inside them. Nadine didn't have a similar plan that would work for her clothing that hung in the closet, so for the most part, that stayed in place. She would just have to make it a part of her final haul. The items inside her dresser drawers were a different story. Damon could see the clothes in her walk-in closet, but he never went through her drawers. Nadine was able to begin putting several items in bags and tuck them away in her car as well.

During her lunch break on Tuesday, she was at the post office setting up her mail forwarding. Nadine was in the parking lot before it dawned on her that she hadn't made a solid plan about where to have her mail forwarded. Her first thought was Sophia's home, and then Trina's. But, by the time she got to the front of the line, neither of theirs was the address that she put on the paperwork.

As she spoke to one of the clerks, Nadine felt like God had sent a ministering angel. She never told the clerk outright that she was an abused wife who needed to leave her husband without giving him notice, but somehow, the lady seemed to know. She directed Nadine to step to the back so that their conversation would be private. There, the woman gave her all the directives she needed on how to have her mail forwarded without the chance of any confirmation notices going to the home she was fleeing.

Tuesday evening, Nadine's heart skipped a beat when she noticed that Damon made it home before she did. That almost never happened. His duties with the city often delayed his arrival. Most days, Nadine would get home nearly two hours ahead of him. Had he suspected something? Had she left clues?

"Oh, God … please help me," Nadine prayed softly while remaining in her car for several moments after parking it in the garage.

Her hand trembled as she pressed the button to turn off the engine, and Nadine fumbled with her purse and attaché case as she exited the car. Her legs felt like rubber bands during her walk to the door as she prepared to enter the house. Nadine took a deep breath and tried to swallow her mounting fear as she turned the knob, and almost froze when she entered the living room and saw Damon and Daddy Deville sitting together looking at something on the screen of Damon's cell phone. It was another rarity. When they both looked up at her, Nadine's mind began racing to find the answer to a question she hadn't even been asked yet.

What if he'd put some hidden cameras in the house? She was aware of the outside security cameras, but what if Damon had had some put inside without her knowledge? What if what they were looking at on his phone was footage of her packing? What if the camera had audio? Maybe they could even hear the most recent telephone conversations she'd been having with Trina. What on earth would she tell Damon if he came at her in any kind of accusing manner?

"Hey, you two," she managed to say, struggling the whole while to look at ease.

"Hey." Daddy Deville sounded normal.

"Hey, come look at this." Damon sounded normal too, but Nadine was still cautious as she walked behind where he sat in order to view his screen. On it, she saw a photo of an overly majestic porch with tall white pillars and concrete lions wearing gold crowns sitting on either side.

"What do you think?" Damon looked up at her as he asked. "I'm thinking of getting our porch renovated like this."

Nadine liked their porch as it was. What he was showing her was a little too flashy for her taste, but she knew better than to let that be her response. Instead, she said, "It's beautiful. When are you thinking of doing this?"

"Real soon. It's a pretty big job, but I want to jump right on it. This porch is going to make our house stand out from all the other houses within miles of us," he gloated.

"It sure would," Daddy Deville agreed.

Nadine didn't quite know how to comment. She'd be long gone before the porch renovation. "When it's decorated, it'll make the perfect Christmas card image," she said, walking toward the stairwell.

"I didn't even think about that!" Damon called out. "Yeah, we have to get it decorated real good for Christmas, and me and you can stand out there in front of it for our photo shoot."

Inside the master suite, Nadine rested her back against the closed door. She had just made herself even more depressed. Her birthday was just days away, and Thanksgiving and Christmas wouldn't be very far behind. What on earth was she thinking? Downstairs, she had a husband who was planning to make her home even grander than it already was. The Christmas cards that would go out from the mayor to all city employees and other city officials would be stunning this year. How could she even think of leaving at a time like this?

A chime from her cell phone indicated the arrival of a new message. Nadine was already holding it in her hand, and she immediately saw that Damon was reaching out to her from downstairs.

What is Bradley's personal cell number?

The message immediately took Nadine aback. Surely, after all the horrible things Damon had said about Bradley, he wasn't about to call him and ask for any favors. A proverbial lightbulb switched on in Nadine's brain.

"That's why you suggested that we all go bowling together Saturday!" Nadine looked at the screen of her phone as if she could see Damon's face there. "You should be ashamed of yourself!" she added in a harsh whisper.

Why? Nadine typed the single word response and hit the button to send it before she had time to give it a second thought. Within seconds, she heard heavy footsteps charging up the stairwell, and immediately, the fear she first felt when she pulled into the driveway returned with a vengeance. Nadine sat on the bed and barely had time to brace herself before the bedroom door flung open.

Damon's first word was the vile one he always called her when he wanted to be as offensive as possible. He followed that with, "What you mean, why? Don't be asking me why I want something; just give me the number!"

"It was just a simple question, Damon. I didn't mean anything by it," Nadine said.

Grabbing the attaché case that she had laid at the foot of the bed, Damon quickly hurled it in her direction. Nadine released a high-pitched yelp but didn't have time to duck. Fortunately for her, he wasn't aiming directly at her. Instead, the leather case slammed against the wall beside her. It knocked her lamp off the nightstand in the process, and the glass base of the lamp shattered as it hit the floor.

"Damon!" she said through a gasp. "This crystal lamp was a part of a set. This is an expensive wedding gift that you just broke!"

"Shut up! You just be glad I didn't break your stupid face! I done told you about questioning me. Now, send me Bradley's number like I asked."

"It's really not necessary for you to speak to me like that," Nadine said as she reached for her phone.

"When I asked nicely, you didn't send it to me. You don't know how to obey until I get mad. I'm so sick of y'all stupid females. Y'all always doing stuff to make us mad and then you act like we're doing you so wrong. I guarantee that crazy White girl did something just like that, and that's the reason she's dead now. If she had kept her stupid mouth closed, she'd be alive today. Sometimes, I think y'all just walk around with a death wish, and when we make that wish come true, the world turns on us and makes us look like devils."

His harsh words were like hot irons on Nadine's ears. There was so much more that she wanted to say but keeping her thoughts to herself seemed like the better choice. Damon was essentially praising a killer for brutally slaughtering his girlfriend for simply having a voice. As far as Nadine was concerned, continuing to talk was certainly not in her best interest.

As soon as he received the text message that gave him what he wanted, Damon stormed out of the room without saying another word. When the door slammed behind him, Nadine's fingers worked fast to send a quick note to Trina. Her best friend's reply was brief but straight to the point.

No more messages or calls from this phone. Delete this and any other texts regarding Damon. Starting now, only use your new phone when communicating with me, Sophia, and Olivia. I'll call you on the new line later.

Chapter 20

Now Or Never

Wednesday morning, Nadine felt that she was becoming paranoid. It was apparent that Damon didn't have cameras in the house, otherwise he would have called her to the carpet by now. Still, just the mere fact that the thought had rushed so quickly to her mind yesterday made Nadine feel the need to take necessary steps to be sure he wasn't spying on her in some other way.

At 9 a.m., she was pacing in the lobby of a repair shop while a good friend of Bradley's, who was a mechanic, swept her car for any tracking devices. While she waited for him to give her the "all clear," Nadine remembered that her car was attached to Damon's satellite radio account, which could also be a method of tracking her location. One quick call to Sirius was all it took to put an end to that possible threat.

The way Damon had spoken to her on Tuesday gave Nadine new determination to leave. Her sister, her best friend, and her therapist were right. She had to know that she deserved better. By the time Thursday rolled in, Nadine had nothing left that she could sneak away from the house without Damon noticing.

She, Trina, and Sophia had been working together like three highly skilled cat burglars. Every detail had been planned with great risk avoidance, yet none of that provided enough comfort to lull Nadine to sleep that night. There was no clock on her bedroom wall, but as she stared up at the ceiling through the darkness, Nadine swore that she could hear every second as it ticked away.

Oh, God. Please let me be doing the right thing.

Her anxiety was creeping back in. Was it because she and Damon had been intimate before he fell asleep? Was it because the last thing he said before the light snoring began was that he loved her?

Nadine was still awake at daybreak when Damon's alarm went off. He had an early breakfast to attend with other city officials from all around Atlanta. Her day of escape couldn't have fallen on a more perfect day. Nadine didn't have to get up this early, so she moved around a bit as though Damon's alarm had slightly stirred her. She turned her back toward him and kept her eyes closed in hopes that he would buy her act.

While Damon walked around the room, in and out of his closet, and in and out of their master bath, Nadine didn't move a muscle. At times, she even held her breath. He needed to believe she was still sound asleep. It seemed to take a lifetime for him to finish preparing for his appointment, but in the end, her performance worked.

At the sound of Damon trotting down the stairwell to the main floor of their home, she sat up straight in the California king bed they'd shared for nearly a decade. The unmistaken deep sound that the heavy security door made each time it closed got lost among the rhythmic thuds of her own strong heartbeats.

Thump-thump. Thump-thump. Thump-thump.

She couldn't let fear paralyze her now. There was no time to waste. Walking across the hardwood flooring of her massive master suite, Nadine peeked out the window long enough to see her husband's limited edition Bentley convertible exit the automatic gate that secured them from the rest of the world. She watched until it was out of sight before refocusing on her immediate task.

Nadine was on a time clock. Her husband had left, but she knew he would be back. He never went straight to work after these breakfast meetings. Damon was too much of a shallow exhibitionist for that. It meant everything to him to impress others. If he went to a function wearing one suit, he wouldn't dare wear that same outfit to another, even if both events took place on the same day. So, even though today's regular schedule for him only required that he attend a city council meeting following the breakfast gathering, Damon would come home to change into a different suit between the appointments.

Nadine quickly switched from her night clothes to a T-shirt and jogging pants. Her morning shower would have to wait. The garments that she couldn't remove from her walk-in closet previously were first on Nadine's list. By the armloads, she placed them in suitcases and large garbage bags. A select few pairs of shoes had previously been left behind for daily use too. Nadine made sure not to forget to grab her expensive Christian Louboutin red bottoms. She had allowed them to remain just in case some formal event that would require her to accompany Damon popped up during the week. The knots in her stomach threatened to stop her momentum, but Nadine pushed past them as best she could. Periodically, she paused long enough to grab tissues to wipe away her tears. Nadine felt like she was shifting into a state of mourning, and in a way, she was. Her marriage was dead. As much as she hoped for resuscitation, the line had flattened. Nine years were going down the drain.

As the thought of it all overran her brain, Nadine stopped packing long enough to shake her head. It really was a pity that she had to make her departure in this manner. They should have been able to sit down together with a therapist. Rev. Proctor had an immeasurable amount of respect for Damon. They could have sat down and talked with him. It probably would have even helped them to attend some marriage retreats where they could gain wisdom from people who had faced the same issues and survived.

It was too late for the "could've, should've, would've" scenarios. They had done none of those things. Damon wouldn't hear of it. The very mention of them always made him angry, which just made matters worse.

The Bible said that love bears all things, believes all things, hopes all things, and endures all things, but that was turning out not to be the case for the Deville household. Nadine had loved Damon during all their years together. Through every argument, every fight, every threat, every name-calling session, and every criticism, she had loved him. Even now, as she prepared for her escape, Nadine still loved Damon.

"Strong love will propel you to give someone chance after chance after chance. The power of love has the potential to be quite mind-blowing." The words Olivia had expressed to her in their recent session came back to Nadine's mind. "God sent His only begotten Son to die as a sacrificial offering so that a world of sinners like us can be saved. That's the power of love. But if we don't accept His love, repent of our sins, and live like we love Him, that God who sent His Son to die for us is the same one whose going to say, 'Depart from me, you worker of iniquity. I don't even know you.' How do we live like we love God? By loving Him right back; that's how. And not with our words only, but with our deeds. You love Mayor Deville, Nadine. But when was the last time Mayor Deville loved you back?"

New tears surfaced, and Nadine used her hands to smear them from her eyes. She hadn't felt loved by Damon since very early in their marriage—not consistently anyway. There were moments that she felt loved, but the longer they were married, the longer the spaces grew between those moments. As much as she had put up with over the years, Nadine was sure that her husband had developed an erroneous confidence that he could grossly mistreat her forever, and that she'd tolerate it forever.

She couldn't rightfully be angry at him for thinking that way. Her actions had given him a valid reason.

A sudden noise coming from downstairs caused Nadine to spin around quickly and face her closed room door. Her eyes locked on the doorknob, and while she watched to see if it would begin turning, her heartbeat shifted back into overdrive.

Thump-thump. Thump-thump. Thump-thump.

If Damon forgot something important and had decided to return to get it, she was trapped. There was nothing she could say or do. Nadine looked over her shoulder toward the large windows in her bedroom. The only plan she could think of was to charge toward the glass with all her might and crash through it. Even if she died in the two-story fall or survived it but was left paralyzed by the impact and had to spend the rest of her life in some nursing facility, she would be better off than having Damon catch her trying to leave him.

With no other sounds heard, Nadine summoned enough bravery to walk to the door and ease it open. A quick peek over the banister revealed that a book had been dropped by Daddy Deville. He picked it up and tucked it under his armpit before heading back to his room.

It was then that Nadine realized she didn't have as much time as she'd first calculated. Today was physical therapy day for Daddy Deville. She had less than an hour to get out before the therapists arrived. Once they were in the house, there would be no way that she would be able to get all her final belongings to the car without being seen. She would have to make several trips up and down the stairs, and with having to practically walk by Daddy Deville's bedroom door each time, it was going to be difficult to get out without her father-in-law seeing her.

Nadine found a level of comfort when Daddy Deville opened his bedroom door and she could hear his shower running. She knew that once he stepped into his shower stall, she could take the trash bags containing the remaining items to the car. He would never hear it over the running water.

Oh, how she missed her dad today. She sure could use one of Alex Jackson's hugs right now. Sophia was right. If their dad was alive and discovered how his firstborn daughter was being treated, it might be enough to push him to the point of committing a felony.

Or maybe not. What if it would have been her dad's advice for her to separate from Damon for a while? Alex believed in marriage. He had loved Nadine's self-righteous mother despite her misguided ways. When her mom would leave on work assignments for days, sometimes weeks, at a time, leaving him to care for Nadine and Sophia like a single father, Alex Jackson stepped up to the plate and did what he had to until his wife returned. He didn't like her extended absences, and they proved not to be wise choices because her disappearing acts built reinforced walls between Rose and her daughters, but Alex had stuck it out. What if he would have recommended that she do the same?

"Oh God," Nadine whispered as she buried her face in her hands. She was so torn. If there was any chance that Damon would change, she'd stay and do what she had to do to make it work too. Trina said he wouldn't change, Sophia said he wouldn't change, and even Damon had told her he wasn't going to change. Nadine would either have to accept him as he was, or she could leave, because there were countless other women out there that would love to be married to him. He seemed to enjoy reminding her of that.

Nadine was starting to feel like a drunk woman having a panic attack. Her breaths were shallow, and her legs were unstable. She reached for her new private cell phone and tapped on the saved number that she wanted to dial. Her options of contacts were limited. Only three people knew that Nadine was leaving Damon today.

Olivia answered on the first ring, but Nadine didn't give her a chance to say anything beyond, "Hello."

Even to her own ears, Nadine's words sounded as though they were coming from a frantic woman who was being held hostage and was terrified for her life. "I don't know what I'm doing, Olivia. I'm scared. This has been my whole life for so long that I don't know what I'm going to do if I leave it. What are people going to think of me? He's gonna lie, and they're going to believe him. I might lose everything. What if..."

"Stop it." Olivia was a pro at being firm without being harsh. "Mayor Deville didn't create you, so he can't destroy you," she continued. "That's the kind of power that he wants you to think he has, but it's all an illusion. Whose report are you going to believe, Nadine?"

"God's" she replied through sobs.

"Whose?" Olivia challenged.

"God's." Nadine's voice was stronger that time, but apparently not strong enough.

"Whose?"

Nadine straightened her back, inhaled deeply, and then slowly emptied her lungs.

"God's!" she exclaimed.

"That's right. God's," Olivia said. "You've ministered to others about His love and His power, and now it's time for you to apply it to your own situation. Trust Him, Nadine. Think about what you've endured. Your husband is just a half-step away from severely hurting you or worse. You deserve better than this, and you know it."

The few moments she spent on the phone with Olivia provided just enough strength and motivation for Nadine to dry her eyes and keep making progress.

Confident that ample time had passed for her father-in-law to make it to his shower, she began carrying the trash bags containing her clothing to her car. The bags were large and a couple of them were heavy, but she got it done, only stopping a few times to catch her breath when her body reminded her that she'd had a recent bout of COVID. The coughs had noticeably lessened in the last forty-eight hours, but they still weren't completely gone yet.

By the time Nadine got her suitcases loaded in with the bags, the trunk as well as the back floors and leather seating of her BMW X5 were covered, and she still wasn't quite finished. She needed to return one last time. While inside, she quickly made the bed she was abandoning, and then grabbed a few sentimental framed items that were arranged on shelves in her reading room as well as other spaces throughout the house— things like her college degrees and pictures she'd taken with family members and friends.

With six bedrooms and four and a half bathrooms, Nadine felt like she was running some weird type of marathon. By the time she was finished, she only had one free hand, and she used it to pour a cup of Daddy Deville's coffee in a travel mug before walking out the door for the last time.

For the first several minutes of her drive, Nadine wept nonstop. She knew she was doing the right thing. She knew her sister, best friend, and therapist were right. She knew her daddy wouldn't want her to remain in that situation. She knew she deserved better. And most of all, she knew Damon would never change. But none of that was strong enough to seal her tear ducts.

Nadine had been careful with her life. She'd planned almost every detail. She focused on her education until she reached her highest goal. Then she focused on her career until she reached an impressive level of success. Only then did she consider a lifelong commitment. Nadine had waited until she was forty to get married. She married a man who was prominent in his church as well as his community. He was well-respected and well-loved in both as well. Damon was a public servant who had grown up in a home where both parents were present. Everything about him said he was a safe bet, but Nadine had bet the house and lost.

Just the thought of what Rose Jackson was going to say once she found out about this made Nadine cringe. Her mom's house probably should have been the one she was headed to right now, but it wasn't. And the distance between Atlanta, Georgia and Houston, Texas had nothing to do with it. She wouldn't go to her mother's if she only lived ten minutes away. There were complete strangers that Nadine would choose to talk to about her crumbled marriage before she would volunteer to reveal it to her mother. She loved her mom, but Nadine had no desire to hear the trail of Scriptures and church quotes that Rose would, no doubt, throw at her.

The tank of Nadine's car had been filled with gas on the way home from work yesterday, so she only had one stop to make today before hitting Interstate 20 heading west, to grab her cash box from the storage unit. Everything else could remain there for now.

The drive from Atlanta to Birmingham was typically a two-hour and fifteen-minute drive, but Nadine was pulling into the familiar driveway in two hours flat. She sat in her car and stared at the red front door for several moments before finally getting out. With every step closer that she got, it became more difficult to hold back a new flood of tears. Nadine stood on the front porch gathering herself for a long while before she finally rang the doorbell.

A short wait later, the door opened and Nadine was met with the warm smile that she had long ago grown to love but hadn't seen in far too many months.

"Well, look at God!" her Aunt Pat exclaimed while opening the door wider so her niece could enter. "You were just on my mind, and I just got done praying for you!"

Chapter 21

In Loving Arms

Nadine lay flat on her back staring up at the ceiling. The space she occupied was eerily quiet. All the noises she heard were faint ones coming from the outside. The sound of rainfall had helped to lull her to sleep last night, and although it was no longer raining outside, Nadine could hear the occasional drop that hit the roof from the leaves of the mighty oak tree that stood just outside her window.

Drip!

That was the one hundred sixteenth drip she had counted, but no doubt, there had been far more. And then there were the swishing sounds of the occasional car passing over the wet pavement of neighborhood street and the far-away laughter of children. Their carefree giggles reminded Nadine that while the new school term had begun, today was Saturday and classes were not in session.

Sitting up, Nadine looked around the room. This bedroom always reminded her of an art studio. In one corner, there was a small wooden desk. Nadine remembered the day that Uncle Ross brought the ugly brown piece of furniture home from a yard sale, set it up in the room, and let her help him sand it down and cover it with two coats of white paint. She was around fourteen years old at the time, and Nadine recalled being proud of how professional and beautiful their finished product looked.

Of Aunt Pat's three guest bedrooms, this one was Nadine's favorite, largely because it was unofficially hers. She had spent many days and nights in that room, especially during her middle and high school years. Hardly anything in it had changed over the decades.

The color pallete gave the room an air of refinement despite its simplicity. A black vase holding white flowers graced the corner of the desk. Black picture frames sat on top of the white dresser and chest set. On the wall hung a painting of a little girl and her mother wearing white dresses and white gloves, carrying matching black umbrellas, holding hands as they walked down a sidewalk toward a country church. Even the bedding was decorated in color blocks of black and white, but it had just enough yellow in the pattern to break up the monotony without erasing the elegance.

When they first decorated the room, Aunt Pat and Uncle Ross said Nadine could claim it as hers, and she was welcome to sleep in it anytime she wanted. Nadine had taken them up on that offer more times than she could count, though not lately. Life for Nadine had become very busy in the last few years. While she had come to visit on occasions, she hadn't slept in her room in over a decade.

She felt more rested than she had in a long while. Last night was the first since she contracted COVID that Nadine's sleep hadn't been interrupted at least once during the night by a fit of coughing. Thoughts of her unannounced departure had kept her awake until after midnight, but once she drifted off to sleep, Nadine didn't wake up again until her eyes opened on their own.

Nadine fished her cell phone from the bedside nightstand. It was just after nine o'clock. She had called both Trina and Sophia last night to tell them she'd arrived safely. During her phone call with Trina, Nadine learned that Damon had been frantically looking for her.

"Girl, that nutcase has been calling us like an annoying telemarketer," Trina had told her during their telephone chat last night. "He's called me and Bradley like five times."

"What is he saying?" Nadine had asked. From the very beginning, one of her major concerns had been what Damon would tell people.

"How 'bout he didn't even notice you were gone until he came home from work. When he came home to change clothes between his breakfast meeting and going to his office in city hall, he didn't recognize any changes. But when he got home after work and saw that you weren't there, that's when he started noticing stuff. When he stepped into your closet and saw all your clothes were gone, that's when it hit him like a ton of bricks. He said he asked his dad about you and the old man didn't even know you'd left."

At that moment, Nadine's mind had drifted back to those frantic moments when she'd had to pass her father-in-law's room to get her belongings out of the house before his therapists arrived. She'd been so nervous and anxious.

"Damon was saying all kinds of crazy mess when he called," Trina had gone on to share. "He asked me if I thought he should alert the police. He was saying that you might have been kidnapped." She stopped to let out a short laugh, and then added, "I wanted to say… Fool, what kind of kidnapper lets their victim clean out the closet and pack special belongings before they take them? But I didn't. I just listened and acted just as oblivious as he was pretending to be."

"Yeah." While her one-word response didn't really make sense, Nadine couldn't think of anything else to say. There were no winners here, and while she knew she had done what was necessary to free herself from a horrible situation, Nadine couldn't deny the sadness she felt. Twinges of guilt shot through her heart too. She wasn't feeling guilty because she'd left Damon, but rather for how she had left him.

"Maybe I should have written a note," Nadine had suggested.

"And said what? What were you going to do, Nadine? Leave a 'Dear John' letter? Why? Damon doesn't need to be told why you left. He knows why you're gone. You stayed a heck of a lot longer than any woman I know would have stayed. He can act like he doesn't have a clue, but Damon is fully aware. And even if you had left a letter outlining why you were leaving, you think he would have shown that to people? No. He still would have acted clueless and played the victim. A letter wouldn't have changed anything."

"It wouldn't have changed anything, but after nine years of marriage, I think I owed him that much."

"Nadine, you don't owe Damon nothing."

A knock on the bedroom door brought Nadine back to the present.

"Come in," she called.

Aunt Pat entered carrying a breakfast tray. "I was hoping you were up," she said while placing it on the desk in the corner. "Better get up and eat it while it's hot."

"Oh, Aunt Pat, you didn't have to do that. I'm not that big on eating breakfast, but I definitely could have come to the dining room to eat with you."

"You're already too late for that," her aunt said with a laugh. "I've already eaten. I was up early this morning praying about your situation. I prayed last night that God would give you good sleep, and I prayed this morning that He would give you some clarity."

Nadine smiled at her. "Thanks, Auntie. He answered your prayer for a good sleep. I'm not sure yet about the clarity."

Aunt Pat sat at the foot of Nadine's bed and looked at her. "I'm so sorry about what you're going through. When you were telling me about everything yesterday, I can't say I was totally surprised. God had been putting you in my dreams a lot lately, and I knew something was wrong even though when I called you, you would tell me everything was alright, or you'd dance around a straight answer."

"I didn't think you noticed," Nadine said.

"Sugar, I notice everything. But I have to admit that I didn't think things were as bad as what you told me. There was always something that didn't seem genuine about Damon. His hugs were cold, and his compliments didn't sound sincere. Everything he said or did around me just sounded and looked rehearsed—like he saw me as some voter on his campaign to whom that he would say anything to get me to put a check by his name on the ballot. I know you said you still love him despite everything, but I don't know anything to tell you but the truth. And the truth is, that husband of yours is a politician to his core. Just as conniving as he can be."

Nadine looked at her aunt while she contemplated her next question. Only seventeen years separated the two women's ages, and maybe that was one of the reasons why Aunt Pat had always been easier to talk to than Nadine's mom. Aunt Pat had been married to Uncle Ross for nearly forty-five years. From the start of their marriage until now, Uncle Ross had been a long-haul truck driver who was away from home sometimes two weeks at a time. He was beyond retirement age now, but because his job only required that he sit and drive, Uncle Ross continued to work. He swore it kept him young. Nadine wondered if the weeks that kept them physically separated also served as the glue that held them together. Maybe absence really did make the heart grow fonder. At age sixty-six and sixty-nine, they seemed as happy as ever.

"You look like you've got something on your mind," Aunt Pat said as she returned Nadine's gaze. "Talk … but talk fast. Your food is getting colder by the second."

"It's nothing," Nadine said with a shrug of her shoulders. "I guess you pretty much answered it. I was just sitting here wondering if I really did the right thing. I mean, you and Uncle Ross have been married a long time, and I know every day couldn't have been Sunday. There had to be times when he said the wrong thing or did the wrong thing, but you stayed and worked through it. So, I keep asking myself if I made a mistake."

"You're right. Every day hasn't been all sunshine with me and Ross, but your uncle ain't never said the things to me that Damon has said to you. He ain't never called me no ugly vulgar names. And if he had ever been looney enough to threaten to kill me or pay somebody else to kill or hurt me, we would have been over and done with a long time ago. Yeah, we had to work through some things. Me and Ross had to work through times of not knowing where our next dollar was coming from. We worked through having our first house foreclosed on and our first car being repossessed. We've worked through finding out we weren't ever going to have babies together. We worked through his cancer scare and my gallbladder surgery."

Grabbing Nadine's ankle through the comforter that covered it, Aunt Pat added, "Listen, baby girl. When we stand before God on our wedding day and promise to stay together for better or for worse, in sickness and in health, for richer or for poorer—those are the kinds of things we're talking about. We ain't talking about staying together while we wait to see if one of us is going to make good on the threat to murder the other one. God loves marriage, Nadine," she further stated, "but marriage is supposed to honor Him, and what you and Damon have ain't honoring God. If anybody is being honored in a marriage like that, it's the devil himself. The devil loves a marriage filled with discord and hatred because that marriage goes against everything that God intends for a covenant to be."

Nadine wiped a tear from her cheek and nodded her head. "You're right," she whispered.

Aunt Pat rose from her seated position and made the short walk to the head of the bed to give Nadine a hug. When she released her, she kissed her forehead before pointing toward the desk where the untouched food still sat. "Eat," she said. "You're going to be just fine. It hurts now, but God knows how to restore everything that the enemy makes us believe we've lost forever. And when God restores anything, it's always better than you ever imagined. Go, eat your food. I'll be in the front room after I get the kitchen all cleaned. We can talk some more if you want to."

Nadine watched her aunt walk from the room before she turned her attention back to her phone. She had promised Trina last night that she would give her a call once she'd gotten a good night's sleep. Nadine kicked off her covers and walked toward the desk as she waited for Trina to answer. It only rang twice.

"Hey, girl," Trina sounded out of breath. "Your timing is perfect. I just got in my car to head home. I went to the walking trail this morning. It's been a while since I did that, and I can tell it's been a while too. Whew! I feel so out of shape."

"I've gotten a little off schedule with my walking too," Nadine replied. "Aunt Pat lives in a nice neighborhood though. I'm going to get out and walk it while I'm here."

"How did you sleep last night?" Trina asked.

"Much better than I thought I would. It rained all night here, and I think it helped because I got a solid eight hours before waking up."

"That's good," Trina replied. "I was a little worried about you, so I'm glad you slept well. Damon is still blowing up our phones asking about you. Bradley told me to stop answering his calls, so the last three times he's called me, I let it go to voicemail. Bradley is waiting for him to call his number again. He said that he's going to tell Damon to stop calling us because we don't have any information to share about you or your whereabouts."

"I'm sorry to drag all of you into this craziness," Nadine said just before filling her mouth with the grits her aunt had prepared. It was just the right temperature, not so hot that she needed to blow on it first.

"Listen, baby girl. We are just fine. Don't worry one bit about us. I've been listening to his voicemail messages, and he sounds so perplexed like he is so baffled and has absolutely no idea why you would disappear like this. In one message, he made up some story about how y'all were just talking about renovating the house and using the finished product on your Christmas cards this year."

Nadine took several swallows of orange juice before saying, "Well, he wasn't lying about that. That was the conversation that led to the ugly argument we had a couple of days before

I left. Remember? I called you and told you that he had asked for Bradley's personal cell number so he could get him to price the renovation."

"Oh, yeah; I'd forgotten about that," Trina said. "If he had bothered to include the part where he stormed upstairs and tried to slam you in the face with your own briefcase, I would have remembered. See, that's the kind of stuff I'm talking about. Damon is calling everybody asking about you as though y'all had this great marriage and your leaving has no rhyme or reason to it. Not once, in any of the messages, has he mentioned the cruel things he's said and done to you. He makes it sound like you abandoned him without a cause. I really feel like Damon is plotting to set the stage so that when the word finally does get out, he'll be seen as an innocent victim."

As tasty as her freshly prepared breakfast was, the more Nadine listened to Trina, the more she lost her appetite. She was trying to condition her mind to prepare for whatever fallout came from the spreading news of her sudden exodus, but Nadine's gut feeling told her that there was no way to adequately prepare. Trina was probably right. Damon was going to say or do whatever was necessary to make himself look good. He had to. He was the great mayor of Atlanta. There was no way he was going to tell the truth.

"How many people know now?" Nadine asked cautiously.

"It hasn't become widespread yet, if that's what you mean," Trina answered. "It started out with just you, Sophia, and my family. Now, we know that Damon, Daddy Deville, and Aunt Pat have been added to the list. As far as I know, no one else has been told. But you can bank on the fact that this isn't a secret that will remain hidden. It's going to come out eventually."

Nadine let out a sigh and bit into the slice of toast that had been placed on a saucer by itself. "I've got a lot of stuff that I need to get done," she said while chewing. "I was talking to Aunt Pat last night and she's going to connect me to a family lawyer that can help me start divorce proceedings. There is no turning back from this, so I might as well do what I need to do."

"There's definitely no turning back," Trina agreed. "Even if Damon gets on his hands and knees and begs you to come home, you can't give it consideration. He's prideful, he's controlling, he's an abuser, and you've left him. That's a dangerous mix. You've humiliated him, Nadine. I'm sure he never thought you'd have the strength or courage to leave him after he'd done so much to strip you of your self-worth, but you did. You best believe he doesn't like that. If you go back to him, I'd be scared for what might happen."

Nadine's thoughts immediately went to Rebecca and the consequences she'd suffered for giving in to Danny's pleas for her to give him another chance. When she got free of him, she should have stayed free of him, but he promised to change, and she believed him one time too many. The price she paid was her life.

"No, I can't go back," Nadine agreed. "I'm going to get an appointment set up with this lawyer Aunt Pat is recommending. She said he's a man of faith, and she said now is the time to get him locked in because he's getting married in ten or eleven months, and wedding planning will become priority on his calendar soon. If I get him now, I hope and pray that my divorce can be final before he has to focus on the wedding."

"Where does Aunt Pat know this guy from?"

"He's a deacon at her church. I'll get to meet him tomorrow."

"Oh, you're going to church so soon after arriving?"

Nadine released a chuckle. "If Aunt Pat gets up to go to church, anybody who stays under her roof is going to get up and go to church too. It's not an option at any age."

Trina suddenly released a gasping sound on the other end of the line, and then said, "Guess what?"

"What?"

"I just got a text message from Bradley. He said a breaking news announcement just came on television saying Damon will be doing a live press conference today at noon."

Nadine dropped her fork on her plate, and at the same time, she experienced what felt like her heart dropping to the pit of her stomach.

Chapter 22

Grace For the Race

Nadine stepped out onto the porch and inhaled the fresh air that Monday morning provided. Unlike Saturday, there was no one to be spotted in the neighborhood for as far as her eyes could see. She needed this quiet time alone—not just to exercise, but to think, meditate, and pray. Nadine had stretched before coming out of the house, so she quickened her pace as soon as she made it to the end of the driveway.

What a difference a few hours had made! In the two days that had passed since Damon held his special press conference, Nadine had gone from four or five people knowing about her unannounced disappearance to the likelihood of four or five hundred thousand people knowing about it. Damon had put on quite a performance Saturday. Trina had Nadine on a video call for the entire one-man show. From the kitchen island where she sat on a stool alongside Aunt Pat, Nadine could clearly see and hear Damon as he made pleas for her to return home.

"I don't know why you left or who you left with, baby," He'd said, "but whatever the problem is, we can talk about it. If there's somebody else that has come in to try and break up our marriage, I'm willing to fight for what we have. What God has joined together no man can put asunder!" The preacher part of him came out when he quoted the Scripture, and there were even some replies of "Amen" that came from those who were in the crowd outside city hall.

"Girl, are you hearing this mess?" Trina had asked from the other end of the line.

Before Nadine could reply, Damon continued with, "If your leaving is due to a mental breakdown of some kind, don't be embarrassed. There's nothing wrong with getting professional help, and if that's what you need, I'll make sure you get it."

Nadine remembered wanting to reach through her phone, and then through Trina's television screen, and grab Damon by the throat when he said that part. She couldn't believe he was trying to hint that she could be mentally unstable.

"We will work through this together," he went on to say. "If you're listening to this newsbreak, please call me. I've tried reaching out to you several times, but you haven't answered your phone. I just need to know you're okay. Your friends don't know where you are, your staff members don't know where you are. It's not like you to do something like this, so I'm worried. I can't sleep. I can't eat. Baby, please call so we'll know you're alright."

Damon's voice broke at the end. He lowered his head, and his shoulders were shaking as if he was crying. City council members came to the podium and surrounded him, placing their hands on his shoulders as a means of consolation. Damon's eyes were hidden behind the dark lenses of his sunglasses, so it was impossible to tell whether he had been successful in his quest to conjure up crocodile tears. In any case, it was a spectacle fit for an Oscar.

"Lord, have mercy." Aunt Pat sounded beyond disgusted as she shook her head in disbelief. "This boy is actually trying to make folks think you either ran off with another man or that you've lost your mind." She slid off her stool and walked away, muttering, "It's time for me to go in my prayer closet."

After hearing Damon say that he had made several unsuccessful attempts to reach her, Nadine escaped to her sleeping quarters and powered up her old cell phone for the first time since she left Atlanta. Sure enough, Damon had called her repeatedly. His telephone messages were as unstable as his behavior had been throughout their marriage.

In his first message, Damon had sweetly said, "Baby, where are you? I came home, and all your clothes are gone. Pictures are missing and so are all your hair products and other stuff from the bathroom. What's going on? Please call me."

The next message was left with a marked difference in his attitude. Between the spouting of swear words, he said, "So, you don't think I deserve nothing better than this? Nine years, and this is how you do me? Do you know how crazy all this looks? I know you didn't think this up on your own. You done let Sophia or Trina or some of those other dumb females at the firm talk you into doing this. Y'all trying to make me look stupid, but this is about to backfire on you. I'm going to give you a few hours to call me back. If you do, we can talk about this and forget it ever happened, but if you don't, you best believe that you're the one that's going to be looking like a jackass, not me!"

By the next message, Damon's manipulation tactic had switched from profane to pious. "Listen, baby. I just finished praying, and the Holy Spirit told me that He wants us to be together. He said that He's going to be working on your heart and that if you're really a woman of God, and you want to walk in obedience to His will, you will come back."

Damon went on to say, "God had me walk around our whole property this evening, baby. He showed me that this big house, this big yard, and our fancy cars didn't mean a thing if we weren't enjoying them together. So, here is what I'm willing to do," he added. "I'm willing to go to counseling with you. You mentioned us going before, and I didn't realize that was a cry for help. You were trying to tell me you needed help, and I couldn't see it then, but I see it now. So, if you come back, I will go to counseling with you so you can get the help you need."

When Nadine listened to that one, she almost laughed despite her disappointment. She'd heard that last part loud and clear. He was willing to go to counseling so that she could get the help she needed. Damon still wasn't accepting any responsibility. There was no repentance and no remorse. As far as he was concerned, he was totally faultless.

In the last message, his anger had returned. "I know Sophia and Trina got something to do with this now, 'cause won't neither one of them answer their phones. They're not returning my calls when I leave messages either. And when I tried to talk to Bradley, he told me not to call no more. Talkin' 'bout they don't have nothing to tell me. I told you he wasn't nothing but a punk!"

The more Damon talked, the more demeaning he became. "That nigga might as well wear a bra and panties with some high-heeled shoes. He ain't nothing but a spineless puppet that can't even hold his back straight unless Trina's on the other end, pulling his puppet strings! You know what you're gonna do, Nadine? You're gonna mess around and lose a good husband while your so-called friend will still be all booed up with hers. Is that what you want? In case you forgot, you're not in your thirties anymore; you're about to be fifty years old, Nadine. Listening to your friends, you're gonna be old and all by yourself just like your mama!"

That had been a cheap shot, and Nadine couldn't pretend his words didn't hurt. She wept after hearing them. She was well aware that her birthday was two days away, and she certainly didn't need to be reminded of how old she would be. Starting over at this age was not what she wanted to do, but she had accepted the fact that it was what she was going to have to do.

Damon knew how hard Nadine worked to be sure she was nothing like Rose Jackson. It was an intentional low blow on his part. Her mom wasn't a bad person, but she had behaviors that Nadine didn't like and refused to inherit. While Nadine didn't want to be by herself, she'd rather be alone than be with Damon. Now that she was away from him, she could clearly see the things that she had blinded herself to before.

Olivia was right. Trina was right. Sophia was right. Aunt Pat was right. Even Attorney Duncan was right. Damon wasn't going to change. He didn't see a need to. He'd managed to place a generous amount of blame on her, Sophia, Trina, and even Bradley, but not once had he taken even an ounce of ownership. There was only one direction Nadine could walk from this point, and that was "away." Walking away was her only choice, and she was already taking steps.

After church yesterday, Nadine was introduced to Attorney Herbert Duncan, her aunt's legal recommendation. The three of them made a spur-of-the-moment plan to eat dinner together so that they could talk. They had gone to Flemings Prime Steakhouse following Sunday worship, and Nadine couldn't resist satisfying her hankering for something meatless. She ordered the Roasted Portobello & Cauliflower Steak meal and enjoyed every bite.

As they dined, Nadine informed Attorney Duncan of everything that eventually led to her decision to dissolve her marriage. She even allowed the attorney to listen to the voice messages Damon had left her. Attorney Duncan advised her to find a way to save them in a manner that they could be used later if it became necessary.

After hearing her experiences of the last nine years as the mayor's wife, Attorney Duncan used adjectives like "volatile," "wicked," and "obnoxious" to describe Damon. He also considered Damon "sadistic and dangerous" and advised Nadine to be aware of her surroundings, especially over the next several weeks since her husband indicated in his press conference that he was looking for her.

Nadine had gone to sleep last night wondering how much effort Damon would really put into finding her. As the leader of Georgia's capitol, he certainly had easy access to private investigators, but would he go that far?

As Nadine got closer to the end of her morning walk, her mind drifted to the times that she had tried to get Damon to take a road trip with her to visit Aunt Pat. There was always some excuse, something more important that needed to be done that couldn't be postponed or rescheduled. His refusals had upset her back then, but now, as she took the scenic walk around the neighborhood, Nadine was glad she'd never brought him here.

Even as a child, Aunt Pat's home had been a safe place for her. And it was serving as a refuge even now. Damon probably couldn't even remember what city her aunt and uncle lived in let alone have any idea where their house was located. Even if he knew, Nadine was sure it wouldn't be where he thought she had gone when she made her escape from the mayor's mansion.

Forty minutes after beginning her walk, Nadine was ending it. She made her way up the steps to Aunt Pat's porch and sat on the porch swing. Nothing about her life had been easy, it seemed. The distance between her and her mom, the loss of her beloved dad, the struggle to put herself through law school, and now this.

"They say God won't put no more on you than you can bear, but that ain't Scripture and it ain't true."

Nadine looked toward the front door and saw Aunt Pat standing there. She hadn't even heard the door open, but it was like her aunt had read her mind.

"I used to hear that all the time when I was growing up," Aunt Pat said as she stepped out and sat beside Nadine. "And most of the time, people would start it off by saying, 'The Bible says,' so, of course, I believed it. But as I got my own relationship with God and started to read the Word for myself, I searched and searched, and I couldn't find it nowhere. Imagine how I felt when I found out that one of my favorite Scriptures wasn't scriptural at all!"

Nadine's eyebrows rose inquisitively, but she decided not to verbally reveal the fact that she was two days before her 50th birthday, and she was just learning that the quote wasn't in the Bible.

"It only makes sense that it's not there," Aunt Pat pointed out. "If God didn't allow nothing to happen to us that we, in our own strength, couldn't handle, then what need would we have to call on Him? If we had the wherewithal to win our battles all by ourselves, most of us would never pray. We would never seek God's face. We would never know what it's like to place our faith and hope in Him. The truth is, God allows us to come face- to-face with more than we can bear a whole lot of times. What He does not do, however, is allow more to be put on us than we—with His help—can't bear."

Nadine smiled. "You're right. That does make sense."

"All the sense in the world," Aunt Pat said. "And I said all that to say this. God is going to get you through this. You've got a battle to fight, and I don't care how hard it gets, as long as you seek God's face, depend on Him and be obedient to His Word; you can't lose."

A sigh escaped Nadine's lips. "I keep thinking about all the lies that Damon is going to tell and all the people that He's going to make believe that I've done him wrong. I'm not there to defend myself, and so many people in Atlanta love him. I'm going to look like some kind of heartless villain."

"Do you hear yourself?" Aunt Pat asked. "Didn't I just say with God, you can't lose? Do you plan to leave God out of this battle?"

"No, ma'am. I just—"

"Then, case closed," she said emphatically. "I'm not saying it's going to be easy, and it sure ain't gonna be fun. But lies, manipulation, and deceit are not of God. That means Damon's strength is coming from the pits of hell, and while the devil has power, he also has parameters. In other words, he can only do so much. But the God we serve, on the other hand, is omnipotent!"

Aunt Pat suddenly stood up as though she had been struck by a voltage of electricity. She looked at Nadine like she was preaching a sermon to an audience of one. "There is no limit to our God," she continued. "There is nothing too hard for Him to work out. Whatever He allows us to go through, as long as we've got Him, we've got everything we need. I don't care how many folks Damon knows, if you know God, the army on your side will outnumber his every time. You've got to believe that and walk in faith like it's already done. I don't care how bad it gets, as long as you know that you can do all things though Christ who gives you strength, you're going to win."

Although tears trickled down Nadine's cheeks, a smile parted her lips. "Thanks, Aunt Pat. I needed that."

"God knew you needed it too; that's why He had me come out here." Patting Nadine on the arm, she added, "And you know what else God knows? He knows you need to get some breakfast in your stomach. So, come on in here and wash up. These pancakes can't eat themselves."

"I'll be right in," Nadine promised as she pulled her vibrating phone from her pocket. When she saw her attorney's name on the screen, she answered.

"Good morning, Attorney Duncan."

"Oh, please," he said. "Call me Herbert. We're both attorneys, and the mutual respect goes without saying. We can drop the titles."

"Ironic, huh?" Nadine said, wiping the earlier tears from her cheeks.

"In what way?"

"An attorney needing an attorney."

"I don't see any irony in that. It's the details that make it make sense," Attorney Duncan said. "It's not like you're a family law attorney needing a family law attorney. Heck, if I'm ever accused of committing a crime, I'm going to call you to defend me; I don't care how ironic people might think it is. I don't need to be standing there serving as my own attorney and telling the jury how to adopt a kid, dissect a will, seek child support, change their legal name, or terminate a marriage. If I'm on the line to go to prison for a crime I didn't commit, I'm going to need more than just a good attorney; I'm going to need a good defense attorney. And, what you need right now is a good family attorney."

Laughing, Nadine said, "Very well put. I guess you're right."

"I know I am," he replied with a laugh of his own. "Now, let's get down to business. I told you I'd follow up today after I got to the office and had a chance to look over some things. I did some checking with some friends of mine in the Atlanta area, and Mayor Damon Deville is causing quite a stir there. It seems he has some proverbial bloodhounds out on the streets looking for you, or at least that's the way he's making it seem."

"You think he's only pretending to be looking?"

"Well, let's just say, in this technological society that we live in, coupled with the well-equipped people that he has access to, I don't think he's looking as hard as he wants the public to believe. I have a private investigator on my staff, and he's been following the mayor since late yesterday afternoon. I was sent some photos today of your soon-to-be ex-husband looking quite disheveled."

Nadine frowned at the notion. When it came to being seen by the public, Damon never went anywhere looking anything less than like someone who had stepped out of the latest issue of GQ magazine.

"What do you mean?" she asked.

"I mean this man that you described to me yesterday as being obsessed with how he looked in the eyes of the public was seen in a restaurant Sunday evening looking like he was still wearing the clothes he slept in Saturday night."

"What? Wait ... are you sure your guy was following the right person?"

"I'm holding the pictures in my hand to prove it," Herbert told her. "My guess is that he is intentionally letting people see him look this way so that he can have innumerable eyewitnesses to validate the victimization that you're putting him through. He is playing his cards well, Nadine. He's not going to make it easy for you to get the things from this divorce that you deserve."

Nadine sank back on the swing. None of this should surprise her, but somehow, it did. Damon was more devious than she'd given him credit for. "What do I need to do?"

"Do you have anything on your schedule today?" Attorney Duncan asked.

"Just some telephone calls I need to make. I have to check in with my firm, and I'll probably give my mother a call since I haven't even informed her of all this yet."

"Then I suggest you handle as much of that as you can this morning, and then meet me at my office at around three o'clock this afternoon so that we can talk about a strategy of our own. And Nadine?"

"Yes?"

"Let me assure you that you have the best family lawyer in Birmingham on your side. But even with that, as I was reading the Bible during my devotion this morning, I was led right to the ninth chapter of the book of Mark, where a man brought his demon possessed son to Jesus. When Jesus cast out that spirit, the disciples were perplexed and wanted to know why they weren't able to do the same. Jesus told them it was because 'this kind can come forth by nothing but prayer and fasting.' I believe God led me to that Scripture today for a reason," Attorney Duncan said. "Both of us are attorneys, and both of us know the law. But this is bigger than us, Nadine. Mayor Deville is just like the demons that possessed that little boy, and we're not going to be able to defeat him just by using the law. So, suit up in the whole armor of God, my friend. Because this kind can come forth by nothing but fasting and prayer."

Chapter 23

Some Will Never Understand

"I cannot believe that I had to find out about this foolishness through a stinking phone call from Damon! What in God's name is wrong with you, Nadine? You done tore that boy's heart to pieces."

"Mama, you don't know—"

"It don't matter what I don't know; all that matters is what I do know. And what I do know is the Word of God. Proverbs 12:4 says, 'An excellent wife is the crown of her husband, but she who brings shame is like rottenness in his bones.' Nadine, that man had to get up and face a whole city of people and announce that his wife had run out on him without so much as a word of warning. You brought shame on Damon, and God is not pleased!"

"You haven't even heard the whole story, Mama."

"That's 'cause you didn't bother to tell it to me! Nadine, ain't nothing worse than hearing a grown man cry. What kind of woman walks out on a good man like Damon? Lord, have mercy! Y'all young girls wouldn't know a good thing if it slapped you in the face. Do you know how many women would give a kidney and a lung to be in your shoes?"

Nadine closed her eyes and shook her head. Today was her birthday, but Rose Jackson was too busy being concerned about Damon to even remember. Her mom was right about one thing. She should have learned about this from her and not Damon. But so much had been going on, and quite frankly, Nadine had been dreading making the call to her mother for this very reason. She knew Rose would rocket into some kind of religious stratosphere and not listen without jumping into judgment mode.

The reason Nadine had turned on her old phone in the first place was in preparation to call her mother after she'd failed to do it two days ago. But, when the phone powered on, the first thing it did was alert Nadine that she had new messages. The first one was from her mother, and in it, Rose made her displeasure clear. Nadine called her back fully prepared to explain the situation, but her mom never gave her a chance.

Upon hearing Nadine's voice, Rose began charging at her full force, and she didn't seem ready to let up any time soon.

"You're married to the Mayor of Atlanta, Nadine. You are literally the Michelle Obama of Atlanta. What more could a woman ask for? I don't even know what to say."

For someone who didn't know what to say, she sure was saying a lot. But Nadine kept that thought locked in her mind.

"Where did you run off to, and why won't you tell Damon?" Rose asked. "Is he right? Please don't tell me he's right. Is he, Nadine? Did you leave him for another man? May God have mercy on your soul if you did!" When Rose paused to take a breath, Nadine took advantage of the opportunity to be heard.

"Mama, whatever Damon told you is not the truth. I am not with another man. This has never been about another man, and he knows that. There is a lot that I've put up with in the years I've been married to the Mayor of Atlanta that maybe Michelle Obama didn't have to put up with being married to the President of the United States. Clearly, you're impressed by the fact that Damon is a mayor, but him being the mayor means nothing to me if he can't treat me right."

"Treat you right? Look at that mansion y'all live in. Look at the fancy cars that you drive. Look at those name brand clothes and shoes that you wear. What else the man got to do for you to feel treated right? It's funny how you think Alex was the best thing since Jesus when he didn't do none of that for me. Your daddy didn't make near the money that your husband makes, and even when we struggled to pay bills, I didn't leave him. I don't know what your problem is, but—"

"First of all, the only problem I had was Damon, so as of last Saturday, I don't have a problem." Nadine was done with being considerate. "It may surprise you to know this, Mother, but I have the potential to earn more money handling one case as an attorney than Damon earns in a full year as the mayor. Except for special gift-giving occasions, I buy my own stuff, so that car I drive and the clothes and shoes I wear are paid for with my money. That 'mansion' that you spoke of? I pay half the mortgage every single month."

From the side of her eye, Nadine saw her bedroom door open. She had her mother on speaker, and the combination of both their raised voices had apparently caught the attention of Aunt Pat, but Nadine wasn't about to stop now. If she gave her mom the opportunity to speak again, Nadine knew that she might not have the chance to finish what needed to be said. So, even when she saw her aunt step into the room, Nadine continued.

"Mama, when I talk about being treated right, I'm not talking about who buys what. I can handle the struggle to pay bills. I can handle living in a regular house and wearing knock-off brands of shoes and clothes. Married to the right man, I can even handle driving a smoke-spewing, muffler-dragging, gotta-pray-for-it-to- crank-up hooptie. So, yes, although Daddy couldn't buy you or his children the finer things of life, I do think he was a great man. And do you know why? Because even with the little that he had, he was there for us physically, mentally, emotionally, financially, and spiritually. Daddy loved us, Mama. Even when he couldn't buy us all the things we wanted or maybe even needed, we knew he loved us. You knew it, I knew it, and so did Sophia. The reason you didn't leave Daddy is because he never gave you a valid reason to. But if you'd been cussed at, called out of your name, put out of the car in the middle of nowhere, had things thrown at you, or been forced to look down the barrel of a pistol thinking your life would end at any moment, maybe you would have left your husband too!"

By the time Nadine finished, tears were washing her cheeks, and for a short while, all she could hear from the other end of the line was the harmony coming from some gospel choir that her mom was listening to.

"Are you trying to tell me that Damon did things like to these to you?" Rose finally asked.

"No, Mama. I'm telling you that Damon did these exact things to me. He did all of it and more, and it's been going on for almost the whole time we've been married."

There was more silence before Rose said, "I find this very hard to believe. Why wouldn't you have told me any of this before now?"

"I didn't tell you for that very reason. I knew you wouldn't believe me. Why would I make this stuff up, Mama?"

"I'm not saying you're making it up, but I've never heard Damon say anything bad about you. All I'm saying is this doesn't sound like the Damon I know."

"Well, it's the Damon I know, and I lived with him, so I think I know him better than anybody else. The Damon I know not only speaks badly about me, but he speaks badly about my friends and my family. And that includes you, Mama. He'd never say it to your face, and if you ask him about it, he'll lie and deny it, but he's said some very negative things about you, Trina, Bradley, Sophia—all of us over the years. Damon can be very cruel and very terrifying. That's why I left in the way that I did. I couldn't give him notice because he might not have allowed me to leave, and I couldn't tell him where I was going because I was afraid of what he might do if he decided to follow me."

"Okay, that's fine if you don't tell him. But you need to tell me where you are. Don't I deserve to know?"

Nadine released a heavy sigh. "At some point, I'm sure I'll tell you. But not now."

"Why not? You scared of me too?"

"Of course not. I'm not afraid of you, but I am afraid that you might tell Damon."

"You think I'll tell him where you are knowing what I know now?" Rose sounded offended by the notion. "You don't trust me no more than that?"

"I don't think you'd tell him out of malice," Nadine explained, "but I do think it's possible that he'll either guilt you into telling him or scare you into telling him, and I don't want that to happen. I just think it's best that you don't have the information to give him. Where I am now is a temporary situation anyway. Once the dust has settled, I'm going to find a permanent place, and I'll let you know where that place is. I promise."

"I'm your mother, Nadine; this is unacceptable. Damon can't scare or guilt me into anything. I'll find out where you are, whether you tell me or not, so you might as well tell me. I know you've told somebody. If nobody else knows, Trina does. I'm certain of that, so if I have to call and talk to her, I will."

Nadine accepted the tissue that her aunt quietly handed her and used it to wipe her face before responding. "Mama, I'm trying to spare you from getting your feelings hurt. Anyone who knows where I am isn't going to give you or anybody else that information. If you ask, you'll be wasting your time. All you need to know right now is that I'm safe. Anytime you need to call me, you can. I might not answer right away because I turn this phone off to avoid getting overwhelmed with calls from Damon. But if you leave a message for me, I will definitely call you back."

Nadine decided not to tell her mother that she had another phone. It would only lead to another argument when she refused to give her the number.

"I don't like this. I don't like this one bit," Rose grumbled.

"I know, and I'm sorry. But that's the way it has to be for now. I don't trust Damon not to be able to get just the slightest bit of information and use it to find me. And since you took one call from him and showed some sympathy, I know he's going to call you again. So, the less you know, the better."

"Well, I don't know how I can help you if you don't tell me nothing." Rose's tone reflected her disappointment.

"Just pray for me, Mama," Nadine told her. "What I need most right now are your prayers."

As soon as they ended the call, Aunt Pat sat on the mattress beside Nadine and kissed her forehead. "Happy birthday, baby girl," she whispered just before handing her a small jewelry box.

"You always remember," Nadine said while giving her aunt a hug.

"How could I forget? I was in the waiting room fifty years ago, walking the floor that evening waiting for somebody to come out and tell me you had been born." Aunt Pat told her. "You know, lots of fathers didn't go in the delivery room with the mothers back then; that didn't get popular 'til a few years later. But, your daddy said he wasn't about to miss the birth of his first child. I stayed in the waiting room watching the clock and hoping that it wouldn't be too long before you came. I was a senior in high school at the time, and I had to get up the next morning for class. Around about ten-thirty that night, a nurse came and told me that my sister had given birth to a little girl."

Aunt Pat paused, reached out to Nadine, and squeezed her hand. "I also remember when I first went to the maternity ward to see Rose. It was the next day, and your daddy came and picked me up as soon as I got home from school. When we got to the room, Rose was upset because she couldn't get you to stop crying. I told her to hand you to me. The minute she placed you in my arms, the crying stopped. I knew right then and there that you were going to be my special niece. Your mama wasn't amused, but your daddy couldn't stop laughing. That man was always so proud of his smart, ambitious daughter."

Nadine had heard that story so many times that she could almost repeat it verbatim, but she never grew tired of hearing it. She stared at the still unopened present and said, "I wonder if he'd be proud of his fifty-year-old divorced daughter?"

Cupping Nadine's chin with her hand forcing her to look her in the eyes, Aunt Pat said, "Would Alex be proud to see you have the strength to get up and walk away from an abusive marriage? Absolutely. He would probably have one question though, and it's the same question that has all of us stumped. 'What took you so long?'"

"I guess I'd have to give Daddy the same answer that I give to y'all," Nadine said, shrugging her shoulders. "I really don't know. I think I was just hoping things would change. I was praying for things to change, and I was holding on to the faith that God would answer that prayer."

"God was able," her aunt said, "but Damon wasn't willing."

Nadine thoughtfully rubbed the smooth surface of the top of the red gift box. "Thank you so much for this, Aunt Pat. You really didn't have to buy me anything. You and Uncle Ross are letting me stay in your house. That's more than enough."

"Oh, hush up. We always said you were welcome to come and visit us anytime, so the way I see it, this is just an extended visit. That's not the same as a gift. It ain't like we gave you the house or that you're going to stay with us forever."

Removing the top from the gift box, Nadine discovered an Alex & Ani bangle bracelet that had one oval-shaped charm and three heart-shaped charms dangling from it. Inscribed on one side of the oval charm was the word "Niece," and on the other side was the statement, "Bonded by love, connected for life." Etched into each of the three hearts was a single word, but when combined, they read: "You are loved."

"This is so beautiful." Nadine fought back the threat of more tears as she slipped the jewelry around her wrist.

"I'm glad you like it. I've had that in my dresser drawer for about two months. The minute I saw it online, I thought about you. I was planning to send it to you by mail, but when you showed up on my doorstep, you saved me some postage."

Aunt Pat stood up and started for the bedroom door. "I didn't cook any breakfast this morning, but I did cook some vegetable soup, and you're welcome to some of what's left. I made it for Sister Walker, from our church. She's been a little under the weather. I'm about to drive to her house to take it to her and sit with her for a little bit. I'll be gone for a few hours."

"Okay. Thank you." Nadine watched the door close behind her aunt, and then she looked back at the new bracelet that she'd received for her birthday. The birthday that her mother had forgotten. The birthday that would always mark the year that her marriage dissolved.

Nadine walked to the desk in the corner of the room, reached into the drawer, and pulled out the folder that her attorney had given her during their meeting. She thumbed through the pictures of Damon that had been captured by the firm's investigator. There was one of him sitting in Moe's at lunchtime and another of him entering the doors of the shop where Nadine went whenever she wanted to be pampered by the services of a professional beautician.

Attorney Duncan had told her that based on the locations where Damon was making his appearances, it was evident that he was targeting an audience of people who knew Nadine, making sure they saw his so-called emotional decline.

Nadine's attention was pulled away from the pictures by her ringing phone.

"Happy birthday, girl!" Trina screamed jovially when Nadine answered. She sobered a bit when she asked, "How are you feeling?"

"Like I could use a glass of high-priced imported wine," Nadine answered.

"Well, go pour yourself one."

"Yeah, right," Nadine said with a short laugh. "The closest thing Aunt Pat has to wine is cranberry ginger ale. Maybe I'll go out to a restaurant later this evening and treat myself."

"I thought about taking the two-hour drive there to surprise you today, but we're pretty busy around the office this week, and I have a mediation tomorrow morning, so I figured I'd better stay here and prepare."

"I would have loved to have seen you, but it's probably not a good idea for you to come here right now anyway. We're still not sure if Damon has eyes on the street, following people to see if anybody will lead them to me. If that is the case, you would be the first person they would be tracking."

"Probably," Trina replied, "but Damon's mind is on other things today. That attorney of yours does fast work. Damon got served divorce papers this morning."

Nadine sat up straight. "How do you know?"

"Because he sees to it that everything that happens is leaked to the media. It was on the news this morning. Didn't you know he was being served?"

"Well, yeah. Attorney Duncan told me a couple of days ago that he was going to have it done, but I guess I wasn't expecting it to happen so soon."

"Have you checked your other phone lately? I'm surprised Damon didn't try to call you."

Nadine looked at the phone that still rested in the spot on her mattress where she'd left it after ending the call with her mom. "I checked it just this morning, but I didn't listen to all the messages. The first one was from Mama, so I immediately called her back. She was angry that she had to find out about the breakup from Damon. But I think he called her a couple of days ago; her message had been in my box for a minute before I heard it. He hadn't gotten the divorce papers yet."

"Were there other messages on the phone?"

"Two more, I think. Hold on a minute," Nadine said while punching in the code to listen to her remaining messages. She then placed it on speaker so that Trina could hear as well. The first one was from Damon.

"Happy birthday eve, Nadine." His voice was more than sweet, it was sexy. "In about two hours, it'll be your special day, but I need to get to bed because I have an early day tomorrow, so I won't be awake after midnight to say it. I miss you. I had big plans for your fiftieth, and it was going to be special." He let out a sad sigh. "I'm going to keep praying for you Nadine. I haven't totally given up on us, and I don't believe you have either. Enjoy your birthday, and maybe we'll talk soon. Good night."

"Umph," Trina grunted. "Hello, Dr. Jekyll."

The second was from Damon too. It sounded like he was calling from inside his car. The sexiness was gone. He began his message by potently spouting the "B-word," establishing his anger from the start.

"Have you lost your stupid mind?" he went on to ask. "I know I didn't just get served divorce papers in my office at city hall. You ain't got no shame, do you? And how're you gonna ask for anything from me in this divorce? You're the one who left; why should I have to pay you anything? Walking out of my life was your choice. I didn't put you out. You want a divorce? Fine! I'll give you a divorce, but I won't give you a single penny in it. I'm the mayor of Atlanta. You best believe that my legal team is going to make yours look like the cast of 'The Flintstones.' By the time I get done with you, you're going to wish you never messed with Mayor Damon Deville!"

"And hello, Mr. Hyde," Trina said as Damon's call ended. "I hope this attorney you have is a magician or something," she added, "because Damon's coming with his 'A-game'."

"This kind can come forth by nothing but fasting and prayer," Nadine whispered.

"What?"

"Nothing," Nadine said. "I was just thinking about something Attorney Duncan said. He probably had Damon served so quickly because he's about to get married, so he wanted to get this taken care of as soon as possible. When he and I talked, he said he expects this to be a tough battle. He quoted Mark 9:29 and I've been reading that verse for the last couple of days. Maybe God is trying to tell me something. I think I need to start fasting as I head into this divorce with Damon."

"You let me know which days and all the parameters," Trina told her. "I'm going to fast with you. You're not in this by yourself, Nadine. Your fight is my fight."

Chapter 24

You Must Surrender

Nadine jolted into a seated position. Beads of sweat covered her face. If it had not been for the horrible nightmare she'd just had, she would have thought full-blown menopause had been her fiftieth birthday gift from Mother Nature. Her racing heart felt as though it was at Indy 500 level. Nadine reached for the cell phone on her nightstand to shut off the alarm.

Inhale. Exhale. Nadine took slow deep breaths. Those had worked for her in the past, and she prayed they would do the same today.

It wasn't a new dream; it was a repeated one—the one of her being trapped in her car as it sank under water. It was the same dream where she would look out the car window and see Damon standing on the shoreline watching her sink to her death. Just like before, Nadine woke up only seconds before going under. This time, though, it seemed to her that she sank lower before her waking moment came. Had it not been for her alarm clock, she was sure she would have died this time.

Nadine got up and began to strip the bedding. She would throw it all in the washing machine later today while she completed her scheduled tasks.

If the "dead of winter" referred to the coldest part of the season, then right now, it was the dead of summer in Birmingham. August temperatures in the south didn't play games. It was probably already close to eighty degrees outside, and it was only nine in the morning. Yet, as Nadine stood up, she felt her body trembling. The sweat, combined with the air in the home and her twirling ceiling fan, had her chilled to the bone.

Two weeks had now passed since Damon had been served divorce papers, and Nadine was beginning to feel like she was on trial, and every citizen of Atlanta was a selected juror for her case. By all indications, Damon had the upper hand. The people of Atlanta loved their mayor, or at least, they loved the man they thought he was. Nadine couldn't even fault them for that. After all, she had loved the man she thought he was too.

Every major news station and printed media outlet in the city had either interviewed Damon or a member of his public relations team. The one-sided story had been the talk of seemingly every social media group that was linked to Georgia's capitol. Nadine was happier than ever that she had taken refuge outside of the state. There would have been nowhere to hide there. Everywhere she went, someone in the city would have known who she was.

Still, even in a place where she felt safe, the nightmares persist. Nadine's real life felt like confirmation of her dreams. Damon wanted her to die a slow, agonizing death, and he was taking a front row seat so he could watch it all. He had the ability to stop her from going under simply by telling the whole truth of the matter, but he wasn't going to do it. Damon was far too pompous and arrogant to admit to his abusive behavior.

Nadine removed her wet pajamas and dropped each piece on the floor with the bed sheets before walking into the Jack and Jill bathroom that connected her bedroom to the other guest room in the house. For most of the year, neither of the guest bedrooms nor the adjoining bathroom was ever used, so they stayed immaculately clean. Nadine had made them look lived in for the first time in a long while.

The water from the hot shower felt good as it rinsed away the evidence of last night's bad dream. As she washed her body, Nadine also shampooed her hair. She had not sat in a beautician's chair in two months, but over the last few days, she'd made good use of the afro puff attachment that she purchased from a local beauty shop last weekend. She got several compliments on it at church yesterday. It became her, and it blended so well with her own natural hair texture, that she doubted anyone knew it was a hairpiece.

Sonya, Attorney Duncan's fiancé, told Nadine that she looked like Yvonne Orji. Nadine smiled and thanked her, but in truth, she didn't even know who that was. As soon as the opportunity arose, she did a quick Google search, and after seeing a picture of the Nigerian-American actress, Nadine was able to fully appreciate the comparison as the compliment that it was. The fact that she was being likened to someone who was a decade younger than she didn't hurt at all either.

Nadine hadn't experimented a lot with her hair. In the years she and Damon had been married, he had almost demanded that she wear her hair in one style, slicked back into a sleek ponytail. If she styled it differently, he would become suspicious, as if he thought she was changing it to try and catch some other man's attention. Damon's need to control every part of her life had become a dangerous obsession, and until she broke away from him, Nadine couldn't see the whole picture.

As she rinsed the shampoo from her hair and the soap from her body, she tried hard to think of a reason why she had let her life spiral so far out of control. Nadine had always been a smart, strong-minded go-getter. But somewhere along the way, she had permitted love to not only blind her, but bind her as well. At some point after meeting Damon, she had allowed herself to become a prisoner in her own home who was told how she could dress, where she could go, what she could say, and who she could say it to. More than anything, Nadine just wanted this all to be over so that she could regain some sense of normalcy.

"Don't you worry about a thing," her Uncle Ross had told her after church yesterday.

He was preparing to get back on the road after being home for six days. It was good to spend some time with him. To Nadine, her uncle's hugs came second only to those from her dad. Alex Jackson had been the best hugger of all, but she felt a twinge of that same sense of safety and protection any time her favorite uncle embraced her. It would be another two weeks or so before she would see him again, but he had done his best to assure her during the time he was home.

"Sometimes, the things we go through feel like they get worse before they get better. But God is the same yesterday, today, and forever," Uncle Ross reminded her. "Folks will tell you that you never need to look behind you, only straight ahead. But every now and then, I think we all need to look back. When we look back, we realize that there has never been a time that God has failed us. He didn't fail us then, and He ain't about to fail us now. The key is to keep doing right and to trust Him no matter what."

Nadine knew that her uncle was right, but last night's repeated dream of her near-drowning had been way too real. As Nadine stepped from the shower and began to dry her body and hair, she found comfort in knowing that only forty minutes separated her from the first session she'd have with Olivia since leaving Atlanta. Talking with her therapist always seemed to bring greater clarity in times like this.

Nadine could not deny that her life had become a pressure pit over the last three weeks. Their scheduled session three days ago had been postponed to make room for a meeting with her divorce attorney, and the session before that one had been canceled by Olivia because of a family emergency. Nadine's normal appointments were on Fridays, but after missing two in a row, Olivia said they didn't need to wait another full week.

She had cleared the first available slot today, and Nadine could hardly wait for the arrival of ten am.

The chill was gone now. What the shower hadn't thawed, her hot blow dryer did as Nadine ran the attached comb of it through her hair. The high heat helped to straighten her strands enough so that it was the perfect texture for the stuff she added at the end. Nadine stepped into a pair of jeans and pulled a Steph Curry T-shirt over her head before walking out of her bedroom. She found her aunt sitting at the bar in the kitchen sipping on a cup of coffee. There was a banana peel laying on the surface in front of her. Nadine assumed that had been Aunt Pat's breakfast.

While her aunt had cooked breakfast and dinner during the first days of Nadine's stay, it was clear that she was not one to cook fresh, hot meals every day. Even during the time that her husband was home, her Aunt Pat only worked in the kitchen for a couple of days. Most often, whatever they ate was either leftovers from what had been previously prepared, or ordered from the menu of one of the local eateries. Curbside pickup and contactless delivery were clearly two of her favorite things.

"Good morning," Nadine said as she entered the space and grabbed a skillet from the cabinet.

"Good morning," her aunt replied. "What's for breakfast today? Eggless eggs and meatless meat seasoned with salt-less salt and pepper-less pepper?"

Nadine broke out into a laugh. Her preferred, plant-based lifestyle was not shared by Aunt Pat nor Uncle Ross. "You really should try it sometime. It's really good."

"Umph. I'll take your word for it," Pat said. She looked at the clock on the wall and added, "Don't you have a meeting this morning?"

"Yes, ma'am, but I have time to throw this together real quick."

Less than ten minutes later, Nadine was occupying the stool beside her aunt while enjoying a stir-fried mixture of tofu chicken and eggless eggs. She tried to hold her laughter while her aunt side-eyed her in disapproval.

"I heard Deacon Duncan tell you yesterday that he was making some kind of progress," Pat said.

Nadine nodded while she swallowed her food. "He's been having conversations with Damon's attorney," she explained. "They have been discussing the terms of the divorce. It seems that Damon is willing to give me the money for half the value of the house so that he can remain living there and half of the value of the car that is still there and in both our names. But, what he won't agree to is the cash settlement I'm asking for. He doesn't think I deserve it."

"Of course not," her aunt replied. "That's evident in the way he has treated you. When you value anything, you treat it with the utmost care. Our actions speak way louder than what we say. He might've said you meant everything to him, but his treatment of you is all the proof you need that to him, you don't mean much of nothing."

Nadine knew her Aunt Pat's words were true, but they stung too much for her to piggyback on them and extend the conversation. Instead, she changed the subject. "Attorney Duncan said he had an appointment with Damon's attorney at some point this morning. He hopes that some kind of conclusion can be agreed upon. If not, we're going to end up having to go to court, and Lord knows I don't want to go through that. I really don't want to have to face Damon again."

"In the Word of God, just about every enemy God's people ever defeated, they first had to come face-to-face with," Pat responded. "The secret is never to face a demon on your own. You've got to take God with you. When David came face-to-face with Goliath, he didn't tell that giant that he was coming to him under his own strength. He said, 'You're coming at me with your sword and spear, but I'm coming at you in the name of the Lord of hosts.' David knew the battle was bigger than him. Your battle is bigger than you too, but it ain't bigger than God."

Before Nadine could respond, the screen of her phone lit up and chimed to remind her that she had less than five minutes to join her virtual meeting.

"You go ahead. I'll clean up the kitchen."

Nadine kissed her aunt's cheek. "Thank you."

Inside the privacy of her bedroom, Nadine silenced her cell phone, sat at the desk and powered up her laptop. While she still had not had the opportunity to meet Olivia in person, she'd grown to fully trust the therapist. When Nadine talked to Olivia, she felt as if she was talking to a friend. It was kind of like talking to another Trina, but on top of being saved, this one was professionally trained in dealing with trauma.

"Good morning," Nadine said as soon as Olivia admitted her to the session.

"Good morning. It seems like forever since we last met. I'm glad to see that you're looking rested and radiant," Olivia observed.

Nadine couldn't help but laugh. "You wouldn't have said that if our appointment had been set for nine. I was a mess then."

"Well, that sounds like a great place to start. What happened at nine o'clock?"

While Nadine shared the details of her reoccurring nightmare, and how authentic it felt, she watched Olivia's face for signs of change. Her expressions were always hard to read, because she rarely showed any. Nadine could never tell what was going through Olivia's mind unless they were sharing a lighthearted moment wherein the response was laughter. Maybe that was one of the reasons she found Olivia so easy to talk to. Nadine was never made to feel stupid, inadequate, or like she was being judged.

"Were there any differences at all between the two dreams?" Olivia asked once Nadine was finished sharing.

"Not really. I didn't wake up on my own this time like I did the last time. This morning, I was awakened at the very last second by my alarm. Last time, I was somehow able to shake myself awake before I sank under water. If there were any other changes, I can't remember them."

"I understand." Olivia paused to make notes in her notepad. When she looked back into the screen, she said, "There's a lot of turbulence in your life right now, so having dreams like this isn't odd. Even when you had the dream the first time, your life was experiencing instability and disorder, so it wasn't abnormal to have it at that point either. If there are differences in the dreams, however—even slight differences—those could represent something. That's why I asked about any variations. You mentioned that the dream was very vivid, so I wonder if you were to really think about it, you could identify something meaningful. Close your eyes for a minute and revisit the details."

"Right now?" Nadine asked.

"Yes."

"I really don't want to relive that if I don't have to. I've been trying my best all morning to erase it from my subconscious."

"I know you don't want to, but you need to. Vivid dreams shouldn't be ignored."

"Have you been talking to Aunt Pat?" Nadine asked with a nervous chuckle.

"No, but it sounds like you're staying in the right home. Apparently, your aunt is a woman who is familiar with scripture. From as far back as Old Testament times, God dealt with mankind in dreams. Sometimes the dreams were good and sometimes not so good, but when God chose to use them, it was to deliver a message. So, just for a moment, close your eyes, and think about your dream. Think about the details."

Nadine took a deep breath, and then followed the instructions. She could feel her own body tense as she withdrew snapshots of the dream from her memory bank. In both dreams, she was already in the car and sinking when she became aware of her surroundings. The moments before that, she was in the car riding alongside Damon on the way to what she thought was a romantic getaway. She'd drunk something he'd given her that had apparently knocked her out keeping her unconscious while he maneuvered the vehicle to the bank of the river and pushed it in.

In both dreams, by the time Nadine regained consciousness, her lower body was already covered as water from the river entered the car. She would sit there helpless, screaming for Damon to come and rescue her. But in his silent response, he would just watch as the car slowly sank with her inside. If there was any difference in the dreams at all, it was that last night she was screaming louder. Nadine recalled the image of herself leaning forward in the seat to get a good look at Damon while she pleaded with him to …

"I was on the passenger's side!" she suddenly blurted, her eyelids jetting upward.

"You were on the passenger's side?" Olivia seemed unclear as to what that meant. "Damon was driving, so you should have been on the passenger side, right?"

"Yes, but not in the first dream," Nadine explained. "I mean, in the first dream, yes, he was the driver while we were on the highway, but when I came to, he had forced me in the driver's side of the car to make it look like I'd been driving the entire time. Damon had made it look like I had somehow lost control of the vehicle and driven off the roadway and into the river. He was staging it to look like an accident."

As she spoke, Nadine felt breathless, like she had just awakened again. "The difference is, last night, I was on the passenger's side; I hadn't been moved. In the first dream, I was able to turn my head to the left and look right outside the driver's side window seeing him standing at the ledge watching me sink. In last night's dream, I had to lean forward and look from the passenger's side through the driver's side window to see that."

Silence hovered for a few seconds before Olivia's voice broke through it. After laying her pen and pad to the side, she said, "Before we end today's session, we're going to pray about that difference because I believe it's significant," she told Nadine. "In my spirit, I feel like that small change is a message from God. In the first dream, you were in the driver's seat. You were the one sitting in the position that represents control. In the second dream, you remained in the passenger's seat—the seat that entrusts someone else to take you where you need to be."

Olivia leaned forward as she continued speaking. "I believe that's God's way of telling you that He needs you to stay in the passenger's seat and save the driver's seat for Him. You may not see him there. You may not even feel as if He's there. But He is there, and He needs you to trust Him. This will not be an easy transition that you're going to go through with Damon, but in the depths of my very soul, Nadine, I feel that God is telling you to take your hands off the wheel, get out of the driver's seat, and stop trying to figure out how He's going to deliver you."

Nadine felt tears filling her eyes. She tried to swallow the overflow of emotions, but they defied her will, and she broke into an uncontrollable sob. While she could still clearly hear Olivia, she could no longer clearly see her. Tears had all but blinded her vision.

"In the same way that Damon's actions forced you into the driver's seat in your dream, his actions are forcing you into the driver's seat in your reality. You can't let that happen. If he can make you unconscious to who's really in control, he will have you try to do what only God can do. In your effort to control the situation, you woke yourself from your first nightmare. With you out of the driver's seat you couldn't wake yourself. The clock did it. God's time is not our time, Nadine, but His timing is always perfect. He may not have come when you wanted Him to, but the time is right, He rescued you just the same. All you have to do is totally trust Him."

Chapter 25

Ready For Battle

Damon had proven himself to be unrelenting … and not in a good way. Two more weeks passed, and two more failed attempts at mediation had forced them into accepting a date for a court appearance. One of Nadine's worst fears was being realized.

"In my professional opinion, he's just hell-bent on doing whatever it takes to force you to be in the same room with him," Attorney Duncan told her as they sat together in his office.

Nervous energy wouldn't let Nadine stay seated. While her attorney talked, she walked around his workspace admiring mounted awards on the walls and framed photos on his bookshelves. Herbert Duncan had gone to Duke University, where he earned his degree four years before Nadine did at Howard. One bookshelf space displayed an extensive selection of books while another space was reserved for photographs. Most appeared to be framed images of Attorney Duncan with various family members and business constituents. One was an image of him and Sonya making their official wedding announcement. The obviously happy couple beamed from ear to ear while holding up a save-the-date sign for June of next year.

"At this point, Mayor Deville is very much aware that your marriage is irreparable, but he has no intention of letting you just walk away." Attorney Duncan's words got Nadine's full attention. "You rejected him, and even more, you embarrassed him."

Nadine looked at him with widened eyes. "What have I done to embarrass him? I left him, yes, but I moved clear to another state. It's not like I hung around to be a constant reminder of our failed marriage."

"Apparently, none of your friends back home told you about this," Attorney Duncan said while simultaneously reaching into his drawer and retrieving a magazine. "Or, maybe they just haven't seen it yet."

Nadine walked toward his desk for a closer look. It was one of the weekly gossip magazines that can be found near the checkout counter of grocery stores. Damon's face was on the front cover and the accompanying caption read, "Damon Deville or Demon Devil?"

Nadine gasped and grabbed the magazine from her attorney's hand. "What's this? Who wrote this? What is this about?"

"I don't know who the source is, but the mayor's abusive behavior has been leaked. This article is written based on a reliable source's account of your rocky marriage."

"What reliable source? Before coming here, no one knew the details except Trina and Sophia, and neither of them would waste their time talking to a rag magazine. I know my aunt and uncle didn't do it either."

"Well, that leaves me, and I can assure you that they didn't get their information from my office," Attorney Duncan said.

"Then they must have just made up a lot of stuff. You know how the media can be."

"Yes, I do. But this stuff isn't made up. Many of the things that you've said that he did are printed in this article, so somebody blabbed. This 'rag magazine,' as you called it, pays good money to people who are willing to betray family and friends to give them confidential details. They got to somebody who is connected to the story."

Nadine flipped to the page where the article began and scanned the words. He was right; there were details outlined that someone who was in-the-know had to reveal. "I can't believe this," she whispered. "This is crazy."

"Yes, it's crazy, but the Word of God says, 'All things work together for the good of those that love God'," her attorney quoted. "This crazy article could work to help your case. I don't know what the intent was of the person who betrayed your trust, but their unauthorized disclosure of this information may have been just what you needed. Up until now, all that the people of Atlanta had to go on was your husband's sob story of being callously abandoned by a wife he'd done nothing but love. This can open their eyes to the fact, or at least the possibility, that they haven't been hearing the whole truth."

Nadine closed the magazine and stared at the cover. "But Demon Devil? That's so harsh."

"Have you looked at your reality lately, Nadine? That's harsh too." Attorney Duncan slid the magazine from her grasp. "One of the biggest mistakes that abuse victims make is keeping a heart for their abuser. We should love everybody with the love of God, and we have to forgive as God says to forgive. But this is no time to feel sorry for your soon-to-be ex-husband. You want to talk about harsh? Look at what you've endured and what you're still enduring at the hands of this man."

"I know, I know." Adding a heavy groan, Nadine threw her head back and looked upward. "I just want this to be over. Lord, help me!"

"I think maybe He already has," Attorney Duncan said while holding up the magazine as a visual reminder. "I don't think it's a coincidence that your hearing is four days away, and this issue hit newsstands four days ago. This feels a lot like God's divine intervention to me."

"I guess I was just hoping for something amicable. This totally killed the chance for that."

"Didn't you tell me earlier today that your therapist instructed you to stay out of the driver's seat?"

Nadine plopped in the chair across from his desk and began massaging her temples with her fingers. "Yes."

"Then, do it," Attorney Duncan ordered. "I have a newsflash for you, Nadine. This wasn't going to be amicable anyway. This was going to be a nasty fight for us without this article, and it probably still will be. But prior to now, the only bright light we had was that I was able to convince the court to allow your hearing to be held in Marietta. It's about an hour away from your husband's throne, and you have a much better chance of avoiding any bias there. But now, we also have the advantage of people getting a glimpse into what you lived with for all those years. With this article, they have something to consider other than the manipulative lies of Mayor Deville."

Nadine nodded slowly. She wasn't oblivious to the truth of what her attorney was saying, but the thought of walking into a room where she'd have to faceoff with Damon was almost tormenting. Why couldn't he have just let the divorce be settled through the mediation?

"Your husband's need to control you is still very much intact." Attorney Duncan said the words as though he'd read her thoughts. "Mayor Deville couldn't manipulate you into going back to him through his many phone calls, so what he's done is manipulate the system so that you'll have to meet him in a courtroom. He knows that you wanted this to be handled through mediation, and that's why it wasn't. Nothing about this is going to go your way if he can help it."

"How long will the hearing last?"

"There is really no way to gauge that. On paper, it doesn't look like it should last long. The only issue on the table is the monetary settlement. He's already agreed to the stipulations of the property. Once again, it's about control. He could easily agree to give you half the value of the house and the shared vehicle because he gets to physically retain the items. To the eyes of the public, he's lost nothing there. But you're also trying to get six figures out of him, and he doesn't think you deserve that, so he's not going to just hand that over."

"What's your professional opinion, Herbert? Be honest with me. What do you think my chances are?"

Her case file had been lying on his desk, and Attorney Duncan picked it up as he answered her. "We have proof that the mayor's father received a settlement of over a million dollars from his previous employer. Injuries he received while working there were a direct result of the company's negligence and ultimately led to him needing double-knee replacement surgery. From the settlement, he gave six figures to Mayor Deville in addition to placing the mayor's name on his personal bank account. That means free access to his father's money at any given time."

Attorney Duncan placed the folder back on his desk. "When this windfall came, you had already been married for eight years. Had the money come at any point prior to your marriage, I'd say your chances of getting any of it would be pretty much nonexistent. If you had walked out on the marriage within days or even weeks of him getting the money, I think the court would have frowned on that too. With things as they are, I'd say you have a good chance. But, even with it being a good chance, it's going to be a fighting chance. Mayor Deville is going to make sure that."

The drive to Haynes Street in Marietta was the quietest two hours of Nadine's life. She and Aunt Pat had ridden with Attorney Duncan, and the jazz music that played over the radio was the only thing that kept the ride from being silent.

Upon their arrival, the three of them had been escorted to a room where they were told to await further instructions. Attorney Duncan took advantage of the time by looking over his notes. Not wanting to disturb him, the women sat quietly. The room's acoustics, coupled with the lack of conversation, made amplified other noises.

"My Lord!" Aunt Pat exclaimed. "Is that your stomach growling? Did you eat breakfast this morning?"

Nadine released a soft giggle. "No, I didn't. I've been fasting for the past two days."

"Well, I guess that shuts me right on up," Aunt Pat said as she smoothed out her skirt. "I ain't about to say nothing against you fasting."

The door to the room opened, and at the sight of her best friend and sister, Nadine jumped from her chair, tears immediately spilling from her eyes. The last few months without seeing either of them, had been rough.

"I'm so glad to see you guys," she said, delivering a tight hug to both.

"Don't start with all that crying, big sis," Sophia warned. "I promised myself I wasn't going to do that today."

"Me too," Trina said, while at the same time wiping a tear from her cheek. "By the way, I'm not crying because I'm seeing you," she added. "I'm crying because I'm hungry!"

Nadine laughed. "Well, you're the one that said you wanted to know what days I was fasting so you could join me."

"I was okay with those one-day deals, but when you decided to do the last forty-eight hours straight, I wasn't ready!"

"Ladies, let me have your attention." Attorney Duncan's voice put an abrupt end to their reunion celebration. "I want to thank each of you for agreeing to come and support Ms. Jackson in this hearing today."

"Ms. Jackson." Trina applauded as she repeated the words. "See, I like you already, Counselor. You automatically knew to cut that fool's last name right on out of there."

Attorney Duncan smiled at her response. "Well, I didn't exactly take for granted that she would be reverting to her maiden name. She told me of her plan to do so once the divorce became final, so now seems like as good a time as any to recognize that." He turned his attention back to everyone. "Once again, thank you all for coming and agreeing to speak on behalf of Ms. Jackson. Our last person should be arriving any moment, and at that time, I'm going to review a few important things with all of you before our case is called."

Nadine looked around the room. Aunt Pat, Trina, and Sophia were the only three people she was expecting. When the room door opened, Nadine turned to see a woman that up until that moment she had only viewed through a computer screen.

"Olivia!" she said through a gasp of breath.

"Hi, Nadine." She walked toward her. "I just want you to know that I'm only here for moral support. Our confidentiality agreement will be honored. I'll only bend or break it at your request. I just wanted to be here in case you need me."

New tears were pushing behind Nadine's eyeballs as she accepted a warm hug from Olivia. "Thank you," she whispered in her therapist's ear.

"Ain't God good?" Aunt Pat asked.

"Yes, ma'am; He sure is," Attorney Duncan agreed. "Now, listen up everybody, I can't express how important it is that you all remain professional during today's hearing. Lies will be told, and false accusations will be made. I can say that without a shred of doubt. To cling to any level of integrity, the mayor will have to stick with the things—true or false—that he's been saying all along about the marriage, and about Ms. Jackson personally. Whatever is said, I don't want any rude outbursts from any of you. Is that understood?"

"You won't get none from me," Aunt Pat said. "That devil won't get under my skin."

"I certainly understand," Olivia said.

Sophia sighed. "Okay. I understand too."

Attorney Duncan looked at Trina who stood silently side eyeing him. "Mrs. Richards?"

"I can't make that promise," she said. "I'll do my best, but if that fool says the wrong thing about my friend, I'mma use his own necktie to choke him half to death."

"Don't say stuff like that," Nadine scolded. "People might think you're serious."

"I'm very serious. If I thought I could get away with it, I'd set his drawers on fire with him still wearing them. So, if I just choke him 'til he passes out, I think that's being quite cordial."

"Mrs. Richards, no matter what Mayor Deville says in this hearing, if you react in that manner or any other way that disrespects the court, you're going to do your friend more harm than good," Attorney Duncan explained. "I'm not going to let you sabotage my client, so you need to let me know right now if we need to let you sit this one out."

Nadine grabbed her best friend's hand, and her eyes were pleading. "Come on, Trina. I need you in the hearing with me.

Please say you can hold it together. All Attorney Duncan is asking you to do is the same thing that you and I both have asked countless clients of ours to do. If anybody can do this, you can."

"Trina," Olivia chimed in, "if you can't hold your temperament for this hearing—especially knowing how important it is to Nadine's case—then you and I need to add some additional topics to our sessions."

Trina raised her hands in surrender. "I'll behave. I promise. If Nadine comes out of this victoriously, it'll be well worth suppressing my revulsion of Damon."

"We're going to need more than self-control and our own strength to get us through this mess," Aunt Pat said. "Deacon Duncan, is it okay if we pray?"

"Absolutely," he replied.

The sound of light knocking made them all turn toward the door. When it opened, a court official ducked his head in the room. "The Deville versus Deville case is up next. I need everyone in this room who is a part of it to follow me."

"Hold your horses, sir," Aunt Pat said. "We were just about to pray. You can come on in and join us if you want, or you can stand at the door. But, none of us are following you until we talk to God."

"We're on a schedule, ma'am." He paused to look at his wristwatch. "I can give you two minutes."

"Good, 'cause all I need is one."

The man quietly stepped back into the hall and allowed the door to close behind him.

Aunt Pat wasted no time. "Lord, we come before you today acknowledging that you are the only true and living God, and besides you, there is no other. You have control over everything and everybody, including the judge that will be presiding over this hearing. Lord, please give him supernatural wisdom, knowledge, and understanding so that he can detect the lies and see through the deceit of the enemy. We ask that you grant divine favor to your daughter, Nadine, today. Be her strength and her fortress. Don't let her fasting and prayers be in vain. Show yourself strong and mighty and give us victory. When you do, we promise that we won't take any of your glory. We will testify of your goodness and your mercy. Work it out as only you can. In Christ's name, we pray. Amen."

As if he'd heard the chorus of amens that came from those in the room, the court official opened the door again, signaling that time was up.

The uncomfortable silence returned as Nadine followed her attorney out into the hall. The others fell in formation behind her. It was a relatively short walk to the courtroom entrance, but to Nadine, it felt like miles. As soon as the double doors swung open and Nadine walked inside, her eyes locked onto Damon's. His charade continued. He'd let his hair grow longer than normal, and it appeared he hadn't shaved in at least two weeks. As she walked past him toward her seat, Damon's lips curled into a sneer.Nadine suddenly felt as though she was locked in a car and on her way to sinking deep in Lake Taguloo. Just like in her dreams.

"Oh, God ... please help me," she whispered.

Now that you've finished reading The Power of Love, write a review on the Amazon or Goodreads listing to help other readers find the book that is best for them.

Instagram: @ChaseBoykinsTheAuthor

Facebook: @ChaseBoykinsTheAuthor

www.ChaseBoykinsTheAuthor.com

rebel queen

We hope you loved Chase's book as much as we have loved preparing it for you! With a combined 20+ years in publishing, we know how to help anyone write, launch, and market a book. So, if a book is on your bucket list, we're the team to take it from brain dump to bestseller.

RebelQueen.co
marti@rebelqueen.co
Facebook and Instagram @rebelqueenbooks

www.ingramcontent.com/pod-product-compliance
Lightning Source LLC
Chambersburg PA
CBHW070436300726
48975CB00007B/1950